El Flaco
Dark Republic Book Three

D.L. Young

The characters and events portrayed in this book are fictitious. Any similarity to real persons, living or dead or undead or even just hanging on in a coma, is purely coincidental and not intended by the author.

Copyright © 2018 David L. Young

All rights reserved.

ISBN-10: 0-9908696-6-0
ISBN-13: 978-0-9908696-6-5

For Brooks, John, Stuart, and Gary,
my other brothers

CHAPTER 1

Ernesto "El Flaco" Guzmán races the motorbike over the nighttime streets of Dallas, leaning into a corner, his knee dangerously low to the pavement, nearly brushing the curb. He comes out of the turn, pulling the bike upright again and gassing the throttle. The engine screams in his ears as he shifts into third gear, then quickly into fourth.

He glances over his shoulder. The pack of a half a dozen motorbikes is still there, hunting him, relentlessly chasing him down. Getting closer.

The city flies past like a dark dream studded with the occasional jewel of light blurring in the corner of his vision as he flashes by. A cooking fire on the sidewalk, a flashing neon sign. Enormous buildings tower over his head, dead giants watching him weave his little machine left and right through a maze of empty streets like a frantic ant. He clenches his teeth, focusing on the bike, concentrating on the machine's weight and balance, the tires' grip on the cement, nudging it faster as he reaches Elm Street.

It's risky, foolhardy even, pushing the bike this hard—with so little light he can see only a matter of yards in front of him. But he can't let them catch him.

He takes another look back. Still there. So close now he

squints at the glare of their headlights. Then suddenly one of them is beside him, inches away.

Puta madre, where did he come from?

Hidden by his helmet, the rider's expression is unreadable as he gestures at Guzmán, pointing frantically at the ground.

Guzmán shakes his head, then smiles as he lifts his leg and thrusts the heel of his boot against the rider's gas tank, shoving hard enough to send the bike wobbling away. The rider wrestles with the handlebars for an instant, but fails to regain control, and in the next moment machine and rider separate, sliding over the street. Sparks fly from the underside of the bike as the rider tumbles to a stop beside the sidewalk. Amazingly, he pops up to his feet and shouts something unintelligible at Guzmán.

Guzmán looks back, sees the chase pack in chaos. Headlights lurch and jerk as riders weave and scramble to avoid the fallen bike, knocking into each other as they do so. Guzmán roars with laughter.

"NOT TONIGHT, CABRONES!" he shouts, his voice raucous with joy as the distance between him and the stalled pursuers grows. "Not tonight!"

A turn to the left, two more to the right, and then they're gone. He's lost them. A smile creases his face, his skin stiff and taut in the cold night air. Still, he doesn't slow, urging the bike faster, revving the engine higher. He leans deep into the corners, feeling the tires wobble as he pushes the machine to its limits. He wants to stay like this forever, feel like this forever, the cold wind in his face, his eyes tearing up so much he can hardly see, dancing on the precipice of his mortality. Whatever this feeling is—joy or terror or maybe both mixed up together—he doesn't want it to end. This is what it means to be alive, truly alive.

Then, as abruptly as it welled up inside him, the euphoria disappears, doused by the sudden flare of headlights straight ahead of him. A Humvee sitting in the middle of the roadway. He brakes hard. The bike swerves and quivers underneath him, but he manages to keep control as he maneuvers around the truck, his knee missing the front bumper by inches. The driver shouts, "Don Flaco!" as Guzmán passes by and steers into an alley.

For a moment, the alley's as dark as midnight, then a flash of lightning illuminates everything around him, revealing every detail of the narrow passageway. Crumbling brick walls, piles of garbage, puddles of standing rainwater. And not of least importance, the alley's dead end, bearing down in front of him. Guzmán brakes hard, but he's too close to stop. He lays the bike down, tumbling away from the machine in a sprawl of arms and legs. The motorbike slides away and slams into the concrete wall, bursting apart into a mess of flying metal and rubber and plastic.

Guzmán rolls to a stop, his back thudding against a steel trash bin, knocking the air from his lungs. He lies there for a moment, catching his breath, staring up at the starless black sky. His knees and elbows burn and ooze blood, but otherwise he's uninjured. He sits up and squints into the Humvee headlights that have come to a stop a few meters away, illuminating him like twin spotlights.

He spits in disgust. "Puta madre," he mutters. The chase is over. They've caught him.

From beyond the blinding light a door slams shut. A figure appears, silhouetted by the glare, and approaches, stopping a couple feet in front of him.

Guzmán rubs his smarting elbow and sneers up at the man hovering over him. "I had them beat tonight."

The figure waves a hand back at the truck, and someone in the passenger seat turns off the headlights, leaving only the soft yellow glow of the hazards. Guzmán blinks and the details of the figure's face take shape: the wide nose, the bushy mustache, the grave expression that somehow conveys both concern and disappointment.

Chavez, Guzmán's faithful lieutenant and right hand,

reaches down to help up his fallen patrón. "Vamos, jefe," he says, holding out his hand. "Lots of work to do."

A drizzle begins to fall. Guzmán sighs and remains sitting, a stubborn child pouting in the rain. Chavez stands there, patient and waiting, until finally his jefe takes his hand and reluctantly stands.

* * *

"These games are risky, jefe," Chavez mutters, glancing at his patrón in the rearview, his tone and gaze those of a disapproving parent. Raindrops ping and patter against the roof of the Humvee as Chavez pulls the truck out of the alley.

Guzmán sighs. "Exercises, hombre, not games. Estos son mis ejercicios." In truth, he also thinks of them as games, but he isn't going to give Chavez any satisfaction, especially after the old spoilsport interrupted one of his better runs. "They keep me sharp. Battle-ready, as the gringos say." A pair of pickup trucks join them, taking their usual security positions in front and behind.

Chavez grunts. "You could wear a helmet at least."

Guzmán waves his hand. "Bah, you're worse than a wife, hombre." For months old Chavez has been pestering him about the dangers of these motorbike games of tag with his soldiers, but Guzmán loves the chases, loves gathering up the best of his riders and having them come tearing after him like a pack of wild dogs. He usually gives himself a fifteen-second head start, but tonight, feeling brash, he'd cut it to five. Sometimes they catch him, cornering him in an alley or dead end street. Other times he bests them, evading them entirely. What moments they are, these frantic, glorious, adrenaline-fueled minutes racing through the dark veins of the city! The motorbike chases have become his escape, an old outlaw's momentary reprieve from a new life that has traded adrenaline and excitement for tedium and paperwork.

A young bodyguard, one of Chavez's fresh recruits from the Dallas locals, sits in the passenger seat. He passes a roll of white cloth to Guzmán, seated in back. "For your arm, don Flaco." Guzmán takes it and winces as he dabs blood from the raw skin of his elbows. Outside, the rain has stopped. The Humvee slowly rolls forward over the smooth, even streets. It hardly feels like moving, Guzmán muses as he wraps the cloth around his arm. Six months living in the city, and he's still not used to the feeling of driving over paved avenues. Probably never will be, he decides, after a lifetime rattling and bouncing over old dirt roads, nearly forgotten trails, and open countryside.

He lowers his window, breathes in the freshly washed night air. Small knots of people loiter on the walkways, the sidewalks that used to move, ferrying citizens and robots all around the city, though now they stand as still as their concrete predecessors. Faces glance up at the motorcade. Blank stares, empty expressions.

Guzmán grunts. "Remember when we first took the city? We couldn't go anywhere without getting mobbed." The good times, he recalls. Those intoxicating days that felt like the happy afterglow of lovemaking with a beautiful woman. Cheered everywhere he went. Men wanting to shake his hand, women throwing themselves at him. Seems like a lifetime ago now, though it's been barely half a year since they took the city.

Chavez pushes a button, closing the rear window. "They're just used to seeing you now," he offers. "In the camps, we were always moving, away for months sometimes. Your people hardly ever saw you. But here, settled in, they see you every day. It's different now."

The Humvee's motor rumbles as they roll through the rain-dampened streets. As they approach the City Hall building, the walkways clot with people. Guzmán studies their faces, but he can't decide what it is he sees. Resignation? Frustration? Indifference? Whatever it is, it's something far removed from the wide-eyed fervor he saw—and *felt*—not so long ago, when they'd squeeze together by the hundreds under a tent in some desert town to listen to him give a speech, hanging on his every word, cheering him on.

"Yes," he mutters to himself. "It's different now."

*   *   *

The City Hall building stands twenty stories tall, its half dozen spires twisting and curving upwards, organic and patternless. The structure's built of a self-repairing semiporous concrete Guzmán's engineers told him provided heating and cooling without air-conditioning machines. Greenery covers much of the building, catching rain and recycling wastewater. The city's architecture was designed by the AIs for maximum comfort, self-sufficiency, and durability, with minimal upkeep. Made to last a thousand years, one of the native Dallasite engineers boasted while giving Guzmán and his retinue a tour of the building.

Flanked by Chavez and the new recruit, Guzmán approaches the entrance. As usual, there's a crowd out front, hundreds strong, congesting City Hall's wide plaza. Tonight, though, the throng appears larger than usual.

"Híjole," the new bodyguard gasps. "Look how many."

Chavez tugs on his patrón's arm, pausing the trio at the edge of the plaza. "Maybe we should get back in the truck and drive around back, jefe."

Guzmán yanks his arm away. "Nonsense, compadre. I'm not going to hide from my own people." But even as he strides forward into the crowd, outwardly defiant, he swallows hard in anticipation. Chavez and the bodyguard hustle to keep up, regaining their positions alongside their obstinate chief as he crosses the edge of the plaza. A silence slowly falls over the murmuring crowd as faces turn toward Guzmán in recognition. The throng gently parts for the three men as they make their way toward the entrance.

"Buenas noches," Guzmán says, nodding politely. A few return the greeting; fewer still reach out to shake his hand. Most stare at him, their expressions those of the helpless, the disillusioned.

"We have thieves in our building, don Flaco," a tiny old woman in a threadbare poncho complains. "And no one does anything about it."

He stops and bends down to the woman, nodding respectfully. "I'm sorry, señora. I'll have someone look into it."

"They took my virgencita and my rosary," she moans. "The ones my grandmother gave me."

"Lo siento," Guzmán repeats, then turns to the bodyguard. "Send someone to her building, compadre. Tonight."

"Sí, jefe," the young man responds.

The old woman's protest is the first crack in the dam, releasing a rushing flood of complaints.

"We have contaminated water, don Flaco," a woman holding a baby pleads.

"The food market on Young Street has *pickpockets*," a man behind her whines. "We never had pickpockets in the camps."

"What about the power, don Flaco?"

"Yes, will the power *ever* come back?"

Here, the answers do not come to him as easily as they did in the camps. But he stays among them, caught in the knot of their worry, listening and reassuring them he'll do everything he can. A hand closes around his forearm.

"Don Flaco," Chavez urges. "We have business that can't wait."

*   *   *

From his office on the top floor, Guzmán stands with his arms crossed, peering down at the crowd behind the tinted glass of his window. "Did you see their faces, compadre?" He frowns, shakes his head. "The way they looked at me?"

Behind him, Chavez grunts. "Since when have you been so preocupado about the way people look at you, jefe?"

Guzmán shifts his gaze to his loyal right hand's reflection in the glass. The old bull sits at a desk, hunched over stacks of papers. A pair of reading glasses sits low on his nose as he concentrates on his work. Messy piles cover the desktop. Weeks, maybe months, of stratified tedium.

"They fix the comms out west?"

Chavez replies without looking up from his work. "Not yet."

"What's the delay? It's been, what, three days?"

"We're sending a radio crew out in the morning." Chavez looks up, placing his hand atop one of the stacks. "Apartment grants for the Delta Building. Did you sign these yet, jefe?"

Guzmán shrugs. "I don't remember."

Chavez sighs. "I know it's not the most inspiring work, don Flaco, but it's necessary. It takes time to get everything in order, especially after the way the city was left."

Indeed, Guzmán muses. Six months ago, they victoriously claimed the city…and inherited the mother of all messes. And it was a mess of their own making, truth be told. When Dallas' AIs were rendered inoperable by Soledad Paz—the act of sabotage that allowed his troops to take the city—the thinking machines were irreparably destroyed. The Dallasite technicians tried for weeks, but they couldn't bring them back to life, leaving Guzmán in charge of a shell of a modern metropolis, its power grid damaged beyond repair, its flying drones grounded, its robots frozen in place, its moving walkways stilled. The infamous Dallasite dependence on technology Guzmán had so mocked from his camps in the dusty western desert was no longer a laughing matter. The native Dallas engineers and technicians, without the help of their AIs, couldn't manage to turn the lights back on.

And so the glory of Guzmán's victory faded quickly into an endless tedium of administration and paperwork. Rubber stamps and pens replaced bullets and guns. The near-constant debauchery of his nomadic life as a rogue warrior replaced with long nights alone with Chavez, signing papers by the hundreds, managing housing disputes, and seeing to the endless minutiae that came with running a settlement of skyscrapers.

Guzmán stares out the window, the soft susurration of shuffling papers behind him. He pictures the fat preacher, Reverend Wright, still out there somewhere, alive and conspiring against him at this very moment.

"Jefe," Chavez calls.

Guzmán doesn't move or reply. *Are you out there, you old crook? Waiting for me to come after you?*

"Jefe," Chavez repeats, louder.

Guzmán snaps out of his reverie. Far below him, the crowd mills in a slow, swirling eddy. He sees their faces again in his mind's eye. The disappointment in their eyes, the frustration in their voices. Madre de Dios, does he know how they feel. He lets out a long breath. *Not the most inspiring work, but necessary.* Maybe old Chavez is right. There's still so much to do, so many duties that require his attention, his focus. Who would have ever guessed a pile of unsigned papers would trump hunting down your enemies?

He sits down at the desk across from Chavez, and his lieutenant passes him a pen and nods to the largest stack. "I stamped those already, you only need to sign them."

Guzmán eyes the pile of papers. "Por Dios, there must be five hundred."

"Four hundred thirty-eight," Chavez answers, "but that's just the first batch."

Cracking his knuckles, Guzmán settles in for a long

evening. Necessary work, he reminds himself as he signs the first document and sets it aside. Tiresome, monotonous, but necessary.

CHAPTER 2

"Yuck," Steffa complains, her face wrinkling up as she chews. "Can I spit it out yet?"

Soledad Paz gazes out the window of her penthouse condo, watching the city slowly come to life twenty stories below. Steffa's voice seems far away as Soledad peers down at the food vendors wheeling their portable kiosks out into the plaza and setting up for the breakfast rush. Merchants and dealers and peddlers are unrolling the small plots of rugs on which they'll display their wares. Hand-crank radios, batteries, engine parts, tools, jewelry, clothes, shoes, toys. In another hour the city's central plaza will transform completely, from an empty lot to a bustling marketplace, choked with pedestrians and goods from every corner of the Republic.

"Can I spit it out yet?" the girl repeats, louder.

Soledad finally turns to face her, finding the girl's face twisted into an exaggerated grimace of disgust. "I'm not going to tell you you'll get used to it, gorda, because I never did. I still hate chewing hierba myself." She checks the clock on the wall. "Yes, it's been long enough. Here you go." Soledad holds a napkin open for the girl, who spits out the leaves into it.

"Bleh," Steffa whines, with all the drama an eight-year-old can muster. "Yuk, yuk, yuk."

"Go ahead and finish your breakfast."

The girl gobbles down her eggs and toast. "More?" she asks, her cheeks still bulging with barely chewed food, her chin shiny with yolk. Soledad folds the napkin, wipes the girl's face clean. Poor creature. Even after six months of regular meals, she still eats like a refugee, as if her next meal might be days away.

"Sure," Soledad answers, moving toward the kitchen.

After the girl has finished her second serving of eggs and fourth piece of toast, Soledad clears the dishes from the table and sits across from Steffa once more. "All right, let me take a look at you," she announces, using the same words as always, signifying the start of their reading lesson.

She stares into the girl's eyes. The child's pupils are large and dilated, her irises thin green rings around pools of black. Soledad nods in recognition. The hierba's taken hold. She sighs, once again questioning her decision: whether her own reading skills, deciphering truth from lie, are something that could...or should be taught. But it's a rough, mean world, and any talent that could give the girl an advantage over the herd isn't something to be wasted.

Time to start the lesson.

"I had chicken for dinner last night," Soledad says, her expression blank, her voice neutral and steady.

The girl frowns. "That's too easy."

"We always start with easy ones," Soledad answers. "You know that." Was she as impatient as Steffa when she was first learning how to separate a man from his stories?

"What did you see?" she asks the girl. "Did you notice anything in my face when I said that?"

Steffa shakes her head. "It wasn't your face. It was how you said it."

"How so?"

"Your voice."

"What about it?"

"There was a little shake in it."

The lesson continues. Soledad notches up the difficulty slowly, moving from obvious lies to more challenging half-truths, omissions, and small exaggerations.

"I had a poodle named Pepper with gray fur," she says, though she always thought of Pepper's fur as *dark* gray. The girl shakes her head immediately.

"Twitchy eye," Steffa says, grinning proudly.

"I did not," Soledad protests.

"Did too. Did too," the girl argues. "I saw it."

Damn. So little gets past her. The girl's a natural reader.

The child watches Soledad closely, then she tilts her head to one side. "Is this how your mama taught you?"

The words are a sharp jab to Soledad's insides, unexpected and painful. She stares at the girl, stunned.

Steffa's lips quiver, her eyes water. "I'm sorry, Sol. I'm sorry."

Soledad turns her gaze sharply away from the girl and stands up from the chair.

"I just forgot," the girl whimpers. Tears flow down her cheeks, and the whimper escalates into a wail. "I'm sorry. I'm sorry!"

Magnolia the nanny bursts into the kitchen, her old wrinkled face knotted with worry. "What's wrong, child? What's wrong, my dear?" She kneels down next to the sobbing child and runs a soothing hand over the girl's hair.

Soledad swallows, watching as the girl throws her arms around Magnolia's neck and buries her face into the soft white refuge of the nanny's thick hair. "There, there," Magnolia coos, rubbing the girl's back.

The nanny looks up at Soledad and lifts her eyebrows, silently asking what happened. Soledad hesitates, finding that she can't easily answer. Finally, she mouths the words *my mother*, and the nanny gives her a small nod of understanding. A month back, Steffa asked about Soledad's mother during her lesson. *Do you have the same color eyes as your mama?* It was the kind of out-of-nowhere question a child of eight can suddenly ask, in no way related to the topic at hand. A surprised Soledad tried to mask her feelings, but it was too late. The girl—having already chewed the hierba, the bitter-tasting desert plant that enhanced her innate ability to read people—saw everything. Steffa was so traumatized by what she perceived, she immediately burst into a crying fit. And on that day, too, Magnolia thankfully intervened, comforting the girl as Soledad sat at the kitchen table, her mouth agape, feeling gut-kicked.

Soledad approaches the girl and takes one of her hands into hers. "It's okay," she assures her. "It's all right." The bawling girl reacts by yanking her hand away and gripping Magnolia's neck even tighter.

The nanny gives Soledad a wistful smile. "I've got her. She'll be fine."

Awkwardly backing away, Soledad removes the girl's breakfast plate from the table and busies herself with wiping the dish clean. As she cleans up, she gives a silent thanks for Magnolia's presence in their lives. The nanny was hired shortly after they came to live in Dallas, and Soledad originally planned for her to stay with them for a mere matter of weeks, until Soledad became comfortable caring for Steffa on her own. Now, half a year later, Magnolia's still here, and Soledad can't fathom what she would do without her. When Steffa bounces off the condo walls out of boredom, it's Magnolia who always manages to calm her down. When the girl acts out, crying or throwing a fit or pouting, it's Magnolia who intervenes after Soledad's efforts to deal with the headstrong child invariably fail. As time passes, Soledad finds herself trying less and less, knowing that Magnolia will swoop in and let her off the hook. And when the nanny invariably does just that, Soledad always feels an unsettling mixture of relief at the intervention, tinged with guilt over her own shortcomings as a caregiver.

She finishes washing the dishes, placing her own plate

and Steffa's into the drying rack. Behind her the sobbing eventually subsides. Then she feels a tug on the back of her shirt. Soledad turns and sees the girl standing next to her, looking up, her eyes puffy and red.

The girl sniffs and wipes her nose with her sleeve. "I'm sorry I made you so sad."

"You didn't, gorda." Soledad strokes the girl's hair. "You didn't make me sad."

The child starts to say something but stops herself. Soledad stiffens under the girl's gaze, then looks away. For a moment, she forgot Steffa had chewed the hierba, that the girl could see every unconscious giveaway etched on her face, uttered in her voice. Her pain and sadness and melancholy, flashing like a neon sign.

"Well," Soledad corrects herself, looking down at the drying plates. "I know you didn't *mean* to."

"Why don't we go play cards?" Magnolia suggests brightly.

"Yes," Soledad agrees, still turned away from the girl. "We've done enough reading practice for today."

Sensing the girl's hesitation behind her, she turns to face the child, forces a smile, and tousles her hair. "Go on, now. I'm okay."

Magnolia takes the girl's hand and gently turns her toward the hallway leading to her room. "You remember how to play Go Fish, don't you?"

As the nanny shepherds the girl from the kitchen, Soledad smiles painfully at the woman. "Thank you, Magnolia." The nanny smiles back and nods sympathetically, and then Soledad is alone in the kitchen.

She moves back to the window, absently watching the growing bustle of the marketplace. Thin wisps of smoke waft up from the food kiosks. Awnings spread over the brick in a colorful canopy. More people arrive. The city wakes.

She was about Steffa's age when she lived in Dallas with her parents. Her mother would take her to this same market every Friday morning. The vendors stocked up on Fridays, her mother told her. To get ready for the weekend crowds. This made Friday mornings the best time to shop, her mother claimed, and she was right. The fruit stands were always overflowing with oranges and avocados and tomatoes. The fabrics and shirts and pants were unwrinkled and folded up into neat stacks. The merchants were cheery-faced and friendly, giving away samples of chocolates or other treats, anticipating the rush of weekend sales.

It was a different market, all those years ago. Then, robots of all shapes and sizes rolled through the crowd: tall two-legged ones with shopping bags strapped to their backs, running errands for their owners who sent them in their stead; sturdy, boxlike bots with multiple arms, helping a vendor refill his stock; bulky, slow-moving sweeper bots with yellow blinking lights, cleaning the streets.

Today, far below her window, there isn't a single robot to be seen in the market or anywhere else in the city. Dallas' famed robots have become something that now exists only in her memory.

Like her mother.

A knock on the door behind her. "What is it?" she calls, eyes still fixed on the plaza.

"Disculpe," says Paco, the door guard, poking his head into the room. "Una señora para verla."

"Who?" She isn't expecting anyone.

"La comerciante." The trader. There's only one trader presumptuous enough to drop by this early.

"Fine," she says, though she's in no mood for visitors. "Let her in."

She turns as the visitor brushes past the guard and steps into the condo. The guard shuts the door, leaving them alone.

Indigo Cruz stands in the entryway with her hands on her hips, surveying the spacious room. "Not bad. Not bad at all, Reader Soledad," she says, nodding appreciatively.

"When did you move in?"

"A couple weeks ago," Soledad answers, admiring Indigo's outfit with a similar critical approval. Pants with thigh pockets, red cowboy boots, black shirt covered with a hunter's vest. Everything spotless and unwrinkled and expensive-looking. The look suits her, Soledad decides. Functional yet becoming. Wealthy trader chic.

"New threads?" she asks.

Indigo smiles, opens the vest wide, pivoting on her heel like a runway model from an ancient fashion vid. "The spring line from the hottest designer in Waxahachie," she jokes, lifting her chin and striking a pose.

Soledad smiles back at her. "I heard you went back to your old turf."

"Only for a few days. Wanted to make sure those greenies hadn't run everything into the ground." She joins Soledad over at the window, and a low whistle escapes her lips. "Nice view you got here."

"And did they?"

Indigo shakes her head. "Quite the opposite, truth be told. They're thriving, the little bastards. Opening new trade routes, expanding the old ones. They've got more runners and undertraders than ever." Her tone is one of a proud mother.

"Trade's good all over, I hear," Soledad says.

Indigo nods. "You hear right. And we've got your don Flaco to thank for that. Amazing what a little freedom of movement can do for commerce."

Soledad can't remember a time—prior to these last months—when Texans could travel across the Republic without having to worry about being spotted by gunbirds. For generations, the Dallasites' air force of killer drones patrolled the airways at high, unseen altitudes, raining terror from the skies, assuring Dallas' primacy with the brutal authority of high-caliber bullets and air-to-surface missiles. Few dared to journey across the vast, empty plains and deserts unless there was an absolute, life-or-death necessity. If the turf lords or highway bandits didn't get you, so the general wisdom went, the gunbirds out of Dallas surely would. Only the traders—who kept a constant vigil for drones with their portable radars, sharing the gunbirds' routes on their network shortwave radio frequencies—managed to navigate the wastelands between cities and dangerous territories in relative safety.

But with the drones permanently grounded—their control systems rendered inoperable when the AIs were destroyed—Texans found themselves suddenly free to move about as they pleased. And now, six months after the fall of Dallas to Guzmán's forces, the business of the traders thrives like never before.

"I thought maybe you might decide to stay there," Soledad says.

"Why would I do that?"

Soledad shrugs, looks back down to the plaza. "Not exactly the city on a hill around here anymore."

Indigo gazes through the glass, taking in the view of the city. "True, but Big D is where all the best action is. What kind of trader would I be if I didn't go where the action is?"

The action meant *her* action, of course. As a thanks from Guzmán for her role in helping overthrow the Dallasites, Indigo received a lucrative trade concession. A small percentage of all commerce coming in and out of the city belongs to her. Passive income, she told Soledad one day over beers, smiling with drunken satisfaction. Sweetest setup ever.

Far below, the early shoppers are beginning to arrive, busy ants wandering the winding trails among the food stands and carts and displays.

"You should have seen it before," Soledad says. "Spotless streets, robots everywhere."

"That's right," Indigo says with a sharp sideways glance. "I forgot you grew up here."

"Only until I was eight."

"Still, must've been amazing in those days."

For a long moment, neither speaks as they watch the swelling rivulets of shoppers flowing into the plaza. Years ago, Soledad held her mother's hand tightly in this same market, the noisy crowd pressing in around her. *Don't let go*, her mother told her. *I don't want to lose you.*

"I can't stand this city," Soledad murmurs.

Indigo turns to her. "Bad memories?"

Soledad nods. Months ago she confided in Indigo, telling her the story of her parents' betrayal, how her mother wanted her dead. She wasn't sure why she'd told Indigo so much, why she'd revealed her most intimate horrors to someone she barely knew. Maybe she'd needed to get it off her chest, or maybe it had been a moment of weakness, of poor judgment. Maybe it had simply been the mescal.

Soledad stares blankly at the market. *But you* did *want to lose me.*

Indigo gently places her hand on Soledad's shoulder. "You know one of the worst things you can do when you negotiate a deal?"

Soledad doesn't answer, twisting away from the trader's touch.

"Thinking about the deal you got scammed on the day before," Indigo continues. "Clouds your judgment, looking backwards." She taps the side of her head with a finger. "Poisons your thoughts."

"I'll remember that," Soledad grumbles, suddenly wanting to be left alone.

"The past is the past. No use dwelling on it."

Lost in thought, Soledad barely hears her.

"What the hell's going on down there?" Indigo asks, moving closer to the window.

Something's happening in the market. The crowd of shoppers scatters, rushing for side streets. Vendors, too, are abandoning their stalls and kiosks at a run. Pandemonium.

"Shots?" Soledad wonders aloud.

"I didn't hear anything," Indigo answers.

As she scans the emptying plaza, Soledad detects a low, drumlike THUD-THUD-THUD. "You hear that?"

"Hear wha—"

"Shhh!"

The thudding sound grows louder. Indigo's brow knits in concentration as she listens. "It sounds like a…"

"A what?" Soledad asks, raising her voice above the thickening sound. She can feel it now, a palpable force on her skin, a pounding in her ears. In front of her the window quivers, reverberating from the now-deafening THUD-THUD-THUD.

"DOWN!" Indigo shrieks, her voice barely audible. She yanks Soledad to the floor. Both women cover their heads reflexively, as if the building itself might collapse on them.

At the corner of her vision, Soledad glimpses something outside the glass. She raises her head and looks, the condo vibrating violently as the belly of a helicopter appears. The thundering machine is so close Soledad can see the tire tread of the landing gear. A pair of chain guns hangs underneath the carapace like small cannons. Bundles of rockets sit beneath small wings.

The chopper slowly floats away from the building, toward the center of the city. The intense sound of its rotors fades. The two women stand back up, breathing heavily, staring at the departing copter with open mouths. Behind them, the door guard bursts into the room, pistol drawn.

Soledad shows him her palms. "We're fine," she insists, her heart throbbing in her chest. "Fine."

Magnolia appears behind the guard, carrying Steffa, the girl's arms and legs wrapped around her like a frightened baby monkey.

The guard's eyes go wide as he sees the chopper. "¿Qué chingados es eso?"

"My thoughts exactly," Indigo says, straightening her

vest. "I didn't think Guzmán had any choppers."

"He doesn't," the guard says, holstering his pistol. "Not like that, at least."

Outside the window, the helicopter descends, disappearing behind a pair of buildings. Soledad and Indigo exchange looks.

"City Hall?" Soledad asks.

Indigo nods her answer. "We should get over there."

*   *   *

An armored Humvee carries Soledad and Indigo toward the city center, slowly snaking its way through eerily empty and quiet streets. A security detail of four surrounds the vehicle, jogging and brandishing M-16s, alert eyes moving back and forth, warily scanning for danger.

The door guard didn't want the pair to leave the security of the building, but Indigo overcame his objections, browbeating him, assuring him he'd be working as a street cleaner within a day if he delayed them another minute. Eventually, the guard relented, sending a security detail with them.

Now Soledad sits beside Indigo in the backseat of this armored chariot, gazing out the darkened window. The taste of hierba lingers in her mouth, coating her tongue with a bitter stickiness. She hurriedly chewed some leaves as they left her building, and now she feels the first tingling sensations of its effect. Soft tendrils move through her mind, gently waking her awareness. In another fifteen minutes, her perception will be wide open, dilated like a camera's aperture on the widest setting, and she'll see everything. Every subcutaneous muscle twitch, every change in breathing pattern, every minute vibration in a voice. Everything others can't see or hear, she'll detect easily, parsing lies from truth, reading intentions and emotions in countless giveaways invisible to anyone without the innate talent and the chemical help of the hierba's leaves. Invisible to anyone but a reader.

The truck moves through the city's valleys. Towering buildings of glass and steel rise to the sky on every side. People emerge cautiously from the alleys and doorways, their faces turned upward with worried expressions, as if expecting another monstrous air machine to appear at any moment. The driver turns the Humvee around a corner and brakes to a stop.

"Ay mamita," he utters, staring at the strange scene in front of him with his mouth agape.

Soledad gasps. The helicopter sits in the center of City Hall Plaza, surrounded by a dozen armed, body-armored soldiers. Strange-looking helmets like mirrored globes cover their heads and faces. Curious onlookers gather in alleyways and crowd building entrances, their curiosity outweighing their fear.

"Ever seen armor like that?" Soledad asks the driver.

"Never."

"Let's go the other way," Indigo suggests.

"Yes, ma'am," the driver answers, shifting the truck into reverse and retreating to a side street, escorts trotting alongside. As the Humvee turns, Soledad gets a full view of the side of the chopper and the large white letters emblazoned along the tail.

Oh, Christ. She places her hand over her mouth.

U.S. ARMY.

CHAPTER 3

Guzmán paces back and forth along the basement wall, seething. "Right in front of my office," he hollers into a handheld radio. "How the hell can they land right in front of my office without a single maldito shot being fired?"

A dozen armed soldiers fill the small, cramped room, illuminated by a single lightbulb dangling from the ceiling. Chavez stands next to his jefe, chattering into his own radio.

The explanation comes back as a profusion of apologies that do nothing to quench the flame of Guzmán's outrage. The last thing his troops at City Hall—and across the entire city, for that matter—expected or planned for was a threat from the air. American drones have patrolled the border like vicious, airborne guard dogs since Secession, shooting up anyone who dared to cross the border, but never once has the US made an aerial foray into Texan airspace. With a thousand other problems to solve in his newly captured city, Guzmán didn't bother to set up ground-to-air defenses for what seemed to be a nonexistent threat.

Disgusted, Guzmán clicks off the radio and tosses it to a soldier. How could he have been so blind? So inept?

"This is what happens," he snaps at Chavez, "when you spend all your time sitting on your ass in an office, signing papers." He taps the side of his head. "You take your mind off what really matters."

Chavez lowers the radio from his mouth. "Jefe, we have to go." He jerks his head toward the door on the far wall, the entrance to a half-mile tunnel excavated for emergencies exactly like this one. Twelve blocks to the east, at the underground passage's exit, armored trucks idle and security forces wait, ready to whisk their leader to safety.

"Are they still in the chopper?" Guzmán asks.

"Jefe, we can't risk staying here—"

"Are they STILL IN THE CHOPPER?" Guzmán repeats.

Chavez stares at his jefe a moment, as if he's debating whether or not he should answer. "Sí," he finally admits.

Guzmán folds his arms across his barrel of a chest, lifts his chin defiantly. "Entonces no me muevo. I'm not going anywhere." Don Flaco's not going to run like a scared child, not without knowing the score, not without knowing what these gringos are after. He fixes his eyes on Chavez. The room goes silent, and for a long moment neither man speaks. Then Chavez lets out a long, slow breath, his shoulders slumping almost imperceptibly into acquiescence. A half-smile emerges on Guzmán's face, one side of his mustache lifting upward.

From the escape tunnel behind him, the rebel leader hears shouting.

"Puta madre," Chavez exclaims. "They found the tunnel!" He signals Guzmán's bodyguards, who grab his jefe by the shoulders and begin to hustle him away.

Guzmán pulls his arms free. "Wait, wait." He puts a finger over his lips, quieting his crew. The voices grow louder, recognizable now.

The escape tunnel door flies open. A dozen shotguns rise toward the doorway.

Soledad Paz and Indigo Cruz stand in the doorway, breathing heavily, staring wide-eyed at the weapons trained on them.

A soldier appears behind the two women, shoulders past them. "I tried to stop them, don Flaco," she insists, her face twisted in frustration. "But they wouldn't—"

"It's fine," Guzmán says, waving the soldier quiet. "Go back to your post." Then to the rest of the room: "Stand down, compadres." The soldiers lower their guns.

Guzmán nods at the two women, trying to mask his anger but not entirely succeeding. "Welcome to the party."

"Now turn right back around," Chavez barks. "We're leaving."

"Like hell," Guzmán snaps.

"Who came in that copter?" Soledad asks. "What do they want?"

"We don't know," Guzmán answers. He tells them what he does know: that the helicopter appeared out of nowhere and landed in front of City Hall; that not a shot was fired by either his troops or the chopper; that whoever's inside is still there, waiting for who knows what.

"They want to talk," Indigo says, prompting incredulous looks from Guzmán, Chavez, and the soldiers.

"Talk?" Guzmán blurts.

"Claro," Indigo insists. "They appear out of nowhere, playing the big shot, showing off their big, bad war machine and hotshot soldiers. They're trying to set the stage, showing up like this in the middle of your turf."

In the middle of your turf. The trader's words prick Guzmán like a bee sting. How had he not planned for something like this? *Soft, you old bastard. All this sitting around's made you soft.*

"If they weren't here to talk," Indigo continues, "they could have settled this with a single rocket shot from ten thousand feet in the air." She shrugs. "We've got no gunbirds in the sky protecting us. It's not like we could do anything about it."

Guzmán stares at the trader, whose words manage to pierce through his outrage and the adrenaline pumping through his veins. It dawns on him that she's right. No other explanation makes the least bit of sense. Jesus, he thinks, he really is losing his touch. Something so obvious right in front of his eyes and he failed to see it.

He takes a deep breath and nods appreciatively at the trader. She never seems to lose her cool, Trader Indigo. Always sizing up a situation with uncanny accuracy. At first he wasn't sure what to make of her, but in the past months she has become a valued voice within his inner circle, and not only for her sharp assessments. She also possesses a keen, profound understanding of the vast hinterlands of the Republic, its countless turfs and towns, its fragile economics, its thin scattering of resources.

He chews on her assessment, rubbing his beard stubble in contemplation. "So they want to talk."

His anger dissipates as a flood of curiosity overwhelms him. Why *are* the Americans here? What do they want? What do they want *with him*? He's never met a gringo before, a real *American* gringo, but he knows enough history not to trust one.

"Jefe, I don't like it," Chavez offers.

"A trap?" Guzmán asks. "That's what you're thinking, compadre?"

Chavez nods.

Old Chavez, cautious and careful as always. He may be right, though. But whether it's a trap or not, Guzmán needs to act, needs to change the game. Right now, hiding out like this, he's playing *their* game, and it doesn't sit well in his gut. He's not going to be one-upped by gringos on his own turf. No, señor.

He turns to Soledad, close enough to see the look on her face, the dilation in her pupils that has nothing to do with the darkness of the room. "Hierba?" he asks, a flicker of confidence igniting somewhere inside him.

She nods.

A smile creeps across Guzmán's face. The gringos may have surprised him with their first move, but he's not without tricks of his own.

"Let's go meet these gringos," he announces. "Vamos."

CHAPTER 4

Anxiety and fear. Those were the main vibes Soledad felt moments ago in the dank air of the basement. Anxiety and fear, registering clear and obvious on every involuntary twitch of the soldiers' eyes, on every minute twinge in their voices. Don Flaco was the exception. With him Soledad sensed anxiety, yes, but also a strong undercurrent of curiosity, and, strangely, eagerness. Now she makes her way through the twisting hallways and up flights of stairs with Guzmán's wide frame marching in front of her. Chavez and Indigo follow behind, the soldiers forming a protective barrier around the four of them.

She notices the vigor in don Flaco's quick, purposeful steps. The rush of a ravenous man hurrying to a buffet.

Soledad can't remember the last time she was able to observe Guzmán, to read him in the same way she's read countless others on his behalf, helping him separate truth from lie, friend from foe. Don Flaco has always been careful to avoid her when she's under the hierba's influence. Notoriously secretive, he's always kept his motives to himself, his cards hidden, from her and the rest of his inner circle. But even with all his caution, there have been times, like now, when he couldn't avoid being around his reader while her perception was wide open, and in those times Soledad gathered as much as she could about the man and his way of thinking. What he liked, what he hated, what excited him, what bored him. Most importantly, what touched his innermost core, the wounds and tender spots everyone tries to hide, the vulnerabilities and self-truths that can't escape the finely honed, inescapable perception of a trained reader. But despite her powerful skills, she still feels as if she's only seen the tip of the Guzmán iceberg, that the greater part of the man remains submerged, hidden to her.

"My office," Guzmán huffs. "They're set up in *my* office. The cojones these gringos have."

Behind Soledad, Chavez grumbles something under his breath. A minute later, they exit the stairwell on the tenth floor, where a single American soldier stands guard at the door of Guzmán's office. His mirrored helmet glints in the sunlight slanting in from the hallway window. Across his midsection, he holds a large rifle, his finger on the trigger guard.

"Gringo roadblock," Indigo mutters. The entourage stops.

"Tranquilo, muchachos," Guzmán tells his soldiers. Soledad senses their tension rising. Small neck muscles tighten with stress. Rib cages expand, sucking in nervous breaths.

"Only Guzmán," the American soldier's voice blares, amplified through his helmet.

"I need my three advisers," Guzmán answers.

"My orders were clear, sir," the soldier responds. With his face completely covered by the helmet and his voice altered, Soledad can't read him. He might as well be a robot, she thinks, and for a panicked moment she wonders if the soldier actually *is* a robot. Do gringos use robots instead of flesh and blood soldiers? What if they do? The soldier then shifts his weight from one foot to the other, and Soledad exhales in relief. A conspicuous, all too human giveaway. The soldier's just a man after all.

"I'm not coming in without them," Guzmán adds, his voice firm and unwavering.

A tense minute of silence passes as the group waits for a reply. Soledad feels the soldiers' unease hanging in the air, thick and heavy, causing the hairs on her forearms to stand up. From beyond the office door, the faint sounds of murmuring voices break the silence.

"Anyone ever tell you look like a big lollipop in that helmet?" Guzmán calls over to the American.

Around her, don Flaco's soldiers chuckle, and the tension in the hallway eases. The object of Guzmán's joke doesn't respond, but Soledad notices an annoyed shift in the American's posture. Definitely not a robot, she thinks.

Finally, the soldier apparently gets the okay from his superiors. In his electronic voice he announces that don Flaco's advisers may enter. The door behind him opens, and he steps to one side for the four to pass.

Inside, three men and a woman stand shoulder to shoulder. The woman and two of the men wear military fatigues, and they watch the Texans with sharp stares as they enter the room. The third man is dressed in a sharply pressed suit. Wide lapels with an American flag pin, tapered pants, shiny leather shoes. The man himself is trim, fiftyish, thick blond hair combed straight back from his tanned face. The man smiles, revealing a perfect set of pearl-white teeth, and waves the group inside like a host welcoming guests to a dinner party.

Soledad blinks and stares dumbly at them. *Americans. Actual gringo Americans.* She's seen them in bootleg movies, but she's never met one in person before.

The suited man greets them. "Come in, please, come in."

The man's air and manner feel at once familiar, reminding Soledad of the hustlers and wannabes she vetted for Guzmán during their nomadic years in the western desert. She read an endless stream of fast talkers

30

who sought an audience with don Flaco, looking to sell land or a cache of weapons or their turf's loyalty or, most often, looking to land a deep-pocketed partner for some once-in-a-lifetime moneymaking scheme. Nine times out of ten they were either flat-out lying or stretching the truth so far—exaggerating the benefits of their can't-miss, one-of-a-kind opportunity—they might as well have been.

Guzmán enters the room last. The suited man's eyes light up, his smile widening. "Señor Guzmán," he beams in gringo-accented Spanish. *Seeeen-your.* "Es un placer. Such a delight to meet you."

"Mucho gusto," Guzmán responds, nodding politely.

Introductions follow. Hands are cautiously offered for shaking. Decorum observed with tense, uneasy cordiality. The woman is a general named Bennett. Short-cropped white hair and the clear, sharp eyes of a hawk. She presents Captain Quinn, a man who looks ten years her junior, maybe mid-forties. Soledad gathers that Quinn is the general's right hand, just like old Chavez for don Flaco. The other uniformed man is Garcia, the whitest of the white group, despite his surname. A fair-skinned redhead, freckled and visibly anxious, he doesn't appear to be out of his late twenties.

The man in the business suit presents himself last. "And I'm Roman Kennedy with the State Department," he says, bowing his head with what strikes Soledad as false humility, "at your service."

State Department. Soledad searches through the encyclopedia of her mind, trying to recall the State Department's role from the history books of her childhood library. Part of the executive branch, same as the president, if memory serves. Foreign relations, among other things.

Guzmán presents his three companions without titles, simply giving first names, an informality that visibly amuses the Americans. Soledad suppresses a grin at their reaction. *First point, don Flaco.* It's an old ploy, an opening move in a chess game she's seen him play a hundred times: assuming the role of the simple peasant, the uneducated brute whose proficiencies begin and end with fighting and warfare. El indito ignorante. The American named Kennedy (such a gringo name!) seems especially taken in by Guzmán's act. His eyes shine with the confidence of a man who thinks he's won the argument before the first word has been spoken.

"Shall we sit?" Kennedy suggests, waving a hand at the long table next to the far wall.

Soledad takes a seat near the end, where the angled view will allow her to watch the gringos' faces unobtrusively, moving from face to face with only the slightest shift of her gaze. Still, it's a less-than-ideal setup. She's usually not in the room during a read, where her quiet, incessant staring might make her subjects self-conscious and less readable. Under normal circumstances, she'd be hidden behind a one-way mirror or tucked away unseen into some concealed space. But clearly these are far from normal circumstances, so she has little choice but to try to be discreet. And staring at someone *discreetly* is no easy task.

Kennedy, obviously the one in charge, sits in the center, opposite Guzmán, with General Bennett to his right. Quinn takes his place next to the general, and as he sits he places a book-sized wooden box on the tabletop. It reminds Soledad of the jewelry cases sold in the bazaars, only nicer, with a smooth lacquered finish and inlaid rosewood flowers. Nearest to Soledad is the redheaded Garcia. His green American eyes dart back and forth, his flaring nostrils suck in deep, anxious breaths.

Kennedy reaches over for the box and slides it across the table to Guzmán. "This is for you," he says, with an air of formality.

Guzmán eyes the offering suspiciously. He doesn't move to touch it.

"It's a gift," Kennedy adds. "From your American

cousins."

Soledad watches as her patrón slowly reaches for the box and opens the lid. Inside, there's a roll of white silk cloth. Guzmán removes the cloth and unfurls it, revealing a foot-long twig with long, slender leaves sprouting from both sides. He picks it up between his thumb and forefinger, examines it, then looks over at the Americans, his face clouded over with apparent bewilderment.

"An olive branch," Kennedy clarifies.

Guzmán nods thoughtfully, his fake confusion so convincing that even Soledad nearly buys it. He knows, of course, what an olive branch looked like. His vast grove of manzanilla trees in the hill country had been one of the most prized spoils of his rebellion. Soledad remembers the weeks he spent walking the rows of trees, watching laddered workers collect the plump green harvest. His farmer's interest in the oil-pressing process.

The heavy-handed symbolism of the Americans' gesture surely isn't lost on him, either. Guzmán has always had a fascination with history, with the lessons to be gleaned from the past: the blunders he could avoid; the shrewd tactics he could replicate to his advantage. Soledad has borrowed dozens of historical texts from Guzmán's extensive library over the years.

"A gesture of goodwill," Kennedy continues, "from our country to yours."

"Gracias," Guzmán replies, laying the branch on the table.

"And on behalf of my country, I'd like to offer—though somewhat belatedly, I confess—our congratulations on your victory over the Bullocks. An amazing military success, don Flaco. One for the history books."

Guzmán nods again, acknowledging the compliment. "Gracias," he repeats.

The American's flowery words have no effect on Chavez, seated next to his jefe. He stares at the Americans, his body language tense and wary. On his face he wears his normal scowl. His *perma-frown*, as Indigo had once called it, a poke that amused Soledad as much as it annoyed Chavez. Soledad moves her gaze to Indigo, who she perceives to be the most relaxed person in the room. Or perhaps the least stressed, Soledad corrects herself. The trader inhales and exhales in slow, calm breaths. Her facial muscles are loose, her eyes steady. It takes a lot to fluster the wily Indigo Cruz, a quality Soledad has come to admire over the last months.

Kennedy clears his throat. "Things are changing in the States, don Flaco."

"For good or bad?" Guzmán asks.

"For the good, I hope."

"But you're not sure?" Guzmán adds, leaning forward on his elbows.

Kennedy lifts his eyebrows thoughtfully. "You can never be sure of the future, I find, no matter how inevitable it may seem. Tomorrow always keeps some surprises you can't envision today."

Soledad watches the gringo carefully. He leans forward, matching Guzmán's posture. "I can see you're a direct man, don Flaco. A plain talker, like myself."

Lie. The gringo strikes Soledad as a word-spinner, about as far from a plain talker as you can get.

"Do you know how long it's been since the States has had formal contact with Texas?" Kennedy asks. Guzmán shakes his head, though Soledad suspects he knows the exact number of years and months.

"Seventy-eight years last month," Kennedy says.

"A long time," Guzmán observes.

"Seventy-eight years," Kennedy repeats, "until this morning." He taps the tabletop for emphasis. "Until this *very* moment."

"So why now?" Chavez blurts out. "Why are you here?" The outburst prompts a harsh look from his jefe.

Kennedy's face lights up, as if he's been waiting for this

exact question. "Because, unlike in years past, now *we can*."

The gringo's eyes sparkle. "Let me explain what I mean." For decades, he begins, the Bullock clan exerted total, unchallenged control over the Republic. With their hegemony over the Texas economy, they enriched themselves and their loyalists, living an existence of comfort and leisure in their well-protected Dallas stronghold. And with their drone air force, they kept a constant, brutal vigil on the Republic's countless towns and turfs, eliminating enemies and potential threats with impunity. It's a history lesson Soledad and her companions, born and raised in the shadow of the Dallasite regime, know far better than Kennedy does.

"No small number of my colleagues thought they'd remain in power for a hundred years more," Kennedy explains. "But then you came along, don Flaco, and changed everything."

It hadn't been quite as simple as the American's words imply. Soledad was there when it all went down, when Dallas fell. A few strokes of luck had helped, and more than a few sacrifices. A pang of sadness cuts through her at the memory of Lela, the soldier who'd been her bodyguard, her confidant, her substitute mother, murdered days before the fall of Dallas.

"The Bullocks never wanted anything to do with the States," Kennedy says. He recounts several attempts by the US to establish informal, back-channel communications with the Dallasites, only to be rebuffed on every occasion.

Guzmán straightens up in surprise, then glances over at Soledad. She stares blankly back at him. She doesn't cough or sniff or clear her throat, the three prearranged signals they'd agreed to earlier if she detected a lie or near-lie exaggeration. The gringo's telling the truth.

Kennedy notes Guzmán's reaction. "I understand Americans reaching out in good faith to Texans may come as something of a surprise to you," he says. It's as large an understatement as Soledad has ever heard. The *very idea* of

Americans being anything other than downright *hostile* toward Texans—even wealthy Texans named Bullock— seems unimaginable.

The States' contempt for the Republic was a constant theme in the lives of all Texans. American hate was at the center of Texan folklore for generations, the foundation upon which their nation's sad tale was built. Soledad has read the accounts in histories from Guzmán's library: the breakdown in diplomacy in the years leading up to Secession; how relations immeasurably worsened after Texas declared independence. There were even calls for war from a zealous American minority. But despite the heated rhetoric on both sides, for the first few years after Secession, ties between the two countries remained strained but salvageable.

Then the Crisis changed everything.

During the Great Carbon Crisis, as the history books called it, global energy markets suffered a swift, unprecedented contraction, crippling the world economy for decades. And Texas, still on wobbly financial legs in its first years as an independent nation, was devastated, its economy collapsing in a matter of weeks. A mass exodus ensued, and millions of Texans fled northward, seeking jobs where there were few to be found. And like Mexicans of an earlier era who'd crossed the Rio Grande searching for a better life, Texan refugees traversing the Red River were vilified as job stealers and vagrants, scapegoated for all the ills of an anemic, faltering economy. In Washington, D.C., laws were passed to protect American jobs and the integrity of the nation's territorial boundaries. Walls were erected along the States' southern border, drones were dispatched to patrol from the air, and thousands of soldiers were stationed in hastily constructed compounds in Oklahoma, New Mexico, and Arizona. In a remarkably short time, Texas became culturally, economically, and politically cut off from its motherland to the north.

For decades, what a gringo like Kennedy would refer to

as the *non-engagement model* remained unchanged. With the memory of the desperate years of the Crisis still fresh in the minds of voters, no politician dared to even hint at the possibility of reconciliation with the rogue nation.

"But times change," Kennedy says, "and over the years even hardened positions can soften."

Guzmán scratches his beard stubble. "So what is it you've come to offer?" He gives the general a sidelong glance. "Or maybe demand is the right word?"

"Don Flaco, I'm here to explore the possibility of a new openness between our two countries, but only with the Republic's full and voluntary cooperation. We don't want to force anyone to do anything." He nods to the general. "General Bennett is here in a diplomatic capacity, nothing more."

Not lying. Don Flaco looks at Soledad, lifts his eyebrows. She doesn't make a sound, her face still, eyes unblinking.

"But if I may shift topics for a moment, there is one matter that concerns us," Kennedy adds.

Here it comes.

"And what's that?" Guzmán asks.

"It's more of a who than a what, I'm afraid," the gringo says.

Guzmán lifts his chin dubiously. "What do you mean?"

"Well," Kennedy drawls, "if I can be frank, don Flaco, while your faction holds the most territory, it appears that Rev—"

"His *faction?*" Chavez snaps, indignant.

Guzmán lifts a hand, quieting his second-in-command. "It's all right, compadre. He's talking about the preacher." Then to the Americans, he says: "Wright holds Houston, yes, but that's where his influence ends. And he won't hold it for long."

Kennedy and the general exchange a confused look. "I think you mean he only *used* to hold Houston, correct?" Kennedy asks.

Guzmán narrows his eyes at Kennedy. "Why do you say that?"

The gringo clears his throat. "Well, don Flaco, we are aware that Reverend Wright's contingent holds more than Houston."

"Considerably more," the general adds, the bluntness of her tone a counterpoint to the careful diplomacy of Kennedy's.

Again, Guzmán turns to Soledad. Again, she offers no reaction. They're not lying.

Guzmán shoots Chavez an incredulous look. "¿De qué están hablando estos gabachos?" he asks, his voice notching upward in frustration.

Chavez shakes his head. "Ni idea, jefe. Tiene que ser un truco." Like his patrón, Chavez thinks the Americans are playing some game with them.

An extended silence follows, an awkward quiet finally broken by the general. "Don Flaco," she says, "when was the last time you spoke to your people in the west?"

Chavez breaks in. "That's none of your business."

"Cállate, hombre," Guzmán barks, then to Bennett: "A few days ago. We've had some radio trouble."

Bennett and Kennedy give each other a meaningful look. "They don't know," Bennett mutters, the words followed with a disappointed sigh. "They don't know what's happened."

"Don't know *what*?" Guzmán snaps. Soledad notices the tiny veins under his eyes flushing with color, becoming more visible as don Flaco's temper rises.

Kennedy shifts in his chair. "Don Flaco, I'm not sure how to tell you this, but two days ago you lost most of your western territory to Reverend Wright."

Soledad's hand rises to her mouth. *Not lying!*

"Bullshit," Guzmán spits back at Kennedy. "This is some gringo bullshit." He springs up out of his chair, sending it flying backwards and smacking against the floor with a loud whack.

"No es posible," Chavez insists, also rising up defiantly. He slams his palm against the table. "Not possible!"

Soledad looks over at Indigo, still calmly poised in her chair, watching the gringos with her poker player's cool, trying to figure out what to make of them and what they're claiming. The trader casts a furtive glance in Soledad's direction, lifting her chin with a small, barely perceptible movement, asking the question Soledad doesn't want to answer.

Yes, Indigo, they're telling the truth. These gringos are telling the truth.

CHAPTER 5

A picture is worth a thousand words.

The phrase pops into Guzmán's head, an expression he recalls from a gringo book in his library. He's never understood its significance until this moment, as he runs his eyes over dozens of hard copy photographs covering every square inch of his office table. Images laid out by the redhead Garcia, taken by high-flying American surveillance drones.

"They took San Angelo first," Garcia says, motioning toward the photos on the far end of the table. Guzmán recognizes San Angelo in the images. Fisher Lake to the northwest. The Concho River snaking its way through the middle of town. "Search algorithms picked up the dust cloud kicked up from all those vehicles," Garcia says. "That's how we were first alerted to their offensive."

A dust cloud three miles wide, the young soldier explains, tapping another photo, this one depicting a high-altitude view of a rolling fleet of vehicles racing across the desert. A steel cavalry hundreds, perhaps thousands, strong. Speechless, Guzmán stares at the photos as Garcia continues telling the story.

The armada came out of the Houston area and headed

northwest at high speed, skirting around the northern edge of Austin and then making a beeline to San Angelo. Garcia steps along the length of the table, touching each photo as he comes to a new part of the story. After San Angelo they took Midland and Odessa, then they grabbed Fort Stockton along with several of the largest natgas fields in the western desert. It took them only a single day to capture the western third of the Republic, a gambit achieved by overwhelming force and what Garcia suspects was an ingenious radio-jamming strategy.

Guzmán looks over at Chavez. The old warrior's forehead creases in concentration as he dubiously examines the imagery. Then he glances at the reader again, hoping for a sign from her. They lock eyes for an instant, but she doesn't give him any of the signals they've agreed on. She only looks away. *Carajo.*

Garcia finishes speaking and the room falls silent. Guzmán doesn't lift his gaze from the photographs. He feels the Americans' eyes on him, waiting for him to say something. He feels the uneasy stares of Reader Soledad, the trader, and Chavez, awaiting his reaction. It's as if even the room itself is holding its breath, unsure what to expect from the famously volatile don Flaco Guzmán.

Guzmán breathes in deeply through his nose. Without looking up, he says: "Would you please let my advisers and me have the room for a moment?"

"Of course, of course," Kennedy answers immediately, as if relieved to be excused from the sudden uncomfortable pressure permeating the room. He ushers his compatriots out the door, shutting it behind them.

Guzmán broods over the photographs, clenching his jaw. Then he straightens up and moves to the window. Far below, the gringo helicopter sits in the plaza like some huge insect.

No, he can't buy it. Won't. The story these gringos are trying to sell doesn't make sense. Where would the preacher have gotten so many vehicles? And is it even possible to take so much territory so quickly? Maybe nothing has happened at all. Maybe the pictures are fakes and it's all some gringo scheme. Maybe the communication problems with the radios are just that: communications problems and nothing more.

"It's bullshit," he grumbles.

Behind him, Chavez bickers with someone on the other end of his hand radio, demanding updates and answers. Guzmán turns to find Soledad and Indigo conferring with each other, their voices low and worried.

"It's bullshit," Guzmán repeats, louder. Chavez and the women stop talking. "It can't be true," Guzmán insists, trying to convince himself as much as the others.

Soledad blinks, pauses before speaking. Ever since he's known her, she's always hesitated before giving him bad news. "They weren't lying, don Flaco," she states. "I wish they were, but I didn't see anything."

"Maybe you missed it," he suggests pointedly. "Maybe they're better at lying than you are at what you do."

If his reader's offended by the jab, she doesn't show it. She simply shakes her head. "No," she says gently. "I'm sorry, don Flaco, but I'm sure about it."

A sick feeling rises inside him. She's never steered him wrong before. Not once. God damn that gift of hers! As improbable as it seems, as much as he doesn't want to believe it, he can't deny what Reader Soledad sees.

¡Puta madre, puta madre, puta madre!

He looks down at the mess of building permits and housing applications and commercial charters strewn across the desktop. This desk. This *goddamned* desk he's planted his ass behind for countless hours, growing soft and lazy, signing endless stacks of papers, when he should have been out hunting down that fat preacher instead.

Furious, he bends down and grasps the underside of the wood in a firm grip, a hand on each side. Then like a weightlifter, he yanks it up in a single motion, groaning with the strain, flipping the desktop onto his shoulder. A chaos of papers flies into the air, scattering across the floor.

"Don Flaco!" Chavez shouts.

"Holy shit," Indigo exclaims, quickly stepping back and pulling Soledad with her.

Guzmán pivots to the window and launches the desk with a heave, sending it flying through the glass. Shards explode outward, raining down onto the plaza below. He stumbles forward, his momentum nearly carrying him out with the desk. He teeters on the edge, and for a moment he sees himself falling after it, his angry momentum pulling him out and downward. Then from behind Chavez clutches onto his upper arms, steadying him. The wind whips Guzmán's hair as he watches the desk descend, tumbling end over end. It crashes onto the pavement, splintering into a thousand pieces.

*   *   *

Guzmán gazes ruefully at the jagged hole where his office's window used to be. "That was a good desk," he laments, making a halfhearted sign of the cross at the broken window. "Que descanse en paz." He takes a couple puffs from his pipe, his hand cupped around the bowl, where tobacco glows and softly crackles. He nods at Soledad. "We stole it from the preacher in Conroe, remember?"

The reader nods, her expression dropping. Guzmán regrets the reference instantly. *You old fool.* Of course she remembers Conroe. How could she forget it? They lost Lela in Conroe.

He paces back and forth alongside the conference table where Soledad, Indigo, and Chavez sit, their expressions tense in the uncomfortable afterglow of their patrón's fury.

Paces and turns. He goes back over every word the Americans said, taking long, thoughtful inhalations, filling the room with the sweet-smelling haze of his veracruzano tobacco. The preacher. He never should have waited to go after the damned preacher.

"It's my fault, jefe," Chavez confesses. "If we've really lost the west, it's because of me."

Guzmán waves a dismissive hand. "Nonsense, compadre."

"I should have left more soldiers, better radio networks, more—"

"Enough of that," Guzmán interrupts. The decision to keep the bulk of their army in Dallas was one they both considered carefully, but ultimately it was Guzmán's call. They weighed the options, considered the alternatives, known the risks. But in the end, securing the capitol was given priority, a task that required thousands of troops, a tradeoff that meant the west would have to make do with a minimal deployment of soldiers. And, yes, they knew Wright was still out there, alive and holed up in Houston with his Fundie faithful. But that was hundreds of miles away, and the preacher was broke and smarting from his defeat at Conroe, where he'd lost hundreds of fighters and a fleet of vehicles to Guzmán's forces. A threat from Wright didn't seem anywhere near likely. It would take years for him to rebuild his mad army. Or so they thought at the time.

"You think the gringos are helping the preacher, that this is some kind of trick?" The very idea gnaws at his Guzmán's gut.

"Claro," Chavez answers. "Between a brown-eyed Mexican and a blue-eyed Christian, who do you think they're going to help?"

"Maybe," Guzmán says, turning on his heel, though he doubts things are as simple as that.

"I didn't sense that," Reader Soledad counters.

Guzmán stops pacing. "No?"

The reader shakes her head. "They struck me as sincere, like they were genuinely interested in…"

"In what?" Guzmán prompts.

"In helping us," she says.

Chavez grunts his disagreement. "Imposible."

"What else did you see?" Guzmán asks the reader.

Reader Soledad's eyes take on a faraway look, as if she's focusing on some distant point beyond the building's wall. "I didn't see any lies, but they were being very careful with their words. I sensed there's more they want to tell us, but they're not sure if they can trust us. Not yet, anyway."

"That it? ¿Nada más?"

"That's it," the reader replies.

Guzmán then lifts his chin at Indigo. "Trader, what's your take?"

Indigo shrugs. "If they really want to help us, it's easy enough to find out."

Guzmán nods, considering the trader's words. A grin slowly emerges. He knows what to do.

"Compadre," he bellows to Chavez, "bring the gringos back in."

Moments later, the four Americans shuffle through the doorway, their eyes drawn to the shattered window. They exchange uneasy glances among themselves.

Guzmán removes the pipe from his mouth and smiles magnanimously, the gaping hole directly behind him. "Friends, I'd like to show you something."

*   *   *

"Wow, this is *vintage*." Garcia holds up the protective tarp with one hand and runs his other along the nosecone of a Reaper Mark X. He looks back over at General Bennett, his expression that of a child who's just found a long-lost toy. "We used these as trainers in flight ops school. I could take this bird apart and put it back together again in three hours."

It's been months since Guzmán has been to the old airport on the outskirts of the city, to the cavernous hangar where hundreds of mothballed gunbirds sit gathering dust.

When they first took Dallas, he and Chavez would come out every morning, pressuring the technicians to get the drones up and running. But no matter how they cajoled, bribed, or threatened them, the crews were never able to get the machines operational. It became the single-most disappointing frustration of his Dallas victory: the slow realization that the fleet of drones he'd captured would never become airborne again. It was like having an arsenal of guns without a single cartridge of ammunition. The AIs, he'd disappointedly learned, had run the show. They'd performed ongoing maintenance with specialized robots, they'd modified the operating systems as well as the surveillance and engagement algorithms, and they'd undertaken the myriad tasks required to keep hundreds of drones airborne twenty-four-seven. With such expertise at the Dallasites' disposal, human hands had become obsolete tools, rarely touching the machines. The men and women running the Dallas security apparatus took the roles of strategists and priority-setters. At some point the human expertise in drone operation had been lost entirely, if indeed it had ever been there in the first place.

Chavez flicks switches on the wall, and the enormous space lights up section by section, revealing long rows of aircraft wrapped in canvas cloth, their bodies hidden except for the wheeled landing gear protruding from underneath, giving the aircraft the appearance of poorly wrapped presents.

"Grounded since we took the city," Guzmán announces, his voice echoing off the hangar's aluminum walls. He turns to Kennedy. "But I guess you know that already."

Kennedy nods, flanked by Bennett and Quinn. Soledad and Indigo hover near the fascinated Garcia, who removes the canvas entirely, revealing the whole of the aircraft's truck-sized fuselage.

Guzmán fixes Kennedy with a cool stare. "Help us get them flying again."

The answer comes quickly, as if Kennedy expected the question. "I'm afraid that kind of decision is outside my charter, don Flaco," he says diplomatically.

Rubbing his beard stubble, Guzmán says: "You're here to build new relationships, yes?"

"Of course," Kennedy answers, "but—"

"Then this can be your first investment in our friendship," Guzmán interrupts. "I can't think of any better way to show us that you're truly our friend." He glances over at Chavez, finds the old bear smiling.

Kennedy clears his throat, visibly searching for the right words. "If it were up to me…" He pauses. "Things are more…complicated than perhaps I might like them to be."

"Complicated how?" Guzmán presses.

"Don Flaco," Kennedy says, recovering his composure. "Put yourself in my place for a moment. You'd like to reach out to someone you've never met in person, although your two families have a long shared history. This history can be the foundation you build a relationship upon: common ground, shared values, and so forth. Would a wise course of action be to place your complete trust in this person immediately? Would you, for instance, lend this virtual stranger a large sum of money? Or would it be more prudent to first build trust step by step?"

Guzmán eyes the gringo. It's a smart answer. The right answer. The same answer he'd give if the situation were reversed.

Damn. Well, it was worth a shot. He would have loved to rain hellfire from the skies on that preacher's head, but the wiser part of him knew the gringos wouldn't simply say yes. Killing Wright won't be an easy task. But then nothing worth doing ever is. He stares at the gunbird as Garcia pulls the tarp back over the nosecone, covering the aircraft once again.

"So then what's the first step?" Indigo asks, breaking the silence.

"Well," Kennedy replies, "my colleagues and I believe building goodwill in person, face-to-face, is imperative."

"Which is why you're here," Guzmán observes.

"Indeed. In my experience, the politics of the personal can be a quite powerful tool. And we all know what a persuasive, charming presence don Flaco possesses. Not just anyone could have garnered such dedication and loyalty from so many."

Guzmán readies himself for whatever card the gringo's about to play. You don't kiss someone's ass like this unless you're leading up to something big.

"Unfortunately, my friends," Kennedy continues, pursing his lips in a way that strikes Guzmán as rehearsed, "not everyone back home shares my colleagues' and my enthusiasm for a new openness between our countries." The American pauses for a moment, then lifts an index finger. "But," he says with sudden brightness, "with your help, don Flaco, I believe we can win a lot of hearts and minds."

Por Dios, this gringo can talk.

Kennedy continues, extolling the virtues of diplomacy and meaningful engagement, a kind of sales pitch that stretches on, his words floating close to the topic without penetrating it, a cautious hummingbird hovering near an unfamiliar flower. Still, when he finally gets to the point, even though he's hinted at it for the last few minutes, the ask still hits Guzmán like a splash of cold water.

"Don Flaco, we'd like to invite you to visit the United States."

CHAPTER 6

Located in a sprawling villa on the northern border of Main Street Park, Blue Horizon was once the most exclusive nightclub in all the Republic. Even for the richest Dallasites, admission into its darkened corridors and well-appointed private rooms was no easy ticket. Only with the right mix of well-targeted bribes and carefully managed connections could one gain access. For the ultra-elites, it was a place to be seen, to gossip, to make deals. For the less connected, those who tricked or cajoled their way in, Blue Horizon was a place to seduce wealthy men and women or curry favor with the uppermost crust of the Republic's power brokers.

Nearly every fixture was imported from the States via the black market or through those special connections that had forever existed between the mega-rich of neighboring countries. The kind of connections that made even the strictest trade embargoes little more than an inconvenience, a fee adder that simply made imports more expensive rather than unattainable. A designer from New York provided all the furniture, low-slung and contoured, upholstered in the latest Chinese microsilk that danced with colors like the rainbow scales of a tropical fish.

Massive Baccarat crystal chandeliers hung in every room. Huge canvases of pre-Secessionist pop art adorned the walls. Warhols and Lichtensteins. Mounted over the main bar was an enormous work from Texas native Robert Rauschenberg, a jumbled collage of colorful magazine photos from another era. Vietnam-era helicopters firing missiles, flying in a landscape of cigarette ads. In the center of the club, patrons lounged in a large open-air courtyard with koi ponds and lush, immaculate gardens lined with pathways paved in Brazilian blue granite.

Now, six months after the fall of Dallas to Guzmán's troops, Blue Horizon is a trashed-out distortion of its former elegance. The artwork is gone, smuggled out when the wealthiest Dallasites, realizing their city was lost to the upstart rebellion, fled the city in a panicked rush aboard overloaded helicopters and private jets, bound for friendly Caribbean regimes. Graffiti and bullet scars decorate the walls where priceless art once hung. Gone too is the stylish furniture, looted by incoming soldiers in the early days of Guzmán's victory. In the courtyard's overgrown chaos, fishless ponds overflow with scum and algae.

Soledad sits alone at a rusted wrought-iron table in a hidden corner of the courtyard, obscured by a pair of thick-canopied Japanese maples. Three security guards hover nearby, keeping watch over her. Behind dark glasses, Soledad's distant, disinterested eyes watch a barefisted boxing match at the courtyard's opposite end, where two enormous men fight in an improvised ring of four metal posts connected by thick lengths of hemp rope. A few dozen spectators surround the ring, shouting and cheering the fighters on.

Soledad fidgets in her chair, wondering how much longer she'll have to wait.

"Enjoying the fight?" Indigo appears, arming her way through a maple branch. One of the bodyguards steps quickly forward, then in the next moment recognizes her and slowly moves back to his sentry post against the wall.

Indigo tosses a folder stuffed with papers onto the table. She spins a chair around backwards and plonks down across from Soledad, then nods at the folder. "That's it. No more gossip and guesses. I've got it all right here." She lifts her chin at a passing waiter and orders two beers.

Soledad stares at the folder. "What does it say?"

"Same as we'd heard in the rumor mill. It says your mother wound up in Barbados, and your father landed in the Dominican Republic."

"How'd they get there?"

Indigo shrugs. "Bribed their way into a refugee visa program like the rest of them, I suppose. But they were still processed by immigration." She taps the folder with her finger. "And that leaves a paper trail. We got copies of their immigration papers and your father's work visa."

The waiter sets down a pair of beers. Indigo raises hers at Soledad. "So mystery solved, I reckon." She sips her beer, then tilts her head at Soledad's lack of reaction. "Thought you'd be relieved."

Soledad keeps her eyes fixed on the folder. "I am, I guess. I don't know." When she began the search for her parents' whereabouts, she was determined to find out where they had escaped to no matter what the cost. And now, several months later, after countless starts and stops and dead ends, after a fortune's worth of payoffs to government clerks across a dozen potential sanctuary countries, she finally has her answers. But it doesn't feel like relief, this numbness that's overcome her. She isn't sure what it feels like.

A chorus of cheers erupts from the far side of the courtyard, drawing their attention. One of the fighters has fallen. A man stands over him, shouting the count, punctuating each number with exaggerated sweeping motions of his hand. The spectators pick up the count, adding their voices. THREE…FOUR…FIVE…

Indigo points a thumb toward the makeshift ring. "Got

any money riding on that?"

Soledad shakes her head, finally swallowing a mouthful from her own glass. Everything else in the city might be falling apart, but somehow the beer still flows and the boxing matches continue to flourish. "Thanks for helping me find out."

The trader shrugs. "Didn't do much more than make sure nobody ripped you off." She lifts her glass again. "But anyway, happy to help."

EIGHT...NINE...TEN.

"How did it go with the gringos?" Soledad asks, moving away from the painful subject of her past and her parents.

"I left the dinner to come here. Don Flaco was passing the mescal bottle around and things were starting to get loud."

"Sounds like they're getting along."

"Why didn't you stick around?"

"When the hierba wears off, I don't need to be there."

At the far end of the courtyard, two men carry away the unconscious fighter, hauling him by the ankles and wrists, chuckling like they just bagged a prize buck on a deer hunt. The victor sits hunched over on a wooden stool in a corner of the ring, elbows on knees, taking large, convulsive breaths. Blood oozes from his knuckles.

"He's going back with them tomorrow morning," Indigo says.

"You're kidding?" It seems like quite a leap of faith, trusting the American strangers enough to leave the security of his Dallas stronghold. "They might throw him in a jail cell for all he knows." She shakes her head. "It's a bad call," she mutters. Indigo doesn't offer an opinion, staring blankly at Soledad.

Another fight's about to begin. A man wearing a black bow tie and a wrinkled blue dress shirt with large pit stains stands in the ring, announcing the boxers as they enter through the ropes. His voice booms, rising and falling as he rattles off the first fighter's record, height, and weight, reminding Soledad of Reverend Wright's melodramatic crescendos and intonations during the sermon she witnessed in Conroe.

"It's a bad call, don't you think?" Soledad repeats, full-voiced.

"You said you felt like they could be trusted."

"No, I said I sensed they wanted to help. That's not the same thing." Soledad shakes her head again. "Hopping on their copter and taking off with a bunch of gringos? Going to their turf? No, too many unknowns. Too many ways for things to go wrong."

"Chavez is going with him."

"Of course he is."

"I'm going, too," Indigo adds, then takes a drink.

Soledad blinks. "*You're* going? Why?"

Indigo swallows, places the glass on the table. "How can you ask me that with a straight face? He set me up with the sweetest trade concession in the Republic. You think I might owe him a favor or two?"

It's the kind of answer she's come to expect from Indigo: the practical, sober realism of a lifelong trader. But then Soledad sees something in Indigo's face, as if she wants to say something more. The hierba's effect has long since worn off, so the look remains a mystery for a couple moments. Until the obvious answer hits her.

Oh shit.

"Don't tell me," Soledad says. "He wants me to come along with a bag of hierba in my pocket."

The trader lifts her glass in salute. "You got it. We be diplomats now."

"Christ." *The United fucking States.* She never imagined she might be able to see it in her lifetime. It's as if she's just heard she'll be taking a trip to Mars.

"You didn't think he'd actually go there without you, did you? That gift of yours is his ace in the hole."

That gift of yours. Soledad's *gift.* She's heard it referred to by that word countless times, by Guzmán, by her parents, by others, but she's long since stopped thinking of it in that way. It isn't a blessing. It isn't something to be cherished. Her ability to see truth, to read people, has brought her far more pain than comfort. For a time she even considered never opening up her perception again. She wanted to see the world like a normal person, through the keyhole view of the conscious mind's limited awareness. She longed for the bliss of ignorance everyone else had.

But then after Guzmán took Dallas, he needed all the help he could get. So much had gone wrong. Her ability to parse truth from lie, to read the true intentions lurking underneath the surface of words, became more invaluable than ever as her patrón wrestled with his new role as administrator-in-chief of the strange, enormous, and thoroughly broken city. So despite her misgivings about her *gift*, she decided to help.

"What do you think he'll do if I say no?" Soledad says flatly.

Indigo's expression drops. "Sorry?"

"You owe him, I get that. But I don't know if it's the same with me."

"You're shitting me." The trader leans forward. "You really thinking about telling him no? Why?"

"Guzmán's losing it."

Indigo settles back into her seat, gesturing to the waiter as the bell rings and another bout begins. "No shit. You don't exactly have to be a reader to see that."

"He's...flailing. He's not making good decisions right now."

"You think this is a bad decision?"

"Right up there with Secession and my parents having a child."

"Come on."

"Seriously. I've never seen him like this. Throwing desks out windows. Racing through the streets on a motorbike like he's got some death wish."

"Like either would be out of line with his reputation," Indigo scoffs.

"Exactly," Soledad replies. "His *reputation*. But his reputation is mostly bullshit. The devil-may-care don Flaco is what he shows to the public, the daring rebel with a smirk on his face. Behind closed doors he's careful and thoughtful. You've been around him long enough to know what I'm talking about. I've never seen him take a big risk unless he's looked at it from every angle, unless he's sure the upside far outweighs the downside. But lately, he just seems…"

"What?"

"Reckless."

The waiter arrives with a fresh pair of beers. "So you're not a flaquista anymore," the trader says, "is that what you're telling me?"

Flaquista, meaning a don Flaco loyalist. It's the word locals used to confirm their allegiance, their devotion to Guzmán's leadership. A way to segregate themselves from those who'd lived in Dallas under the Bullock clan, those of questionable fealty.

Soledad sighs. "I don't know what I'm saying."

Indigo reaches over and lays her hand on top of Soledad's forearm. "Please come. I want you to." Soledad's suddenly aware of the trader's knee under the table, pressing against her thigh.

It's not the first time Indigo has made an advance on her, but it's the first time Soledad feels as if the move is equal parts flirtation and manipulation. She picks up her glass, escaping the trader's grasp. The cold beer sends a chill down her throat.

Across the courtyard a hammer strikes the bell, and another round begins.

CHAPTER 7

The streets are mostly empty as Soledad makes her way back to the condo building on foot, flanked by the watchful trio of her security team. Gonzalez, the woman in charge, tried to talk her out of walking home, but Soledad ignored her, defiantly trudging past the open door of the Humvee that had been sent to pick her up. Her building is ten blocks from Blue Horizon, and a walk in the quiet night air, she decided, would give her some time alone to wrestle with her thoughts, to try to bring some order to the chaos spinning through her head.

Small groups huddle around barrel fires on street corners, reminding Soledad of identical scenes from Guzmán's camps in the desert. Buildings tower overhead, looming and silent. On the lower floors, a scattering of lights flicker in windows, but the largest portions of the buildings remain dark and unoccupied. Residents won't waste precious generator fuel keeping the elevators running, so it's a rarity for anything but the bottommost five or six floors of a building to be used for housing. Once chock-full of wealthy Dallasites, the structures now stand almost entirely empty, enormous husks of steel and glass that for Soledad—despite their still-pristine appearance—already feel like ancient ruins abandoned by peoples of some long-ago time. The city she once called home seems like something from another lifetime.

She replays the events of the day over in her head, unable to make any sense of any of it. The scene of Guzmán throwing the desk through the window pops up again and again. The veins bulging from his neck when he lifts it overhead, the mad rage on his face. The piercing jolt of shattering glass.

He's not himself. Hasn't been himself for months. The Guzmán she served in the desert never lost his temper, never threw a fit like the one she saw today. As she told Indigo, his infamous recklessness was only a pretense, a false trait of his carefully managed modern-day revolutionary persona. In all the countless hours she's spent with him, she's never once known him to be *truly* foolhardy. Until now.

How much does she owe the man, really? Sure, he protected her for a few years, kept her from harm. But during that time she was essentially a slave, unable to come and go as she pleased, never a moment to herself, eyes watching her every minute of every day. He also kept the secret of her parents from her, allowing her to believe they were dead when they weren't, and there was no forgetting that. And she's certainly given far more than she's gotten from their association. Guzmán has been, by a margin as wide as the Republic, the lopsided beneficiary of their relationship.

"It's *her*!" a voice cries.

Soledad looks over. A girl of around twelve gawks from the walkway, her eyes wide, mouth agape. "Look, it's *Soledad*." She points and half a dozen others standing nearby look over, their expressions morphing into identical masks of awed recognition. They repeat her name in excited whispers.

Dammit! Soledad realizes she's left her dark glasses in her pocket, and her head uncovered by her jacket hood.

She forces a smile and says buenas noches, setting off a wave of reverent hands making the sign of the cross, touching foreheads and shoulders with the piousness of pilgrims arriving at a shrine. The standard greeting she gets everywhere she goes these days. In the camps, she was eyed with suspicion and distrust by some, with fear by others. But after the fall of Dallas, the legend of her exploits spread throughout the city, and her status quickly skyrocketed to something akin to a living deity. Awe and adoration began to surround her everywhere she went. Her privacy and anonymity suddenly gone, the strange novelty of her newly found fame quickly became an uncomfortable burden. Strangers accosted her constantly, begging her to foresee their futures or reveal the whereabouts of a long-lost child, as if she were some kind of oracle or fortuneteller. As if she could do such things. To save her sanity, she retreated to the guarded box of her condo building, and on the rare occasions she ventures out, she covers her head with a hooded jacket and keeps her face hidden behind dark-lensed glasses.

She walks on, past the gawking stares, increasing her pace. One more block and she's home.

"Ma'am," Gonzalez says, stopping so abruptly Soledad nearly runs into the back of her, "I think we should go around back."

Half a block away, the entrance to Soledad's building teems with people. At least a hundred people crowd around the lobby doorway.

"What's going on?"

"I don't know, ma'am." Gonzalez speaks into a hand radio, then holds it to her ear as the reply comes back. "They'll open up the back for us."

Soledad watches the crowd for a moment. Even from this distance, she can see the desperation on their faces in the dim glow of the lobby's lights, and the fear.

Gonzalez motions toward a side street that bends around to the back of the building. "This way, ma'am."

Moments later, Soledad's security detail hustles her through the rear entrance and into the waiting elevator. She rides to the top floor and enters her condo, finding Magnolia standing near the window. Steffa is attached to her, clutching her arms around the nanny's waist.

"They've been gathering down there all day long," Magnolia says.

Soledad approaches the window, gazing down at the throng of locals milling about. "What do they want?"

"They want you, my dear," the nanny replies.

"Me? What for?"

"They're frightened about that American helicopter coming in this morning. I suppose they're scared of what it might mean and they're looking for someone to tell them everything's all right."

A ball of dread forms in Soledad's gut. Even if she were built for such things as public speeches—which she's not—what could she possibly say or do to allay their fears? For all she knows, this whole visit from the gringos is some elaborate ruse, some ploy to gain Guzmán's confidence. For all she knows, the crowd's fears are right on the money.

Steffa whimpers, her face buried in the nanny's belly. Soledad kneels down beside her. "Hey, there, girlie. I think you're going to squeeze all the air out of poor Magnolia."

She softly caresses the girl's back. Steffa turns to look, her eyes swollen with tears, her forehead a mess of matted hair.

"She's worried they might come after her," Magnolia says. "I told her that was silly."

"Maggie's right," Soledad agrees. The girl looks at her cautiously, wheels of thought turning behind smart eyes.

"You want to come play cards with me?" Soledad asks.

The girl turns her head away, squeezing the nanny tighter. The reaction jabs Soledad with a sharp sadness. She wishes she could make the girl laugh, take away all her pain. She stands, gazing once more at the churning unease of the crowd far below. So much fear. She saw it on their faces before they hustled her away to the back of the building.

Don Flaco, don Flaco, what have you gotten me mixed up in now?

Turning back to the nanny and the girl, Soledad notices the Virgin of Guadalupe pendant dangling over the girl's shoulder. Lela's heirloom. She brushes it lightly with her finger, feeling the contours of the Virgin's dress, worn nearly smooth from years of pious touches from her late protector.

I hear you, dammit, she says inwardly.

She takes a deep breath, exhales. "Magnolia, can you stay here for a couple nights?"

"Of course," the nanny replies.

Soledad looks down at the top of the girl's head. "I'm going to have to go away for a couple days."

CHAPTER 8

"Puta madre, joven," Guzmán moans, shaking his head at the poor shot grouping on the man-shaped target twenty-five yards away. He drops the empty clip out of the gun and eyes the barrel critically. "Is this a stock sight?"

"I think so, don Flaco," the range manager answers, a pimply-faced kid soldier of around fourteen.

Guzmán tosses the gun aside, holds his palm out. "Give me another one."

The shooting range lies on the outskirts of the city, taking up a wide, flat expanse of switchgrass fields on the banks of the Trinity River. Plywood cutout silhouettes stand, splintered and pockmarked, at varying distances, from twenty-five yards for pistols to over a thousand yards for the long-range rifles carried by Guzmán's eagle-eyed sharpshooters. Small stands with corrugated aluminum roofs offer shade from the already-sweltering sun. Guzmán, the range's only visitor this morning, takes target practice for a solid two hours without stopping, firing off a variety of pistols, rifles, and shotguns. Slowly, his hands become steadier and his eyes become sharper, recalling an almost-forgotten familiarity with each weapon. The range manager assists him, hauling heavy bags full of firearms over his shoulders and feeding his patrón ammunition when his weapon goes empty.

Amazing how it comes back to you, Guzmán thinks, the binoculars pressed to his face as he spies the tight cluster of bullet holes a hundred yards ahead. The target is rounder, fatter than the others, and its silhouette includes the outline of a wide-brimmed hat. A plywood Reverend Wright, complete with a suit of white paint and a red flower drawn onto the lapel. Early-morning sunlight shines through fresh holes in the dummy's belly. Guzmán's grins.

"Excelente," the kid beams. "Well done, don Flaco."

"Gracias." Guzmán hands the range manager the binoculars. "Let's try the AR."

"Sure thing, jefe."

He's been away from the range for too long. He can't remember the last time he fired a weapon before this morning, the last time his wrists ached from recoil and his hands smelled of gunpowder. Was it right after taking Dallas? Yes, that was it. The celebratory bullets he shot into the air after taking the city. After that, he hasn't touched a weapon again until this morning. For too long his hands have been nothing but bureaucratic tools, paper signers, instruments of an administrative machine. The gringos have a saying about the pen being mightier than the sword, but puta madre, the sword is so much more fun to wield!

The kid soldier digs through one of the larger bags, then stops and looks up, his attention diverted to something behind Guzmán. A Jeep rolls to a stop a short distance away, Chavez behind the wheel. He exits the vehicle and joins his jefe under the shooting stand.

"Joven, the AR," Guzmán repeats, ignoring the new arrival. The kid scrambles back to his task, hands Guzmán the rifle, and then moves away to another stand to give the men their privacy.

"Jefe," Chavez says, "we have to get to City Hall. The gringos are waiting."

Guzmán fiddles with the rifle's sights. "Change of plans, compadre."

"¿Cómo así? We're not going with the gringos?"

Guzmán hands Chavez a pair of earplugs. "Some of us are. The trader's going, Reader Soledad's going, and you're going too."

As he finishes screwing the second plug into his ear canal, Chavez furrows his brow.

"I'm not going with you," Guzmán says flatly. He squeezes off a few rounds, then admires the result. "Look at that grouping, compadre. Tighter than a young lover's ass."

Chavez looks as if the round just struck him instead of the target. It takes a long moment for him to find his voice. "Jefe, I don't underst—"

"I'm taking a recon squad out west." More rounds rip downrange. The crudely drawn flower on dummy Wright's lapel explodes into splinters. "Esssso," Guzmán whispers.

"Out west? ¿Al oeste?" Chavez wears the shocked, disbelieving expression of a patient who's just been given a fatal diagnosis. "What good will that do?"

"I'll tell you when I get there."

"But, jefe, you can't—"

"I can and I am." Guzmán lays down the rifle and turns to face his right-hand man. He fixes him with a determined stare. "What if the gringos are lying? What if they're making this all up?"

"But the reader said—"

"I know what she said. But it's my turf and I want to know for myself. I want to see with my own eyes what's going on out there."

Chavez steps forward, lifting his chin. "Then I'm going with you."

"No, compadre. I want you to go to the States with the trader and the reader. We need to know more about these gringos. What are they up to? What do they want with us?"

"But, jefe—"

"The trader's smart, she can smell a scam a mile away. And the more time Reader Soledad has with the Americans, the more she can sense if they're really friends or just enemies pretending to be friends."

"If you want someone to babysit them, we'll send security."

"I'm not asking you to babysit them. I need you there to look after my interests."

"Look after your—"

"Who else can I trust to represent me? Who else *would* I trust with such an important task?" Guzmán grins, knowing he's backed Chavez into a corner. If he refuses to go to the States now, it will be a declaration of disloyalty, an act Chavez is incapable of. A line Guzmán knows the faithful old bulldog would never step over.

Stymied, Chavez breathes in deeply through his nose, his massive chest expanding in consternation. "Why didn't you tell me last night?"

"Because you would have kept me up all night trying to talk me out of it. Am I wrong?"

Chavez crosses his arms, answering with another question. "And who's going to watch things here while we're all away?"

Guzmán dismisses the question with a wave. "Hombre, the bureaucracy you built can mind the store." Shortly after they took Dallas, Chavez set up citizen-run committees to oversee housing, commerce, and security. It was less a bureaucracy than a cobbled-together collection of wizened old men and women, the respected and wholly trustworthy elders of Guzmán's movement, and it kept the city running. "Each of the committee heads knows we'll be gone for a few days. And when I told them last night, not a one of them gave me as much shit as you are right now."

This last was perhaps a step too far, Guzmán thinks regretfully. Old Chavez is only looking out for him, as he has for untold years, since Guzmán was a young, penniless rebel with more balls than brains. But Chavez can't be a part of where he's going and what he plans to do.

The old warrior's expression changes, the annoyance melting away. He fixes his jefe with an unblinking stare and shakes his head like a disappointed father.

"You won't find him," Chavez utters. "And even if you do, you won't get close enough to kill him."

Guzmán shifts his weight from one foot to another, suddenly uncomfortable under the penetrating gaze. The two men stand there for a long silent moment that feels to Guzmán like a standoff of sorts. Then something catches Guzmán's eye in the side of his vision. He shifts his attention to a line of six armored Humvees approaching from the city. He grins at the sight of his squad, seventeen of his toughest, smartest soldiers. He selected them himself last night, alone in his office, contacting each of them via motorboy couriers. And now in a matter of minutes he'll be on the road with them, the city growing smaller in the rearview mirror. The thought sends a flutter of excitement through his insides.

He turns back to Chavez, his voice resolute. "Get to City Hall, compadre. The gringos are waiting."

CHAPTER 9

It's Soledad's first ride in a helicopter, and don Flaco's no-show at City Hall has made it an awkward one. She sits between Indigo and Chavez on a bench seat in the copter's cabin, absently fingering the Virgin pendant Steffa insisted she take as a good luck charm. Opposite the trio, facing them, sit the four Americans, tight-lipped still and bristling from Guzmán's snub.

When Chavez arrived at City Hall and delivered the news that don Flaco wouldn't be coming, for a hopeful moment Soledad thought the invitation would be rescinded or rescheduled. No such luck. After conferring with each other in hushed voices for a couple minutes, the gringos said they'd be delighted to host Guzmán's "delegation," though their expressions betrayed a clear disappointment (and not a small amount of insult) Soledad didn't need any hierba to see.

Then there was Chavez's reluctance when he was informed the copter had no pilot on board, that it was being operated remotely from the States. He crossed himself as he cautiously climbed into the cabin, prompting forced smiles from the gringos that struck Soledad as every bit as patronizing as eye rolls. As the helicopter rose into the air, headsets with mics were donned in the awkward air of don Flaco's absence. Outside the cabin window the sharp, rigid geometry of the city's skyline stood incongruous and faintly ridiculous against the backdrop of flat, grassy plains and the slow, meandering curves of the Trinity River. Soledad's stomach fluttered as the copter gained altitude, giving her a view of the outlying areas around the city. Vast zones of long-abandoned structures—empty shells of homes and shops and low-lying buildings—stretched out around the city. The crumbling infrastructure of a different age, overtaken by undergrowth and unpeopled except for a scattering of scroungers, living off whatever they could scavenge, human buzzards picking at the bones of a long-dead carcass.

Now an endless sea of prairie land passes below them as they fly northward. Sporadic bands of wooded patches appear here and there. Mulberry and elm, Soledad guesses, though they're too high up to know for sure. The landscape releases memories of her childhood, of the time she and her parents spent in Wichita Falls, one of a dozen homes they alighted in when her father surveyed natural gas basins for the Bullocks. Sometimes he'd take her with him on surveys, weeklong camping trips that seemed to her storybook adventures into the wild. He even let her set up the instruments sometimes, showing her how to work the dials, how to interpret the readings that came back from deep in the ground.

Mama never came with them. Even though there was no danger, even though the Bullocks often sent drones to watch over them and keep them safe, Mama always said no. Too dirty out in the wild, too many biting bugs. Eventually, they stopped inviting her.

A screen on the cabin door pops to life. Someone's head appears on the visual, encased in a shiny, mirrorlike helmet that reminds Soledad of the soldiers back at City Hall. Only the lower portion of a human face, everything below mid-nose, is visible.

"Good morning. I'm Captain Riley," a woman's voice announces. "We'll be arriving at our destination in approximately one hour." Her words are flat and even, conveyed without the slightest inflection. The matter-of-fact speech Soledad associates with a professional soldier.

"You'll be passing over the Red River shortly," the woman says. "It's quite a sight."

The Red River. Soledad shudders. The border. The red zone. From the time every Texan is a squalling baby, they are steeped in the grim stories of the red zone. The gringo gunbirds that fly so high and so quiet, you're dead before you can even hear them. The refugees forced out of their towns in turf wars, starving and desperate, gambling their lives in hopes of finding sanctuary in the States, risking minefields and drone routes and snipers with nightspecs. The stories always end the same way. No one ever makes it to the river, much less across it.

Soledad peers down at the flat countryside, at its grasses of dull green and hay yellow. So big and so empty. Emptiness to the horizon. A minute later, small white and yellow dots begin to appear on the landscape. A few here and there at first, then more. Soledad squints, trying to make out what they are. After a few moments it hits her. Tents. Refugee tents.

Minutes pass, and the small groups of tents grow into larger clusters of hundreds, then thousands, eventually forming an enormous refugee city, miles wide. Soledad has seen refugee camps before, but nothing like this, nothing even close to this scale. A chaotic patchwork of tents of all colors, of ramshackle shanties with telltale corrugated aluminum roofs, glittering in the sunlight. Irregular footpaths and roadways run like arteries throughout the camp. From this altitude, she can't make out individual people, giving the sprawling scene below the look of a trash dump. A place for human detritus.

"Sanctuary City." Indigo's voice in her earphones.

"Christ, look at the size of it. Gets bigger every year."

Soledad wonders what it's like down there, scraping out a living among the teeming thousands, relying on charity airdrops from the Red Cross, waiting in vain for years for a refugee visa from the States, the one-in-ten-thousand lottery chance that brings them all here. Clinging onto an improbable, unrealistic salvation that will never come.

People see what they want to, what they need to. Facts be damned, circumstances be damned. If the hierba's taught her anything, it's that the human capacity for self-bullshitting is a well that never goes dry.

Then, abruptly, the tent city ends, its sprawl terminating into a sharp edge, as if sliced away with a god-sized knife. They've arrived at the border. She pictures barbed wire and razor-topped chain link, a fenced-off line of demarcation beyond which lies the red zone, a buffer of empty land on the Red River's southern shore where drones patrol day and night, watching for anyone foolhardy enough to try and make a run for it. Between the minefields, the razor wire fences, the ever-vigilant gunbirds, and the American sharpshooters on the northern shore of the river, the border's been sealed off tight since long before Soledad was born, since the time of the Crisis. Her father used to say a Texan was more likely to set foot on the surface of the moon than on American soil. For generations, the only traffic transiting the border has been the Red Cross, relief convoys allowed safe passage to bring food and meds to refugee camps like Sanctuary City. Well, the only *legal* traffic, she corrects herself. Bootleg runs make it across from time to time, smuggling in arms and tech from the States, highly valued commodities in the wastelands, where the norm is pre-Secession leftovers of rusted-out radios and fifty-year-old bullets. About one in twenty smuggling attempts makes it across, according to Indigo. A suicidal business, the trader once told her. But profitable if you survive it.

Far below, the Red River appears, snaking a wide path

across the featureless landscape, its still waters opaque and rust-colored. As the river passes directly beneath the helicopter, Soledad takes a deep breath, imagining some invisible wall extending up from the waterline, a barrier she's just breached. A few hundred yards beyond the northern shore of the river, there's a massive complex of low-lying buildings enclosed within a square of thick walls, each side running half a mile long. Dozens of rows of vehicles parked in neat lines, a pair of copters on helipads. A military facility, Soledad realizes, noticing the twin fortified towers behind the entrance. She pictures snipers with high-powered scopes, tirelessly scanning the river and its shores for movement. A couple miles to the west, she spots another, similar complex, and beyond it another one. The pattern repeats, and she counts thirteen before they grow too small and distant to make out.

Across from her, Kennedy nods at the trio of Texans and grins. "Welcome to the United States."

CHAPTER 10

"That's it?" Soledad squints at the image on the screen. A cluster of buildings shoots up from a flat expanse of endless plains. Oklahoma City as viewed from the copter's nose camera.

"What were you expecting?" Indigo asks. "Lower Manhattan?"

"It's smaller than Dallas," Chavez scoffs, his gravelly voice thick with condescension.

"Quite a bit smaller, actually," Kennedy says.

The pilot's monotone comes over their headphones. "We'll be touching down in a few minutes."

As they approach the city, the geometry of the metropolitan roadways comes into focus. Concentric circles expand outward from the city's downtown, connected by long, straight thoroughfares like spokes on a bicycle wheel, perfectly symmetrical. Far below, vehicles travel back and forth like toys on a track, reminding Soledad of the ant farms for sale at the Elm Street bazaar. Between the roads lie vast greenways crowded with trees and midrise buildings, spiral-shaped structures that appear equal parts organic and man-made. Lush terraces burst with greenery like vertical, stepped farmlands. Enormous triangular arrays fan out from the roofs. Sun tech, Soledad supposes. She's heard of it, of course, but she's never actually seen the strange-looking panels that gather up power from the sunshine. Natgas pellets, for decades, have been the only permitted source of power in the Republic, the basis of its entire economy. The Bullock clan, whose power, wealth, and authority derived from their monopolistic grip over the Republic's energy supply, had suppressed the use of all other power-generation technologies. Petroleum-based generators, solar panels, wind turbines, hydrogen cells: all outlaw tech, vigorously and systematically eradicated by the Dallasites like a gardener meticulously culling a flowerbed. Soledad had a childhood friend whose father once erected a small wind turbine on his rooftop. Ten feet tall, it had a small propeller about the size of a boat motor's. Her friend's father was certain the setup was too small to be noticed by the drones, but the next day there was nothing but rubble and a missile crater where their house used to be.

They reach the city proper. The helicopter suddenly seems small among the towering buildings. A dragonfly in a pine forest. The architecture calls to mind a smaller Dallas. Massive structures with softly curving lines, green spaces between with crisscrossing footpaths. Here, though, there are no piles of trash, no chaotic street markets. Here the city bustles with efficiency, the way it was intended to. Cars zipping along the roadways, pedestrians moving down sunlit paths. A hive with busy, thriving bees. The idea of Dallas as a dead city again crops up in her mind.

"Tan organizado," Chavez remarks, his voice uncharacteristically soft with wonder. So organized.

Across from them, the Americans' expressions have lighted, losing much of their earlier grimness. Soledad ponders if they're amused by their visitor's reaction to the modern city or if they're simply relieved to be back on their own turf.

The copter descends. Soledad grips her armrests,

clenching her teeth against a sudden lightheadedness. How does anyone ever get used to traveling this way? On the screen she sees what appears to be their landing spot, a ten-story building about half a mile ahead, its roof painted with a large yellow H. The aircraft's descent slows, the landing pad growing nearer and larger. Outside the window, she notices a crowd gathered several blocks to the east. Hundreds of people packed tightly together, choking one of the roadways and spilling out onto side streets. A moment later she feels the soft compression of the skids against the rooftop. The spin of the rotors noticeably slows, and the thrum of the motor decreases. Soledad exhales, releasing her grip on the chair.

The cabin door slides open and a uniformed man greets them. "Welcome to Oklahoma City," he shouts above the whine of the idling engine. The man makes a strange face as he looks past Soledad. She turns, finding Chavez pale, his forehead and face beaded with large drops of sweat.

"There's a bag in the panel in front of you," the man says, pointing, but Chavez has already found it. He holds it to his mouth, his thick body convulsing in dry heaves. Soledad turns away, glimpsing Indigo as she does so, noticing a hint of a grin on the trader's face, a glimmer of laughter in her eyes. She flashes Indigo a disapproving scowl. The trader returns it with a shrug and climbs out of the copter.

"I'm fine, I'm fine," Chavez insists a minute later, stepping out of the copter, refusing Kennedy's helping hand. The uniformed man directs the party toward a rooftop elevator. "This way, please."

As she walks, Soledad scans the cityscape, spotting the crowd she'd seen moments earlier, amassed several blocks away. Underneath the engine noise, she hears another sound, faint and rhythmic. Voices? Chanting voices? Before she can get a good look, she's hustled into the waiting elevator.

*   *   *

Soledad, Indigo, and Chavez sit at a table, waiting, in an office not unlike Guzmán's. Sparse decor, a large wooden desk, a tall window running the width of the room, overlooking the city. Garcia the redhead stands, holding the top of the chair back, drumming his fingers every few seconds. He smiles self-consciously at the trio.

"I'm sorry it's taking them so long," he apologizes again, his third such offering in the last fifteen minutes. Kennedy, General Bennett, and Quinn excused themselves for a few minutes on the way to the meeting room, assuring their guests they'd be along shortly.

The room's door slides open and Garcia's expression brightens with relief. The moment only lasts a second, however, when he turns and sees a robot, not a human, rolling through the doorway. The smell of coffee fills Soledad's nostrils. Garcia sighs, disappointed. A thick, round body of stainless steel and brushed black metal glides into the room, its wheels whirring. Across the front of the chassis, CAFFE MASSIMO is printed in large, overly elaborate letters.

"Espresso? Cappuccino? Coffee? Tea?" the machine asks, its voice singing with a cartoonishly exaggerated Italian accent.

Chavez stares at the thing, the wariness on his face so intense, so comically unnecessary, Soledad has to suppress a chuckle.

"Don't mind if I do," Indigo chirps, straightening up in her chair. "Latte on the menu?" she asks, rubbing her hands together.

"Certainly, ma'am." Inside its silver body, things begin to grind and hiss. "Captain Garcia, would any of your other guests care for a beverage?"

Still eyeing the machine skeptically, Chavez slowly shakes his head. Soledad stands up—"No, thanks." She moves to the window. "I saw a crowd from the roof," she says, "a few blocks over." She glances at Garcia. "What was that?"

Garcia joins her at the window. Small helicopters, one-seaters, glide purposefully through the city's canyons of steel and glass and terraced greenery. Hummingbirds in a garden. Garcia searches the cityscape, brow furrowed. "Some kind of demonstration. I'm not sure." He shrugs. "There's always something going on around here. Downtown, you know."

"Ah," Soledad says, nodding, instinctively wondering if he's hiding something, if he knows more than he's saying. The involuntary reflex to read him reminds her of the hierba she has hidden away. Maybe it's a good time to excuse herself to the restroom so she can chew some.

Then she hears it again. The chanting voices she noticed on the roof.

"What in the world?" Garcia leans forward, craning his neck for a better view. Soledad follows his gaze, then gasps. A block away, a surging crowd spills onto a side street. Within seconds, the block's congested with bodies, flooded with the suddenness of gushing water from a collapsed levee. The mob grows, expands, and even from her vantage point fifteen floors above, its chaotic energy is palpable. Soledad watches, noticing that the crowd's not only growing larger, it's growing *closer*.

Behind them the door slides open. She sucks in a reflexive gulp of air and whirls around.

"We've got to move them." Quinn, the military man from the day before, stands stiffly in the doorway. Soledad gathers from his tense expression, his urgent eyes, that something has gone wrong.

"Move them?" Garcia blurts. "Where?"

Quinn's one-word reply comes quickly. "Out."

A small white light above the door begins to flicker. A disembodied voice announces: "Attention. Attention. Please make your way to the ground floor."

"Dammit," Quinn curses. He waves them over, his hands gesturing urgently. "Come on. Let's go before the stairs get too crowded."

Soledad rushes from the room, where a uniformed soldier stands holding a stairwell door open. "This way, ma'am," he urges, waving her over.

She pauses, turning to Quinn. "What's going on? What is that down there?"

"I'll explain everything when we're out of here." Quinn places his palm on her shoulder, urging her forward. "Now, please, we've got to move."

Soledad enters the stairwell, followed by Indigo and Chavez. "Down," Quinn calls from behind them.

"Down?" Indigo questions. She points toward the ceiling with her thumb. "What about the chopper?"

"It's not up there anymore," Quinn replies. "And the elevators dropped to the first floor when some idiot hit that alarm. Stairs are the only way down." He strides past the Texans into the stairwell, waving at them frantically from the landing. "Come on, please!"

They follow Quinn downward, their footsteps echoing through the stairwell. After they descend two flights, the building's occupants begin to trickle into the stairwell, apparently realizing the elevators aren't coming, and join the hurried descent. A nervous, confused murmur fills the air. They shuffle down the stairs, the tension inside the tight space growing more palpable. By the time Soledad and her companions reach the ground floor, the stairwell above her is clogged with bodies and noisy with the sound of panic.

She passes through the ground-floor door. The high-ceiling lobby is clogged with a swelling crowd of building occupants. Outside the building, it's a mob scene. A line of riot-geared soldiers—or maybe police, Soledad thinks—stand a few yards beyond the building's paned-glass entryway. Beyond them, a crowd of shouting faces and a thousand gyrating arms simmers angrily. Handwritten signs bob up and down, though Soledad's too far away to read them. Then she notices the crosses. Large white crosses, dozens of them held aloft, dancing above the chaos of bodies.

Crosses?

Quinn grasps her by the upper arm. "This way. I've got a car waiting around back." They exit the lobby into a hallway at a jog. They round a corner, and Soledad pulls her arm free of Quinn's grip.

"Tell me what's going on, goddammit!" she insists.

Quinn fixes her with an earnest look. "When we're out of here and safe," he says, breathing heavily. "I promise."

From the direction of the lobby, there's a crash of breaking glass, followed by shrieks of panic. Fear yanks at Soledad's insides. Whatever hell was brewing outside, it's just penetrated into the building.

Quinn grabs her arm again. "Hurry!"

This time, she doesn't protest, matching him stride for stride as they race through the hallway, rounding corners at a full run.

"Attention. Attention," the voice repeats, echoing through the halls, its tone absurdly serene. "Please make your way to the ground floor."

Within moments they exit the rear of the building, where a long, black limousine sits waiting in an empty alleyway. The rear door swings open, and the trio of Texans piles inside, followed by Quinn and Garcia.

"Go, go!" Quinn barks. Two soldiers with shaved heads and dark glasses sit up front. One nods, then presses his finger to an earpiece. "Exiting the alley," he says in a remarkably calm voice, "heading south on Browder."

The limo creeps forward, traveling all of twenty feet before it jerks to a stop, its path blocked by a cluster of angry protesters who seem to have appeared from nowhere. Wedged between Chavez and Indigo, Soledad turns to the back window, only to find more behind them. Faces contorted in frenzied rage, their shouts mixing together into a mad, unintelligible roar.

"They've got us boxed in," Indigo gasps.

In seconds the crowd swells, doubling in size as more arrive, closing in on the limo. Fists begin to pound the vehicle. Hollow thuds of flesh striking steel come from all sides. Fear grips Soledad, the raw animal terror of helpless prey surrounded by predators. She clutches onto Indigo's arm. Bloodthirsty savages shriek at them, faces twisted with madness. Only a thin plate of glass separates her from chaos, she thinks morbidly. From being torn apart.

A crack of automatic gunfire rips through the air. Soledad cowers instinctively, the sudden burst of close-range shots assaulting her ears. Up front, the soldier in the passenger seat fires off a second volley from a narrow opening in the sunroof, his rifle pointed skyward. The mob scatters like cockroaches fleeing a flashlight's glare. The path ahead cleared, the limo, now pitted and dimpled with fist-sized dents, lurches forward.

As the vehicle speeds around the corner, tires squealing, Soledad notices a man on the sidewalk holding a large sign. He shouts angrily at them, adding another dent to the limo's body with a well-timed kick as they zoom past. Her eyes lock on the man's sign in disbelief. It's a photo of a man's face. *Reverend Wright's face.* And beneath it, scrawled in clumsy block letters, SAVE OUR PURSECUTED BROTHERS AND SISTERS...NOW!!

CHAPTER 11

"Por Dios, estoy ciego," Guzmán mutters under his breath, berating himself again as the Humvee pitches sideways into another unnoticed ditch. A bit faster or at a different angle, and it might have been enough to turn the truck over. He grips the steering wheel tighter, concentrating on the path forward.

"Whoa, that was a good one," his passenger laughs. The soldier, a wide-chested, thick-limbed youth named Gonzalo Gonzalez—known to everyone as G.G.—smiles underneath a scraggly beard, the boyish, carefree grin a strange accessory to his imposing physique, a frame made for fighting. Much like a young version of himself, it occurs to Guzmán, both in physical presence and character. Maybe that's why Guzmán chose him, because G.G. reminded him of the lighthearted wanderer he once was himself, half a lifetime ago. The Ernesto Guzmán before gray hairs, before heavy responsibilities, a rifle in his hands, the warm sun on his face, and not a worry in the world.

The convoy races westward, single-file, across the plains of the panhandle, a flat, featureless expanse of hay-colored grasses and sparse clusters of trees and shrubs.

They're three hours outside of Dallas, making good time. A hundred yards to their left, the broken remains of I-20 guide their way, a bread crumb trail of disintegrating concrete and rusted steel rebar, showing them the way west. Generations ago, Guzmán ponders, when the highways were still passable, drivers tore across the plains at twice his convoy's current speed, covering the distance between Dallas and Odessa in four and a half hours. Four and a half hours! And that was in a car or truck. In a plane, it took even less. You were there before you knew it.

But that was the Texas of another time, of another universe. For as long as anyone can remember, the quickest time imaginable between Dallas and the western desert has been a full day's hard drive, a rough, dangerous ride across an unforgiving landscape of countless unseen dangers. Deep gullies covered with switchgrass, waiting to break an axle, cannibal highwaymen hidden in elm groves, waiting to ambush easy prey.

It's a hot morning. Guzmán's arm rests on the driver's door, the sun's blaze baking his skin. The breeze through the open windows doesn't refresh as it might in cooler weather. Instead, it's a constant warm breath blowing on his face, drying his lips, eyes, and nasal passages. Trickles of sweat run down his chest and belly. Still, he thinks as he licks his parched lips and wipes perspiration from his forehead, it's preferable to a stack of papers and a cramped office. Far preferable.

Beside him, G.G. listens intently to a handheld radio pressed to his ear. After a few moments, he drops it to his side.

"Anything?" Guzmán asks.

G.G. shakes his head. "Nada, jefe. Still no word from out west. It's like they fell off the face of the earth."

Guzmán knits his brow. "It's damn strange, joven." No, he then decides, damn strange doesn't even begin to describe the situation. Bizarre. Incomprehensible. Unheard of. Only the most extreme words and phrases seem to fit whatever's going on out west.

The west, he muses. These last months it has been largely deserted. After his victory in Dallas, the vast majority of his followers emigrated to the capital in hopes of a better life. Arriving in droves, they flooded the city, and Guzmán summoned nearly all his troops from out west to help manage the situation and keep the city from falling into total chaos.

Chavez warned him, of course, that such a course left the western desert—along with its natural gas basins that provided the largest part of their energy—desperately undermanned, that their security forces were spread too thin. The west, Chavez maintained, was wide open and vulnerable. But Guzmán saw things differently. Who could possibly threaten him now, he insisted, after he'd taken Dallas? The Bullocks were defeated and gone. The Fundies had suffered an unrecoverable loss of soldiers and equipment in Conroe. The fat preacher had gone into hiding like a scared mouse. There was no one left to challenge him, no clan or turf boss who had anything close to the number of fighters, much less the gear and weapons required to even consider such a move. The security needs of the capital, a prize Guzmán had no intention of letting slip from his hands, far outweighed those of the far-flung west.

No, it wasn't ideal, leaving nothing but a skeleton crew of Odessa-based engineers behind to manage the vast western natgas fields, protected only by a sparse scattering of soldiers. But it was a temporary necessity forced upon them. Once they'd trained up enough new recruits, he promised Chavez, once the situation in the city settled, then he could afford to be more generous with his troop deployments.

Half a year later, the situation in the city hadn't settled. If anything, it had moved in the opposite direction of settled. The once-great capital had become little more than a poorly organized slum, its technology dead, its beautiful buildings spacious corpses, housing a population of disenchanted, restless residents. Most were still loyal flaquistas, Guzmán knew, but less so, it seemed to him, with each passing month. He saw it in their eyes, heard it in their voices: the disappointing reality of the promised land; the lost faith in their savior.

He's felt their disillusionment himself, shared in their frustration. The victory over the Dallasites was an incomplete one for him. Wright slipped away, after all, robbing Guzmán of a satisfaction he'd been waiting a lifetime for. It was like fucking without an orgasm, he complained to Chavez. Not a day passed that Guzmán didn't look at the map pinned to the wall of his office, staring at the Gulf coast, brooding over where the Fundie preacher might be hiding. In the pine forests near Conroe? Or maybe down in the swampy bayous closer to the Gulf? He'd pestered the trader Indigo for daily updates on the chatter over the shortwave radio channels, but there'd never been as much as a whisper of the preacher's whereabouts. Months passed and his restlessness grew. How many goddamned papers did he have to sign, how many housing disputes did he have to preside over, before things would be secure enough for him to free up a cohort of soldiers and hunt down the old crook? They'd trained up hundreds of new recruits, but with *thousands* arriving to the capital each month from every corner of the Republic, it was only ever enough to keep the city from tipping into chaos. From the confines of his cramped office, a settled, peaceful Dallas still seemed far away. An orderly, prosperous one, farther still. The revenge that he'd longed for, that he'd almost tasted in Conroe, might never be satisfied.

Guzmán turns the wheel sharply, cursing under his breath. The vehicle lurches, narrowly missing a deep gulley.

He still isn't sure what to make of the Americans' story. Wright hasn't had nearly enough time to gather up an army. Even if the preacher has been converting Fundies day and night over the last six months, there's the question of training. And gear and weapons and vehicles. By all accounts, the preacher had amassed his entire army at Conroe, where Guzmán's flaquistas soundly crushed them. Wright fled back to Houston with his tail between his legs, his soldiers dead, his vehicles and weaponry destroyed. No, six months is far too little time to build an army when you're starting from zero. Of course, you wouldn't need an entire army to take the western desert in the feeble state Guzmán left it, but if you wanted to live past the massive counterattack that would surely come out of Dallas, you'd need forces numbering into the thousands, well-armed and motivated.

Still, even with so many questions outstanding, he's perversely hopeful that every word of the gringos' story is all true.

The very idea of it, from the moment the Americans told him, ignited something wild inside Guzmán's gut, a feeling he couldn't name if he tried. A heady mixture of outrage, bloodlust, and, strangely, joy. He knew almost immediately there was no way he was going to stay in Dallas, waiting by the radio for some word from out west. And there was no way he was going to talk politics with Americans on their turf, either, not when his own turf was under siege. But somewhere deep inside himself, a place free of self-delusions and rationalizations, he knows the thing that sent him racing across the desert isn't about turf or gringo politics or natgas fields.

It's about the preacher. It's about a long overdue debt. If he doesn't get off his ass and finally repay it, something in his gut tells him he'll never get another chance.

"Boss," G.G. says. Guzmán, lost in obsessive thought, doesn't hear him.

"Boss," the young soldier repeats urgently. "BOSS!"

Guzmán jolts to attention. The Humvee's suddenly airborne, diving nose-down into a deep gulch. He comes up off his seat, momentarily weightless, then strikes his head hard against the roof. An instant later, the truck's front end slams violently against the depression's flat bottom. A loud, sickening crunch of metal punctuates the impact. The vehicle wobbles a short distance, then comes to a stop.

Guzmán and the young soldier sit without speaking, catching their breath as a cloud of brownish-gray dust slowly settles around them. After a few quiet moments, Guzmán finds the voice to ask G.G. if he's all right. The youth nods, says he's fine. In the rearview mirror, another truck comes to their aid, carefully navigating the steep decline.

Pinche distraído, Guzmán scolds himself, the crown of his head throbbing.

And they were making such good time.

*   *   *

"Could have been a lot worse," Ramirez announces, rolling out from under the Humvee. The damaged vehicle leans sharply to one side like a boat about to capsize. "Just need to swap out the shock," he continues, hopping up onto his feet, brushing the dust from his armored leggings, "and we're good."

Guzmán stands apart from the soldiers gathered around the truck. Angry at the delay, embarrassed at himself for being the cause of it, he blows sullen puffs of bluish pipe smoke from the side of his mouth. "Then let's swap it out," he says, removing the pipe from his lips. "Ándale."

The soldiers scramble into action. Expert hands move swiftly, positioning the jack beneath the undercarriage, lifting the enormous machine off the ground, switching out the broken part for a new one. A few minutes later, before Guzmán can even finish his bowlful of tobacco, they've completed their work. Impressed, he steps toward the truck, forgetting his rancor, his thick mustache curving into a wide smile. The proud grin of a commander of a hotshot squad.

He opens the passenger door, steps up onto the running board. G.G. hovers behind him tentatively. Guzmán turns back to the young soldier and chuckles. "Soy tonto, pero no tanto," he jokes. "You better drive the rest of the way, jovenazo."

"Claro, don Flaco," the soldier answers crisply. He trots around the front of the Humvee and climbs behind the wheel. As the engine rumbles to life, Guzmán checks the sun's position.

"You think we'll make it there before nightfall?"

"Sin ningún problema, jefe," the youth responds confidently, popping the shifter into drive. "I'm on it."

The Humvee rolls forward, its nose tilting upward as they exit the gully, pressing Guzmán back into the seat. G.G. steers the vehicle with careful proficiency, zigzagging up the steep incline, feathering the gas like he's made this same climb a thousand times. The kid can drive, Guzmán observes. Scrub bushes make popping noises, their dry twigs snapping underneath the crush of enormous knobby tires. And then they're out, back on level ground among the endless plains. Four of the Humvees sit idling, waiting for the other truck to follow Guzmán's out of the gully.

They've only lost ten minutes of travel time, Guzmán notes with satisfaction, when something catches his attention. In a small grove of live oaks some distance away, small pinpoints of white light burst in its branches. Fireflies, he instinctively thinks for an instant, until the pop of gunfire hits his ears. At the same moment, the window explodes next to his head. Shards of broken glass fly through the cabin as he throws himself down onto the seat.

From somewhere outside the Humvee, a soldier shouts: "AMBUSH!"

CHAPTER 12

Soledad stares at herself in the mirror of the quiet bathroom, water hissing softly from the basin faucet in front of her. She cups her hands underneath the stream, splashes her face, feels the cool wetness against her cheeks. The pendant hanging around her neck stares back at her; she buttons her shirt, hiding it from view.

There's a knock on the door. "Ma'am, you all right in there?" her soldier escort asks.

"Coming," she calls, hurrying into a stall. She leans over the toilet and spits out the hierba she's been secretly chewing, then flushes it away. The plant's bitter taste coats her tongue like a dry paste. She checks herself again in the mirror, focusing on her eyes. There's a slight blurring in her vision as her pupils dilate. A moment later, she feels it: the first sensations of the hierba's effect on her awareness. It's like a valve slowly opening, the feeling of her awareness expanding. She begins to see things in her face, hidden truths revealing themselves. A sheen of anxiety covers her features like a nearly invisible glaze on a clay pot, a patina so thin and translucent only she can detect its presence. And underneath it, there's something else. A kind of heaviness behind her eyes, weighing upon her. She averts her gaze from her reflection.

Her thoughts drift backwards in time, to when Dallas fell to Guzmán's army and he released her from his service. She felt as if the world had been opened up to her, finally liberated from the cage of her servitude. Even with the terrible realization of her parents' cold-blooded betrayal, those heady days following the flaquista victory felt like a time of hope for the future, of ever-improving tomorrows for herself and little Steffa.

How long did that feeling last? A few weeks? A month? Little by little, her optimism faded, a slow leak from a car tire, until one day she woke up and realized it was gone completely. The dream of better days ahead, of darker days gone and forgotten, turned out to be a fleeting one. She'd become a prisoner of her fame, locked away in her top-floor apartment like she'd been locked away in Guzmán's desert camps. She'd traded one cage for another, but maybe the new one was worse since it had been a cage of her own choosing.

And then there was little Steffa. The girl sensed Soledad's malaise, distancing herself from it as if it were a cold she might catch, though Soledad was sure this was more instinct than conscious abandonment. She hoped as much, at least. More and more, Steffa sought comfort in the arms of Magnolia. And more and more, Soledad felt like a third wheel, like a despondent interloper in an otherwise contented family of two.

Her tenuous ties to Dallas, to Guzmán, to her place in the world the dizzying trajectory of the past has thrown her into, feel as if they're being stretched to the breaking point. For this first time it occurs to her that maybe it wouldn't be the worst thing in the world to let them break.

How much does she owe the man? Again the question pesters her thoughts like a flying insect that evades every swat of her hand. He's sent her on this harebrained diplomatic errand while he took off on some even more harebrained mission of his own. None of it makes any sense, but then again don Flaco's not making much sense lately. Maybe she doesn't owe him anything.

Another knock at the door, this time harder. "Ma'am?"

"Coming," she answers quickly, snapping her attention back to the moment. She again focuses on her reflection, and with no small effort arranges her features into a neutral stare, pushing the discord of her own thoughts and the terrifying moments from the limo far into the back of her mind. She takes a deep, cleansing breath and readies herself to go find some answers. If not for don Flaco, then at least for herself.

A minute later, the soldier escorts her down the hallway, where she rejoins Indigo and Chavez in a small, cramped room with no windows and blank walls of dull white. A safe location in a safe building, Quinn assured them minutes earlier, before he excused himself from the room.

"You okay?" Indigo asks her.

"Fine," Soledad answers, taking a seat next to the trader. She glances at Indigo, gives her a small, meaningful nod. The trader recognizes the signal immediately, though she does a skillful job hiding her reaction. Indigo's got her poker face on. To Soledad's right, Chavez breathes audibly, his palms flat against the top of the small, round table. He gives off an obvious, palpable air of discomfort and tension. Even the least perceptive pair of eyes could see in his harsh, uneasy features, in his stiff posture, that the old warrior would rather be anywhere but where he is right at this moment.

The door opens and Quinn returns with General Bennett and Roman Kennedy. Bennett wears the same fatigues from the day before (or, more likely, another identical set), and Kennedy has changed into a dark blue suit, its cut and style similar to the one he wore in Dallas, and a canary-yellow tie. Their faces are grim, their American mouths drawn into tight lines. As they sit down across from the Texans, Soledad perceives a discernible embarrassment, which makes sense. Their guests were almost beaten to death by an enraged mob. Probably not the welcome they'd planned on.

The last to take a seat is Quinn. Flustered and anxious, he's the easiest of the three gringos to read. There's a tightness in the tiny muscles around his mouth, an erratic pulse in the large veins in his neck, and a nearly imperceptible twitch of his eyeballs. All giveaways only Soledad can notice, thanks to her preternaturally strong perception, heightened and sharpened with the hierba's help. Quinn displays all the telltales of a man struggling to regain his composure.

Kennedy clears his throat. "I cannot express how sorry I am," he says, his voice low and resounding with regret, "for the incident that just occurred."

Not lying. The American's voice and eyes project sincerity, a genuine sorrow. Soledad turns her gaze to Quinn. "You said you'd tell me what was going on."

Quinn swallows but doesn't answer, casting an uncertain glance toward Kennedy and Bennett. Kennedy blinks and drums his fingers on the tabletop, his perfectly manicured nails dancing up and down like little motor pistons. The room's silent as Soledad watches Kennedy, who begins to swivel back and forth in his chair.

He's debating with himself, trying to decide how to start, how to explain things. She imagines words and phrases hurtling around his head like papers in a tornado.

In the next moment Kennedy confirms her observation. "Where to begin, where to begin?" he mutters, seemingly as much to himself as the other occupants of the small room.

Soledad glances over at Bennett. The general's unblinking hawk eyes stare back at her, alert and wary. A gringa version of Chavez, she decides, although the woman displays none of Chavez's current awkwardness and discomfort. Her sharp stare notwithstanding, Bennett exudes the quiet confidence of a soldier on her home turf.

"We have ourselves a bit of a...political situation here, my friends," Kennedy finally manages to get out. He addresses Chavez, making the same stupid assumption men always make about who must be in charge. But Soledad isn't the least bit offended, even giving a silent thanks for the slight. It's better for her if the Americans' attention is directed toward someone else. Better if someone other than herself does the talking so she can focus her attention on the read.

Chavez grunts. "Political situation?"

"It may help if I back up a step," Kennedy raises a provocative eyebrow. "Would it surprise you to learn that a great deal of Americans favor a normalization of relations with Texas? That many even yearn for its return to statehood?"

He lets the statement and its heavy significance settle over the room. The trio of Texans sit in stunned silence.

Soledad's gut reaction is instant disbelief. Does this gringo take them for complete fools? As far as lies go, this one has to be right up there with the most unbelievable she's ever heard, and she's heard plenty. Good ones, bad ones, clever ones, ridiculous ones, ones that make you want to roll your eyes, ones that make you want to reach out and slap the liar across the face. She's heard lies of every shape and size and degree of exaggeration. And they all have one thing in common: they never get past her. There's always a giveaway, a clue the speaker unknowingly transmits. Something she can see in the facial muscles, the eyes, the posture, or something she can hear in the voice.

But right now she perceives none of those things. Has she missed something? She concentrates on Kennedy's face, searching for anything that might suggest deception. She listens carefully to the echo of his words in her head. She senses nothing. *Nothing!*

But how? How could it be true? It's like the American just told her the Earth is flat without so much as a batted eyelash.

Indigo speaks up, the first of the Texan trio to regain her composure. "Then why is the border locked down so tight?" she asks pointedly. "Why do you shoot down anyone who tries to get across?"

"Personally, I'd like nothing more than to pull back those positions," Kennedy answers, "but reversing decades of immigration and national security policy isn't something that happens quickly…or without considerable debate."

On this last comment, Soledad catches something. A restrained timbre in his voice, a sudden, involuntary stiffness in his posture. There's much more underneath the word *debate*, some larger meaning. The light behind his eyes, the optimistic glow she recalls from their first meeting in Dallas, seems to have faded into something less hopeful.

Kennedy returns to his storyline. "I know it may be hard to believe, but I can assure you that over the last several years, there's been a significant shift in public opinion vis-à-vis Texas. It can't come entirely as a surprise, can it? After all, when Texas broke away—"

"Seceded," Chavez corrects.

"When Texas *seceded*," Kennedy continues, nodding in acknowledgment, "families were torn apart, lives were irreparably damaged, the ties that bound our peoples together were severed with a ruthless, brutal efficiency. And for a long while, this suited most Americans just fine. But times change, and attitudes and positions soften. The pain and difficulties of nearly a century ago grew hazier in the American memory. And more and more, people began to question—rightly, in my opinion—a perpetual nonengagement model. In fact, public opinion had turned enough that, a few years ago, the State Department discreetly began to extend diplomatic feelers to Dallas."

"To the Bullocks," Chavez observes.

"Indeed," Kennedy concedes. "But our efforts were rebuffed at every turn."

Not a single quiver in his voice, Soledad observes. Not

a single lie or distortion in anything the gringo is saying. Every word of his increasingly engrossing story is true.

Kennedy shrugs. "We're not sure why they refused to engage. Maybe they felt threatened. Or maybe it was simply a question of time, and they would have warmed up to us eventually. But long story short, the Bullocks didn't seem interested in any sort of dialogue with the States."

Soledad glances over at her companions. Raptly they listen, riveted by the American's words.

"And during this period," Kennedy goes on, "we also watched—with a great deal of concern—the rise of Zachariah Wright's influence in the southern portion of the state. Pardon me, of *the Republic*. It seemed clear to us that he had ambitions to supplant the Bullock regime and install his own power structure."

A soldier enters the room, self-consciously hesitating in the doorway, carrying a pitcher of water and a tray of glasses. General Bennett nods at him, and he places the glasses on the table, fills them, and leaves.

Indigo picks up her glass. "Sure seems like you know a lot about the goings-on inside of Texas." She takes a sip. "For a country that's *nonengaged*, I mean."

Kennedy smiles. "Not engaged is not the same thing as *not interested*, Señora Cruz."

Or not spying, Soledad adds silently. Like her companions, she's well aware of the American intelligence presence operating in Texas since forever. The high-flying, untouchable drones taking pictures, the occasional gringo agent caught in some act of espionage. Once she even identified a spy herself during a read, some fast-talker posing as a trader, trying to buy his way into don Flaco's inner circle. She spotted him right away as a fraud, and under a particularly effective torture session Chavez orchestrated, the man gave himself up.

"In any case," Kennedy says, "we became ever more convinced that the Dallasites were underestimating Wright. Understandably, we were concerned about the eventuality of him gaining unchecked power. The Bullocks may have not been a friendly regime, but the idea of having some...*theocracy* run by a madman on our doorstep was simply unthinkable."

"So why not send in a gunbird to take him out?" Chavez suggests.

"The politics of military intervention were...problematic," Kennedy replies, then he casts a meaningful look at General Bennett. Soledad follows his gaze, absorbing the general's demeanor. The tension in the woman's features exudes concern, though she's doing her best not to give anything away. Soledad senses the woman is worried Kennedy's revealing too much to the strangers.

"So we took...*other measures*," Kennedy continues, "to limit Wright's ability to acquire resources."

The general leans forward stiffly. "Roman, we agreed on levels of disclosure."

Kennedy lifts his hand in a supplicating gesture. "General, I'm going to need a bit more latitude. We all know what's at stake and what the timeline is. If I'm going to err here, it's going to be on the side of candor."

Bennett's mouth straightens into a tight line. "My call," Kennedy adds, "and I'll take the hit if it comes to that." His assurance doesn't seem to ease the general's tension. After a moment, though, she gives him a small nod, apparently allowing him to continue.

Indigo speaks up before he can continue. "Trade in the Gulf."

Kennedy looks at the trader. "Pardon me?"

"You stopped trade in the Gulf," Indigo expands. She moves her gaze between Soledad and Chavez. "Wright's bread and butter is seafaring trade. And they shut it all down to bleed him dry."

Soledad nods, recalling what Indigo once related to her about the source of the preacher's wealth. As a youth, Reverend Wright had tirelessly worked the Galveston docks, slowly building his fortune. Indigo called the preacher a born hustler, aggressive and relentless and charming all at the same time. Eventually, he'd amassed enough wealth to insert himself into the local power structure, like some Mafia boss in the Chicago of the history books, buying his way into Houston City Hall. He spent money as fast as he made it, growing his network of influence with an ever-expanding payroll of bribes and payouts. And the world being what it is, there was no shortage of corrupt local officials who were happy to take his money if all they had to do was turn a blind eye to his religious rallies or appoint some Fundie as the local chief of police.

Gradually, over years of careful stewardship, Wright built a considerable empire in southeastern Texas, a beast with a thousand tentacles, doling out an endless supply of payoffs that secured his power, that allowed his movement to thrive. If his high-powered charisma had been the blood of the Fundie movement, attracting droves of desperate souls, then his money had surely been the oxygen, empowering its growth.

But then one day, all seafaring commerce in the Gulf died. The ships laden with goods from Caribbean nations and South America and friendly turfs in the Yucatan mysteriously stopped arriving in port. And the vessels leaving Texas, their hulls heavy with tons of natgas pellets, steamed out of the Gulf and never returned. The flow of Wright's wealth suddenly dried up, leaving him broke and his movement struggling for survival, unable to feed the bribe-hungry beast of his own creation.

"Any historian will tell you it takes more than a loyal following to build an empire," Kennedy says.

"It takes cash," Indigo offers.

"A lot of it," the general adds.

Kennedy pauses, reaching for a glass of water. The interruption gives the Texans a moment to try to digest all they've heard, to get their heads around the torrent of revelations unleashed on them. Astonishment and disbelief begin to give way to curiosity. Soledad can feel it herself, and she can sense the same longing in Indigo and Chavez. Three blind mice, suddenly given the ability to see. Now they want to see everything, know everything.

Soledad furrows her brow. "So you *blockaded* the Gulf of Mexico?"

"Maritime embargo is usually how we phrase it," Kennedy answers. "To the general public, the president called for the action to stop the flow of arms to terrorist groups, which, to my way of thinking, wasn't far from the truth. And it worked. For a time, at least."

Until something unexpected happened. Soledad hears the unvoiced words almost as clearly as if they were spoken out loud.

"Until Guzmán took Dallas," she says instinctively.

"Yes," Kennedy replies, gazing at her curiously. "That's exactly right. We didn't see that coming."

"I don't understand," Chavez inserts. "What does one have to do with the other?"

"Let me put it this way," Kennedy says. "The flaquistas' victory in Dallas may have been the worst thing that's ever happened to Texas."

CHAPTER 13

Two of Guzmán's Humvees are destroyed immediately. One deafening explosion follows another in quick succession, the concussions rocking his own truck violently, the heat blasts fiery hot against his skin.

G.G. pulls Guzmán by the arm, heaving him out of the truck onto the ground, away from the gunfire. "Jefe," he yells, "are you hit?"

"No!" Guzmán shouts back. A short distance away, the two trucks burn. Bright orange flames engulf their bodies, thick columns of black smoke billow upwards. "What was it?" he shouts. "RPGs?"

"I didn't see," G.G. answers. "I think so." The soldier winces as bullets ping and thud against the Humvee's steel.

Keeping his head low, Guzmán reaches into the truck and feels around the front seat for their weapons. Shards of glass prick his naked hand like needles as he finds the M4s and pulls them from the vehicle. He tosses one of the rifles to G.G. just as a high-pitched whoosh zips past the front of the truck. Guzmán catches a glimpse of the rocket-propelled grenade the moment a third Humvee, a short distance away, is hit. The explosion sends him flying backwards, slamming him against the truck's steel body.

The RPG's target, struck in the rear wheel, launches from the ground, tail end skyward, and flips end over end. A chaos of metal, glass, and dirt flies in all directions.

Ears ringing and stunned, Guzmán sits with his back against the truck, his legs splayed out in front of him, the wind knocked from his lungs. He watches the destroyed vehicle, its rear half blown off by the RPG, tumble to a stop. He sucks in large, reflexive gasps of air. A near-constant barrage of bullets pounds the Humvee, sending thudding vibrations through his body, rattling his bones.

From nowhere, the gringo phrase *sitting ducks* pops into his head. They can't stay here. They're caught out in the open, easy targets for whoever's firing RPGs from the cover of the trees.

He glances back at the ditch, some thirty yards away. The truck that was following them out sits motionless, tilted upward, near the top of the rise. The vehicle is empty, its four passengers on their bellies at the edge of the ditch, firing back into the trees, their rifles laying over the lip of the gulley. Beside Guzmán, G.G. squats behind the front of the truck, his rifle shouldered. The soldier springs up and squeezes off a volley of shots, then squats back down.

"We can't stay here," Guzmán shouts. He motions toward the ditch. "We've got to move."

G.G. peers warily at the space between their truck and the gulley. Guzmán knows the soldier's thinking the same thing he is. Thirty yards, all of it spanning open ground. Under heavy fire like this, it's a hell of a long run to make without getting shot.

But staying put is suicide, and the young soldier, giving his jefe a quick nod, seems to come to the same immediate conclusion. "I'll give you cover!"

Crouching low, Guzmán pulls open the back door, removes a pair of helmets, and passes one to G.G. Both men hurriedly cover their heads, fastening the straps under their chins. Guzmán then inches his way toward the rear of the Humvee, his head next to the bumper, and slings his rifle over his shoulder. From the gulley, one of the soldiers spots him and frantically waves him over. G.G. shouts, "Go, go, go!" and springs up from his squatting position. Guzmán hears the barrage of covering fire and sprints, head down, toward the ditch.

Each step takes an eternity, like in a dream. His body feels heavy and slow, as if the force of gravity has suddenly doubled. His vision narrows into a long tunnel that ends thirty yards away. He pumps his arms, taking awkward, crouching strides. For a split second he ponders how ridiculous he must look, a huge man, hunched over, trying to make himself a small target as he scrambles across the grass. He can't hear anything over the pounding blood in his ears, though he's aware of bullets whizzing all around him. Almost there. A few more steps. As he finally reaches the edge of the gulley, a shot finds its target, striking him and knocking him off his feet. Scorching pain explodes through him as he careens headlong down the embankment and lands at the bottom of the ditch, slamming against the hard dirt.

He spits dirt from his mouth, a white-hot flame burning in his left shoulder. A soldier—a sharpshooter named Isabel—clambers down the embankment and helps him to his knees. The world around him spins dizzily.

"G.G.," Guzmán sputters, waving his uninjured arm back toward the truck. "Give him cover."

"Sí, jefe," the soldier shouts, though in the next moment they both realize the order's unnecessary. Above them a figure appears, diving over the rim of the ditch headfirst, then tumbling down the embankment. G.G.'s mass of flailing arms and legs. The soldier turns an ungainly somersault and butt-skids to a stop next to Guzmán.

G.G. turns to his jefe and nods. "Fríamente calculado," he shouts, popping up to his feet. Then his eyes widen as he notices Guzmán's shoulder. "Don Flaco!"

Blood pulses from Guzmán's upper arm, warm and sticky. He tears at the bullet hole in his sleeve, ripping it open wide so he can get a look at the wound. Pain radiates through his shoulder, sending a wave of nausea through him. Bullets ping against the steel body of the abandoned Humvee at the top of the ridge. Somewhere above him, soldiers shout urgently between bursts of gunfire.

Guzmán spreads the fabric open with his fingers. A tear in the shoulder muscle. It's a bloody mess and it hurts like hell, but it won't kill him. And, thankfully, it's a grazing wound—there's no bullet lodged in his body.

Isabel removes a plastic tube from her vest pocket. "For the bleeding," she shouts, tearing off the cap with her teeth and injecting a sticky white fluid into the gaping laceration without warning. Don Flaco clenches his teeth and winces against the fire that suddenly courses through him, but manages to keep his shoulder motionless so she can apply enough coagulant to stop the flow of blood.

Three more of his squad appear, hurling themselves into the ditch, scampering down the embankment. One of them loses his helmet on the way. Guzmán watches it skitter across the dirt like a wounded animal. His shoulder throbs mercilessly. Each heartbeat radiates pain into his neck and chest and down the length of his arm.

"Bleeding's stopped," Isabel tells him, tossing away the empty tube of coagulant.

His left arm dangling, Guzmán clambers up the ridge to the soldiers firing into the thicket of oak trees. Isabel stays close to him. He crawls next to one of the soldiers and peers over the edge. Muzzle flashes erupt from the distant tree line. Sunbaked dirt explodes a foot away from his head.

"¡Cuidado, jefe!" Isabel cries, pressing a firm hand on his uninjured shoulder, forcing him downward.

He looks over at the Humvee parked on the lip of the ridge.

"Is that Paco's truck?" he shouts at Isabel. She turns

and looks, then turns back to him with a nod.

"¿Segura?" he asks, recalling the list of gear he told Paco to store.

"Yes, jefe," she confirms. "I was riding shotgun."

Though still painful, his shoulder is already beginning to numb from the coagulant's anesthetic. Keeping his head low, Guzmán scrambles toward the Humvee.

"Don Flaco!" Isabel cries. "What are you doing?" He leaves her behind, hearing her shouted pleas for him to stop between bursts of gunfire.

With every stride it feels as if someone's jamming nails into his shoulder. He races across the ground in an ungainly step-limp-step-limp sprint, his left arm pressed against his torso as if it were in a sling. Twenty yards from the Humvee, he pauses, noticing fresh pockmarks running the length of the vehicle's body. Nearly one entire side is fully exposed to the incoming rounds.

Caray!

Time seems to slow almost to a stop as he stands there, staring up at the truck from the gulley floor. Shots strike its steel body, explosions of yellow sparks popping like little fireworks. A strange euphoria begins to come over him, the feeling of riding a motorbike at top speed through narrow, darkened streets, the engine screaming in his ears, at the very edge of control. The incomparable thrill of the death dance. Of being so close to his mortality he can sense its heavy presence hovering near him, feel its warm breath on the back of his neck. Smirking at the edge of the great abyss. It's a rush no drug could ever match, a satisfaction no tangled bedsheets could ever give him.

A grin spreads across his face. He forgets the pain in his shoulder and runs forward, his steps light and quick. Behind him, he's vaguely aware of Isabel still hollering, imploring him to stop. He reaches the back of the truck and yanks open the rear hatch. Bullets pound the Humvee as he rummages through the gear. He winces as a shot caroms off the hatch door, inches from his head.

"Not today, Santa Muerte," he laughs, finally finding what he's looking for. "Not today, you greedy bitch."

A whoosh of air rockets over his head. Another RPG, missing its target.

Bad aim, hombre. You should have taken more target practice.

He tucks the grenade launcher and a bag of ammunition under his arm.

My turn.

A hailstorm of rounds slams into the truck. Guzmán scurries away, back to the low-lying cover of the ditch, then clambers up the ridge where the soldiers are gathered and returning fire. Laying the grenade launcher on the ground in front of him, he realizes he's never actually used one of these contraptions before. He raps Paco on the leg, knocking on his body armor like a door. The young soldier turns around.

Guzmán gestures at the weapon. "You know how to work this?"

Paco stares blankly at the fat barrel of the airburst grenade launcher for a second, then shakes his head. They found the weapon in a cache of arms in Dallas last week, some bootlegger's treasure trove. All recent stuff, maybe only five years old. Intrigued by the new tech, on a whim Guzmán tossed it into Paco's Humvee as they were gearing up to leave Dallas. He'd used grenade launchers before, of course, but neither he nor anyone he's ever known has fired one that is less than thirty years old. This model has all sorts of strange toggles and buttons where there aren't supposed to be toggles and buttons.

Guzmán takes four of the short, stubby rounds from the bag and loads them into the cylindrical chamber. He crawls to the top of the ridge and peeks over. The tree line stands a couple hundred yards downrange. Bursts of gunfire fill the air. He ponders the weapon in his hands for a second, then flips what he hopes is the range control switch. On top of the launcher's barrel, a pair of triangles filled with what looks like opaque glass fold up into position. So far, so good. Through the glass he sights the target, lying flat on his belly and steadying the weapon's stock against his shoulder. Little white dots appear in the range finder, painting themselves over the trees like a swarm of invading insects. A green light begins to flash and he moves his finger off the trigger guard.

"Hide from this, cabrones," he mutters as he fires. The recoil sends a jolt of excruciating pain through his opposite shoulder, though he manages to keep his eyes open and looking forward. The round moves through the air slow enough to track, and he follows its lobbed trajectory, watching it climb as it moves away from his position, then reaching its apex and falling back down toward the oak thicket. A burst of bright light explodes above the treetops. An instant later the concussive sound of the explosion reaches him.

Isabel moves next to Guzmán, peering through her sniper scope. "Esssso. Good hit, boss." Then she yells out to the soldiers, ordering them to cease fire.

A quiet minute passes. The prone soldiers peer through binoculars and rifle scopes, looking for movement.

Through the ringing in his ears, Guzmán thinks he hears the sound of a motor. The distinct chug-chug-wheee of an engine being kicked started. And then he sees a motorbike flying out of the thicket, tearing across the plains in the opposite direction. A desperate, foolhardy attempt to escape.

"Yo lo tengo," Isabel bellows, claiming the target for herself. She settles her belly against the ground and positions the rifle on her shoulder. Licking her thumb for luck, she adjusts the sight and takes aim, cocking her head slightly and caressing the stock with her cheek. She fires and the rider slumps and falls, disappearing into the grass. The motorbike travels on, riderless, for a few moments before it starts to wobble, finally tumbling to a stop.

She looks over at Guzmán and nods, her face hard. "I think that's the last one, jefe."

EL FLACO

He lies in the dirt, breathing heavily, fresh waves of pain coming over him. His squad runs over and gently maneuvers him down the embankment. They stand over him, young faces smiling down at him in awe: the last thing he sees before the pain finally overcomes him and he passes out.

CHAPTER 14

"I did not come here to be insulted," Chavez seethes, rising from his chair.

Kennedy shows his palms, a conciliatory gesture. "I didn't mean to offend—"

"You say don Flaco's the worst thing ever to happen to Texas." Chavez glares at the American. "And you say it's not to offend?"

"Please, please," Kennedy implores. "A regrettable choice of words on my part. My apologies. Please, have a seat."

Soledad watches Chavez, his body tense, his face radiating ire like heat from a campfire. She reaches over and touches him lightly on the forearm, encouraging him to sit. He stands there for a moment, then snorts his displeasure as he lowers himself back into the chair.

"Thank you," Kennedy says. "Now, let me explain what I meant by that poorly phrased comment."

Guzmán's unlikely overthrow of the Bullock clan, the American explains, was the wild card that threw the whole game into chaos. Kennedy and his colleagues clearly underestimated the flaquistas, he admits, pegging Guzmán's movement as a regional uprising in the western desert. A local problem, nothing more. The flaquistas' success was a symptom, they concluded, of the Bullocks' growing complacency and fracturing influence. None of the American experts viewed don Flaco's movement as a threat to the incumbent regime, at least not in the near term. Wright and his Fundies, it seemed at the time, were the only legitimate threat to the Dallasites' hegemony.

"And we weren't the only ones surprised by your don Flaco's success," Kennedy says. "When Guzmán took Dallas, it forced Reverend Wright's hand."

Soledad listens to the American's truthful words, inwardly agreeing. Wright may be a lot of things, but a fool's not one of them. After Guzmán took Dallas, the preacher would have known that sooner or later don Flaco would be coming after him next, eager to rid himself of the longtime rival who'd vilified him for years, calling him "a heathen bean-eater" and "a godless desert snake."

"So he took to the airwaves," Kennedy says.

The preacher had run out of time and the Lord's favor, it seemed, so in a desperate gambit, he began to preach his gospel over the shortwave channels, pleading for help from any American Christians who might be listening. His people were being persecuted, and they needed aid from their American brothers and sisters. A bloodthirsty tyrant had taken over his beloved Texas. A Mexican Antichrist who wanted to hunt down and kill every last God-fearing man, woman, and child.

At this, Indigo nearly spits out her water. "He said that? A Mexican Antichrist?"

Kennedy shakes his head and raises his hand like he's taking an oath. "I swear. Those exact words."

Indigo casts an incredulous glance at the American. "And people *bought* it?"

"Hook, line, and sinker," General Bennett answers.

"By the thousands," Quinn adds.

Soledad recalls listening to one of the reverend's early broadcasts in Guzmán's City Hall office. They all laughed,

laughed at the ridiculousness of it, at the exaggerated rise and fall of Wright's voice that sounded more like a caricature of the preacher than his actual person. Guzmán himself was nearly brought to tears, pounding the desk with his palm as the preacher described him as the new pharaoh, living in the new Sodom of Dallas, mixing every biblical metaphor possible in his hours-long, scattered, maniacal rants. They even imagined gringos to the north laughing just like they were at the raving melodrama of this ridiculous backwoods Texan.

Soledad sits there, dumbfounded. She detects no signs of falsehood in Wright's words, but still she has difficulty believing that many Americans even listened to those berserk broadcasts in the first place, much less took them seriously. Had they all been completely wrong? Could *gringos*—educated, smart, sophisticated gringos—have actually been gullible enough to buy the crazy stories the preacher was selling?

Kennedy stands up and gives voice to Soledad's exact thoughts. "We never imagined his ravings would garner anything but ridicule." He moves over to the wall and gestures with his hand. The solid wall fades into transparency, becoming a window and revealing the cityscape beyond. "But it seems we were wrong again."

Far below them, the riot-geared police seem to have finally gotten the upper hand. The unruly crowd dissipates under a thinning fog of what Soledad assumes is tear gas.

The disconnected puzzle pieces in Soledad's mind begin to come together, forming a coherent story. The crazies they just saw outside. The crosses held aloft. The image of Wright on a sign that protested his persecution.

Soledad looks at Indigo and Chavez. The confusion on their faces slowly fades into understanding as they seem to arrive at the same conclusion.

"He puts people's heads on spikes," Chavez blurts. "The gringos want to help a man like this?"

"The ugliness of his movement," Kennedy answers,

"and the terrible things he does in its name are largely unknown outside of Texas." He sighs. "For your average churchgoing Oklahoman, Wright's movement isn't a cult or some kind of violent sect, they're a fellow Christian denomination in need of help."

"Wright has become…something of a political phenomenon here," General Bennett adds, her tone as somber as her unblinking eyes. She explains how the outpouring of sympathy for Wright and his Fundies has gained momentum in recent months, a grassroots movement of support that politicians and public officials can no longer ignore.

"A week ago," the general says, swallowing, "a flotilla of private boats out of Louisiana broke through the blockade and landed a shipment of supplies on the Bolivar Peninsula."

"'The Christian Cajun Navy,' they call themselves," Kennedy grumbles, still staring down to the street. "Can you believe such nonsense?"

It was a game of chicken in the Gulf, the general explains. Tugboats and shrimpers versus warships. And it was the warships who blinked first and gave way. Worried about the political fallout that would surely befall them if they stopped or harmed the privateers, the White House ordered the Navy to stand down and allow them through.

"Big mistake," Kennedy says, finally turning away from the window.

"And just how big was this flotilla?" Indigo asks, leaning forward.

"A couple hundred vessels," Kennedy answers.

Indigo exhales harshly, grimacing as if she's in pain. "And their hulls were full of weapons for the Fundies."

Kennedy confirms with a disappointed nod. "We got pictures from our drones when they unloaded. Guns, grenades, rocket launchers. Ferries full of vehicles."

"Enough weapons and gear for an army," the general adds.

Indigo turns to Chavez. "Enough to take the western desert."

Chavez shakes his head. "Pinches gringos hijos de puta," he mutters.

Bennett picks up the water pitcher and refills Indigo's glass. "Wright didn't waste any time in making his move," the general says. "When we found out he'd taken the west, we asked for the green light to reach out directly to Guzmán." She pauses, then adds regretfully, "Something we probably shouldn't have waited so long to do, in retrospect."

"So you're going to help us?" Chavez asks. "Help us fight them?"

General Bennett sets the pitcher down on the table, looks cautiously over at Kennedy.

"Our options are limited," Kennedy answers carefully. "I'm afraid with so much public sympathy for Wright, direct military involvement simply isn't on the table." He nods toward the window. "You just saw the kind of support he has now. We're starting to see these demonstrations more and more. Can you imagine how bad things might turn if we actually took up arms against him?"

"We had hoped," Bennett says, "to bring Guzmán here so he could help us lobby on his behalf. We know he's very persuasive, skilled at personal politics."

Soledad nods in silent agreement. So many times she's witnessed don Flaco turn a roomful of doubtful lieutenants into ardent supporters. His natural, unforced charisma has been as much a part of his success—perhaps more—as his shrewd military tactics. He's charmed thousands into following him, into buying into his movement. It isn't much of a stretch to imagine him charming American policymakers to earn their favor.

But then he bailed out on the trip to Oklahoma, opting instead to tear off across the plains on some ill-conceived mission. Soledad wonders where that leaves them, wonders if the gringos have a Plan B. Or are she and her companions just supposed to get back on the chopper and fly home now?

For a long moment no one speaks. Outside, tiny copters float back and forth in the near distance like toys suspended by invisible strings. Soledad feels tired, deflated. She was certain the Americans would lie, that they intended to deceive and manipulate their backwoods guests. She feels strangely let down that they haven't. The goddamn truth, that merciless bitch, has let her down once again.

The door opens and Garcia the redhead stands in the doorway, breathing like he's just run there. His face is twisted up in anxiety. He looks at Kennedy and swallows. "Sir, can I have a word with you?"

Kennedy exits the room for a moment with Garcia, then returns, his expression deflated, lips drawn into a tight line as he struggles to hold back what Soledad perceives as disappointment.

Bad news coming. As if they needed any more.

"Twenty minutes ago, the president ordered an end to the blockade," Kennedy announces grimly.

"Good God," Bennett exhales.

"Por Dios," Chavez echoes, turning to Soledad. "They're taking the preacher's side. They want him to kill us all."

"Please," Kennedy implores, "we're not taking his side."

"Caray, ya lo sabía," Chavez insists, crossing his arms and turning to his companions. "I knew it and I told you. Se los dije y no me pelaron."

Kennedy shakes his head ruefully. "It's politics, folks. Simple, brutal politics." Dejected, the American explains how the pressure to lift the embargo has intensified. The public—at least the part of the public that's sympathetic to Wright—has been punching holes in the official story of terrorism in recent weeks, accusing the White House of plotting against the Fundies. Even some congresspeople and senators have taken up the call, openly questioning the motives behind the blockade. Lifting the embargo would undoubtedly help Wright, but keeping it in place had become politically untenable. Wright taking Texas might not be ideal, but for the president and his advisers, such an eventuality would be a lesser evil than taking a big hit in approval ratings. Kennedy lets out a disappointed breath. "Politics," he repeats. "At the end of the day, that's what this is all about."

The tanned American pauses for a moment, and Soledad senses the wheels turning behind his eyes. Possibilities being considered, options being evaluated.

"Maybe there is something we can do," he says, the barest hint of optimism in his voice.

Chavez grunts. "What can you do if the casa blanca is supporting the preacher?"

"As I said," Kennedy insists, "I don't believe the White House is taking a side here. They just can't afford to *look* as if they're taking a side. They're playing it down the middle."

He looks over at the general. "Can we share intel?"

"I'd have to go through channels," Bennett responds, then adds fatalistically: "Who knows what will get approved now?"

"Go ahead and send the request in." Kennedy retakes his seat at the table. "I want to share the best intel we've got. Drone footage and imagery of Wright's forces. Anything that can help."

"Pictures, how wonderful," Indigo scoffs. "A gunbird strike or two might be a bit more useful, don't you think?"

The Americans ignore the jibe. "We've got feet on the ground, too," Kennedy says. "Sending in reports over encrypted satphones."

Indigo turns to Soledad and gives her an incredulous smirk. "Can you believe this shit?" She angrily shifts her gaze back across the table to the Americans. "Pictures from gunbirds and a few pairs of helping hands on the ground? You think that's gonna make some kind of difference?"

The Americans don't say anything.

"The Gulf's back open for business," Indigo hisses, "and that means the clock's already ticking. The help the preacher's getting isn't gonna stop with those Cajuns. He's gonna have more guns and volunteers shipped in than he knows what to do with." She looks at Chavez and Soledad. "All those crazies we met outside, they're gonna start sending him food and gas and arms till it's coming out of his backside. How long you think he'll wait before he marches on Dallas?"

"About as long as he waited to take the west," Chavez cuts in.

"You're right," the general concedes. "No doubt Wright has a lot more help coming his way. But it's not there yet. And he may have taken a big piece of your turf, but we don't think he's got enough arms and personnel to take Dallas."

Yet...enough arms and personnel to take Dallas...yet. Again, Soledad senses an unspoken word on the general's tongue.

She pictures boats of all sizes and shapes, docked at seaside piers along the Louisiana coast, sitting low and heavy in the water, loaded down with weapons and soldiers. Could things have really turned this badly this quickly? She begins to understand what she sensed haunting Kennedy's eyes minutes earlier, that thing underneath his disappointment after hearing Garcia's bad news. She begins to feel it herself. The dread and loathing of war, looming and unavoidable.

"So what are you saying?" Soledad urges Kennedy. "What are you telling us?"

Kennedy folds his hands together on the tabletop, his expression gravely earnest. "I'm telling you that our government, at its highest levels, appears to be warming up to the possibility of Wright eventually being in control of Texas."

Truth.

"And I'm telling you that everyone in this room believes this would be an extraordinarily bad thing."

Truth.

"I'm also telling you that, outside of some intelligence which may be of use to you, we can't offer military support or any other overt assistance. And lastly, I'm telling you there's not much time to act."

Truth.

He takes a long, deep breath. "You have to eliminate Reverend Wright, my friends, and you have to do it quickly."

...Truth...

CHAPTER 15

Ernesto knew that he wasn't supposed to bother Mamá when she had visitas, that he wasn't supposed to bang his little fist on the door. "Ernestito Francisco Guzmán," she'd chide him, leaning down far enough that he could see she was naked underneath the baggy t-shirt, "go outside and play like I told you." But she'd always smile and wink at him so he knew she wasn't really angry.

Visitas. Visitors. That's what she called the men she spent time with behind the closed door of their tiny one-room apartment. There were so many of them, coming and going all the time. One day Ernesto tried to count them all, but he ran out of fingers and lost track.

He tried to be patient like Mamá wanted him to, but it wasn't easy. He played with the other children outside, the boys and girls who lived in the same building, whose mothers also had lots of visitas. They had a fun playground. A collection of old cars and trucks and tractors, their engines removed so the kids could crawl around inside. They'd play hide-and-seek, king of the hill, and car chase, Ernesto's favorite. He always had to sit in the driver's seat, and he always insisted he'd won the pretend races. It was fun, but he liked being with Mamá more, so as he played with his friends he kept an eye on their first-floor door from the playground. As soon as her visita left, he'd run home for snacks and limonada. But before long there'd be a knock—another visita—and she'd shoo him out again, playfully slapping his behind. Vete a jugar, ándale.

Today was Mamá's birthday, so he'd tried his best to behave. Between visitas he brought Mamá fresh churros from the viejito's kiosk and her favorite licuado de chocolate. He hadn't interrupted her once, and he hadn't gotten into any fights on the playground—not any bad ones, at least. Mamá always hated it when he had fights, even though he almost never lost one. She warned him that fighters never ended well, and she didn't want that for her Ernestito.

"Ay, que delícia," she cooed, breaking off a portion of churro and handing it to him. He gobbled it up, the fried dough warm on his tongue and down his throat. "What did I do to deserve such a good boy?" she purred, taking his face in her hands. She kissed his cheeks and hugged him, cradling his head against her chest. He could smell her last visita's sweat on her, but he didn't mind.

A knock on the door.

She held him tighter to her breast and then sighed sadly, a slow release Ernesto felt as much as he heard. A sagging in her chest and a long exhale with a soft, sorrowful moan. He didn't want her to be sad on her birthday, so he decided to leave without having to be told. "I'll go play," he said, releasing his arms from around her.

He opened the door, but this visita didn't let him run past, didn't ignore him like all the others did. This one grabbed Ernesto by the upper arm hard, stopping him cold. He looked up at the man and saw a hard gringo face with a scraggly beard. Angry eyes stared at Mamá.

"Get some clothes on, whore," the man sneered.

Outside, they had gathered up all the children and their mothers. It was the first time Ernesto had seen everyone who lived in the apartment building all together. Sometimes they had parilladas or quinceañeras in the empty field across the street, but even then there were always several mothers who had to work. Visitas could show up anytime, even on Christmas.

Ernesto joined the assembly of residents, Mamá clutching him tightly to her side. She looked worried and so did Linda Gorda, who lived next door. Linda had four little ones, and they pressed against her ample hips and belly, looking scared. Linda asked Mamá if she knew what was going on, but Mamá shook her head no. None of the mothers knew either, and Ernesto could see that the not knowing worried them a lot. More men with hard faces— some white, some brown like Ernesto—stood nearby holding shotguns and rifles. Marta, the woman with no kids who lived three doors down, asked Mamá where Antonio and the other padrotes were. Why hadn't the men protected them? Marta looked as angry as she was scared. What the hell did they take their money for, she griped, if they didn't show up when they were needed? Mamá said she didn't know.

Then a man stepped forward in front of the others. He was young with a big, strong body and a voice that was even stronger. He was dressed nicer than the other men, who were all clothed in well-worn hunting gear and boots. His shirt and pants were clean and new and his shoes held a shine. And he didn't carry a weapon, only a leather bag slung over his shoulder, which he dropped onto the ground at his feet. The man announced in a loud, crisp voice that his name was *Right*, like right and left or right and wrong, which Ernesto thought was a strange word for a name. But gringos sometimes had names that didn't make sense, like Baker or Shoemaker. Those were jobs, not names.

The strangest thing about this man's name, though, was how all the mothers gasped and got quiet the moment he said it, and how his mother drew him closer and her hands began to tremble. That's when Ernesto really began to get scared.

The man spoke in a booming howl, his voice rising and falling. He paced back and forth menacingly, reminding Ernesto of a caged cougar he had once seen at the bazaar. Ernesto's English wasn't that good yet, so he couldn't understand much of what the man said. The words hardly seemed to matter, though. The man's face, his enraged bulging eyes, and the vicious force of his voice communicated plenty. The man hated them all. All the women and their children.

Ernesto couldn't grasp this. The man had never met him or Mamá before, didn't even know them. So how could he hate them so much? He remembered how Mamá had once told him how some people were just born bad. Hay gente chueca, she'd said. Maybe this man was one of those.

As he bellowed on, behind him a few of his men hustled back and forth along the front of the building, darting in and out of the rooms, pouring something that looked like water from plastic jugs onto the floors. Some of the women began to cry. Linda Gorda shouted to the men, begging them no, no, please don't do it. Marta hollered at them angrily, calling them cowards and hijos de la chingada. A strong chemical smell hit Ernesto, burning the insides of his nose, and then he knew it wasn't water the men were pouring from those jugs.

Then the man named Right stopped talking and he leaned down to the bag he'd dropped. From it he pulled a man's head, freshly severed. Blood and gore dripped from the neck as he raised it up high, gripping it by the hair. Ernesto recognized the head as that of Antonio, one of the padrotes, the pimps who were supposed to be protecting everyone. The women began to shriek.

The man stood before them brandishing the head like a proud hunter with a prize game bird, his face crazy like some kind of demon. Flames erupted in the apartment building as the men tossed burning rags into the rooms. Ernesto watched as his and Mamá's home went up in flames, eyes welling up with tears. Their bed, their food, their clothes, all burning. Every meager possession they owned and the only home Ernesto had ever known, all of it being consumed by fire.

And then the man raised his voice even louder, booming over the noise of the growing bonfire, over the shrieking cries of the women and children.

"For the wages of sin is DEATH," he roared, a monster standing before a raging inferno, "but the gift of God is eternal life in Christ Jesus our Lord."

In later years, whenever Wright's name came up or the reverend made an unwanted appearance into Ernesto's thoughts, this was the moment that always came first to mind. The horrific spectacle of a madman, a devil disgorged from hell.

The last thing the man shouted was that the women's wickedness would find no sanctuary here. Then he and his men left as suddenly as they had appeared, Ernesto's home still ablaze. That night all the families slept outside, huddled together, frightened and shivering. The padrotes never showed up, and the next morning they discovered why when one of the children went for a morning pee, finding a dozen heads set atop tall spikes in the nearby woods.

After the incident, Ernesto and his mother moved from Houston to the west, like a lot of the other mothers did. Out west, she assured Ernesto, she could work without worrying about men like that showing up. The journey there took weeks. Ernesto would later remember the time as an endless suffering of blistered feet and a hunger so intense it made him sick.

They finally resettled near Del Rio. But despite his mother's promises, their lives never returned to what they'd once been. With the arrival of so many women like Ernesto's mother to the western desert, where the scattered population offered far fewer prospects than populous Houston, customers were scarce and infrequent. Sometimes she'd go for days without a single visita. Problema de oferta y demanda, she told Ernesto, smiling painfully. Supply and demand, she'd then say, teaching him the English words. They moved from place to place, trying to find somewhere that had more visitas, but it was the same in every dusty, sunbaked town. With each failure, Ernesto's mother seemed to grow weaker and more fragile. The girlish bounce in her voice went away; the spark in her eyes faded.

Life deteriorated into a scramble for survival. At eight years old Ernesto became the family breadwinner, his mother having surrendered to indifference. He stole food from the markets or people's homes. He taught himself to shoot with a revolver he'd robbed from a sleeping drunk. He used the gun to hunt small game, mostly desert hares and snakes. Good meat if you knew how to cook it right.

Impressed by his audaciousness, the town boys looked up to him, followed him. They sarcastically nicknamed him "El Flaco," the skinny one, because he still had the chubby cheeks and round belly of a toddler. The town boys were the earliest of his admirers, the first flaquistas, who in the decades to come would eventually number in the tens of thousands.

The spark never returned to his mother's eyes. She seemed to age decades in the two years since they had been forced to leave Houston, her hair graying, her body growing ever frailer. She died in her sleep, her beloved Ernesto lying next to her. He remained with her body for days in their tiny squatted room in Del Rio, until the smell aroused the concern of an elderly couple who lived nearby. They dragged him from the room screaming and crying.

The couple, whose names Ernesto didn't know, tried to comfort him. They fed him stew as he sat huddled on their threadbare couch, and murmured that it was just his mother's time. Ernesto looked at them like they were crazy.

"Bullshit," he said, using one of the first English words he'd learned from a green-eyed boy back in Houston. "That man named Right killed Mamá." He stared past them, a seed of vengeance already growing in the fertile ground of his broken heart. "And one day I'm going to kill him."

*   *   *

"Don Flaco…don Flaco…"

Guzmán opens his eyes and the blackness recedes, dissolving into a perfect blue sky. For a disorienting moment, he's still in his dream memory, still in Del Rio, still ten years old. His head hurts with a pounding throb. Slowly, his awareness returns. He's lying on the ground, looking skyward, with a hell of a headache. He rolls to one side, pressing the bulk of his weight onto his injured shoulder, sending a painful reminder jolting through him. With a groaning curse, he rolls onto his back again.

G.G.'s head pokes into his field of vision, staring down at him, grinning. "How you feeling, boss?"

"How long was I out?" Guzmán croaks.

"Not long," Isabel answers, leaning over him. "Not even a minute."

"Help me up."

Woozy and aching, he gets to his feet with G.G.'s help. Isabel looks him up and down, her sniper rifle slung over her shoulder. A soldier of few words, she nods at him grimly and he returns the gesture.

The rest of the squad, what's left of them, are scattered about the area. Isabel has some of them assessing the damage to their convoy: the loss of life, the injuries, the damage to their gear and vehicles. The other half search through the distant thicket of trees, making sure all the ambushers have been eliminated, salvaging whatever they may find.

His wits recovered, curiosity pushes its way through the pounding in Guzmán's head. He wants to see their attackers. His hand clutching G.G.'s shoulder for support, he heads toward the oak thicket on wobbly legs. As they approach the tree line, Isabel gives him the bad news. Three of the six Humvees are destroyed or irreparably damaged. Of the seventeen soldiers they left Dallas with, eight are dead, and two have gunshot wounds—neither life-threatening, a small blessing amid the disastrous ambush. Only seven somehow managed to avoid injury.

By the time they reach the thicket, Guzmán's head has almost cleared and his legs have steadied. He passes through the brush, finding five bodies, motionless and bloodied and sprawled out in unnatural positions atop a bed of fallen leaves. Memo busily rummages through the pockets of the dead for anything useful, and Astrid piles up all the plundered gear. Automatic rifles, a decent amount of ammunition, and a pair of grenade launchers. Three men and two women. The men all sport telltale tattoos covering their bodies. Bible verses, images of Jesus, large ornate crosses. The women all have waist-long hair woven into pairs of braids.

Guzmán shakes his head. Fucking Fundies.

"Jefe," Memo says, squatting next to one of the bodies. "Mira."

The woman's lifeless eyes stare upward; her mouth hangs slightly open. Still clutched in her hand is a radio microphone, its curly rubber cord disappearing beneath her back. Memo rolls the woman onto her side, revealing the remains of a small shortwave radio. The device is broken into pieces.

Memo picks up a casing panel, examines it, then tosses it aside. "Looks like it was shot right through."

Guzmán kneels down next to the woman, looks at the radio mic in her hand. One side of her face is grotesquely swollen and her teeth are visible through a large, meaty hole in her cheek. A shrapnel injury from one of the grenades he fired.

"Did you call your friends," he asks her, "before your radio busted? Did I kill you before you called for help?" When she doesn't answer, he looks up at Isabel. "¿Qué piensas?"

"We have to go back," she says flatly. "We've got dead and injured."

Guzmán turns back to the dead Fundies. Dappled sunlight shines through the canopy of leaves and branches, falling over their bodies. "Bury our dead," he tells Isabel, "and then take one of the trucks and get the injured back to Dallas."

Isabel's expression darkens in confusion. "*One* of the trucks?"

"I'm taking the other two."

"Jefe," she protests, "we don't know if they called for help on that radio. You can't just go and—"

"I'm taking the trucks and that's it." He doesn't remove his eyes from the dead woman, though he doesn't see her. The images from his dream memory haunt his senses, blaring fresh and horrible. The monster roaring, the inferno behind him, the trophy head raised up high. He can see every detail of the reverend's face, hear the madness in his voice as clearly as if he were here in the thicket with him. And worst, he can smell Mamá, the sickening stench of her death in their tiny squat.

"Don Flaco," Isabel pleads, "we can have more trucks and personnel here in a few hours. You don't have to—"

"¡Basta ya!" he snaps. He's waited years, decades. He convinced himself other things were more important. Winning territory. Growing his army. Slowly, carefully, he expanded his power, eventually gaining the whole of the Republic. And to what end? Wright's still out there, still alive, blood pumping through his veins, every beat of his heart an insult to his mother's memory.

He's done with waiting, done with playing the hero, done with worrying about everyone and everything else.

Done with everything except the killing.

CHAPTER 16

Guzmán doesn't feel crazy. A crazy person, after all, does crazy things. A crazy person wouldn't, for example, have made sure the bodies of his fallen soldiers were taken back to Dallas. A crazy person wouldn't have cared, would have instead left them out there to rot in the sun. And a crazy person wouldn't have given two shits about their shortwaves being destroyed in the ambush. But being stuck with nothing except short-range hand radios—their communications with Dallas effectively cut off—*does* bother Guzmán. He planned on calling Chavez and Reader Soledad to learn how things were going with the gringos, and now he can't. And if he were *really* crazy—stark, raving crazy like that bug-eyed hustler with the shaking hands who wanted to sell him the Rio Bravo—the five soldiers accompanying him wouldn't have volunteered as quickly as they did. Of course, G.G. shrugged and said what the hell, living forever's overrated anyway, but the kid was always making jokes like that.

Still, making a mental list of reasons why you're not crazy is exactly the kind of thing a crazy person might do, isn't it? And if taking six trucks and seventeen soldiers on a mission into the unknown was so risky that it nearly sent old Chavez into hysterics, then what other word could describe the decision to push onward with only two trucks and five soldiers? Seems like crazy more or less fits the bill, as the gringos say. And if that's what this is, then fine, that's what it is.

Isabel sits beside him, piloting the Humvee over the grassy expanse of the north central Texas plains, expertly maneuvering the machine around dips and arroyos Guzmán doesn't even notice. Sharpshooter's eyes, he thinks. She doesn't miss a thing. It's midafternoon as they travel westward, following the lead Humvee a hundred yards ahead. The enormous vehicle, fitted out for rough country with its huge knobby tires and oversized suspension, rolls along at a steady pace, gently rocking back and forth over the uneven ground. G.G. rides in back, absently spinning the barrel of an old six-shooter he calls his lucky piece.

Time passes and the flat green plains begin to lose their color, dissolving into dull browns and grays. Lush prairie grasses thin out and clumps of thick-leafed shrubs start to appear. Tough, drought-resistant plants that sit low to the ground, their stubborn roots anchored deep into the hard dirt. The terrain begins to undulate with the gentle rise and fall of low-lying hills. In the far distance, plateaus emerge like rust-colored tabletops pushing above the western horizon. They'll be in the desert soon, Guzmán notes, a flutter of anticipation rippling through his insides. Where the preacher is.

A voice comes over the hand radio, Paco from the lead Humvee. Drowned in crackling static, his words are unintelligible, but his excitement comes through plain enough. G.G. puts on the speaker to his ear.

"What is it?" Guzmán asks.

G.G. listens, his expression knotted in concentration. After a moment, he nods, then puts the mic to his mouth. "Got it," he calls back. "I'll tell him."

The young soldier lowers the radio. "They spotted a

motorbike."

Guzmán whips his gaze around and peers out the windshield. "Where?" He scans the terrain, sees nothing.

"About two clicks to the west."

"Pull us up even with them," Guzmán orders Isabel, fumbling through his gear bag for his binoculars.

"Jefe," she says cautiously, "con todo respeto, it's safer if we hang back."

"I know it is, niña," he snaps back. "Now acelérate."

With a reluctant press of the driver's foot, the truck gains speed and draws closer to the lead vehicle. Guzmán, binoculars in hand, clambers over the seat and shimmies up into the turret. A warm wind hits his face as he emerges from the top of the Humvee. Below him he hears Isabel chastising G.G. He shouldn't be out in the open like that, she scolds. Why didn't you stop him from getting up there? G.G. throws the question back at her. Why didn't *you* stop him? You can tell him as easy as I can. Like he'd listen to either of us anyway, he adds.

Guzmán presses the binoculars to his face and scans a barren vista of muted browns, of scrub brush and small, leafless trees with gnarled, deformed-looking branches. He sees the dust plume first, a distortion of kicked-up dirt in the near distance, ahead and a bit to the left. A moment later the motorbike appears, topping a small hill, then disappears over the other side.

He slaps the hood of the vehicle and calls down to G.G. "Five points to the left, two clicks ahead."

The young soldier relays the message to the other Humvee, and both drivers adjust their course. The two vehicles travel side by side, a fifty-yard gap between them. Guzmán waves to Esteban, his counterpart in the other turret. Esteban waves back, his long black hair flying out like a flag behind him.

"Does he see us?" G.G. calls up.

Guzmán spots the motorbike rising over another hill, then it disappears again as the land dips. The rider's moving at a decent pace, but not a panicked one. He doesn't seem to be running.

"No creo," he calls down. "Pásame la radio, joven."

G.G. reaches up with one tanned arm and Guzmán brings the radio to his mouth. "Bring this fish in, nice and easy," he orders. "He doesn't know he's hooked yet." They'll stop the rider and find out if he—or she, from this distance it's impossible to say—knows anything about what's going on out west.

The Humvees separate, the drivers putting a half-mile distance between the vehicles, flanking the motorbike on either side as they slowly close the distance. Guzmán watches through the binoculars, searching for the giveaway billow of dust, then radioing course adjustments to the drivers when the motorbike peeks above a hill or ridge. The chase reminds him of an old gringo novel from his library, a story about hunting whales, how the fishermen would patiently follow the enormous animals in a flock of small boats, waiting for a shadowy glimpse of their prey beneath the waves or a telltale spout from a blow hole, like a dust cloud in the desert. The captain chased his obsession to the farthest oceans of the world. In the end that whale got the better of him, and the tortured captain died unavenged.

Guzmán laughs to himself. Maybe if the captain had been a Mexican with a .50-caliber machine gun, things would have turned out differently.

Time passes and they cut the distance to less than a mile. When they're close enough, they'll pull alongside and fire off a few warning rounds into the air. Then he'll either stop or try to run. If he's smart, he'll stop.

Half a mile ahead, the motorbike rises into view. They're so close now Guzmán can make out the model of the bike, a Yamaha. He also notices something odd about the rider's jacket sleeves. He looks through the binoculars and realizes the rider's actually wearing a vest. What Guzmán thought were sleeves are tattoos covering both bare arms. On the back of his helmet is a crudely drawn cross.

The rider's a Fundie.

Guzmán starts to remove the binoculars from his face, but then notices a change in the rider's posture. The Fundie turns and looks directly behind him. In the next moment an enormous plume of dirt shoots high into the air from the motorbike's rear tire. *The fish finally sees he's been hooked*, Guzmán thinks, and then the Fundie and his vehicle disappear from view over the far side of the hill.

"¡Ya nos vio!" Guzmán shouts down to Isabel in the driver's seat. He slaps the roof with his palm—"He's running! Go! Go! Go!"—and braces himself against the sudden lurch of acceleration as he radios to the other driver.

A giddy smile comes across Guzmán's face. *The chase is on.*

He bounces back and forth in the turret as the twin Humvees tear across the rolling countryside like coyotes after a hare. Through the binoculars the terrain jumps and shakes as he searches for their prey. A minute later he spots the motorbike, flying over the top of a ridge high into the air, a grasshopper startled from the grass. The skilled rider has already put another quarter mile of distance between himself and his pursuers.

A stark landscape stretches out in all directions. The rider has nowhere to hide, no forests he can get lost in, no nearby towns he can disappear into. But he's got a good machine and he handles it well. Over this kind of terrain, he can certainly outrun them, and in fact he already is.

Guzmán feels a tug on his pant leg. He looks down, sees G.G. holding the hand radio. "Esteban's asking if he can engage the target," the youth shouts upward.

"No," Guzmán answers. "Tell him to hold his fire." He smiles down at the soldier. "Why should he have all the fun?"

G.G. smiles back. "Roger that."

Isabel pushes the Humvee faster, but still the gap widens. Guzmán quickly settles in behind the .50-cal, flips the switch on the range finder, and peers down the scope. Even with the laser crosshairs, at this range and with all this bumping around, a well-aimed shot will be next to impossible. A few rounds intended as a warning could easily take out the rider or blow up the bike. But with each second, the motorbike pulls farther downrange, farther away. Another minute passes and the joy of the chase gives way to a growing worry that the rider might escape them and report their whereabouts to his superiors. He has to take the shot.

Guzmán fires. A rooster tail of dirt explodes up from the ground to the left of the bike. The bike speeds on, undeterred. *He's got ice in his veins, this Fundie.*

Guzmán aims again, trying to compensate for the Humvee's constant jostle, and squeezes off another quick burst. The shots strike the ground behind the rider's back tire. The bike swerves madly and vanishes over the hill.

Moments pass and the Fundie rider doesn't appear again. G.G. radios the other Humvee, but Esteban hasn't spotted him either. Guzmán scans back and forth across the landscape. He can't find anything. No machine, no dust clouds, nothing but low hills and scrubby brown shrubs dotting the bleak countryside like countless scabs.

Time moves with excruciating slowness. Sweat drips from Guzmán's forehead, dampening the binoculars' rubber eyepieces. For as far as he can see, there's nothing but a vast emptiness extending to the horizon. Worry begins to bloom inside him. If the Fundie escapes them completely, they're screwed. Their little two-vehicle caravan, no matter how well-armed and manned, won't get very far at all if they can't keep their presence a secret.

Another minute passes and geography intervenes on Guzmán's behalf. The rolling terrain begins to level out into flatlands. His view of the near distance becomes less obstructed by hills and ridges.

"Come on, come on," he mutters, bouncing around the turret, peering through the sweat-slicked binoculars, "show yourself, you little rabbit."

Two miles out, he spots the hazy blur of a dust cloud, and then finally the motorbike itself speeding across the barren countryside. "Floor it!" he shouts to Isabel, slapping the roof so hard his hand tingles with a painful sting. The driver obeys, stomping down on the gas and throwing Guzmán momentarily off balance.

Steadying himself, he drops the binoculars around his neck. His eyes tear in the rush of warm wind. He bellows course adjustments down to Isabel. G.G. calls the other Humvee, tells them they've spotted the rider.

Gradually, the tiny two-wheeled vehicle gets bigger. Guzmán grins. They're gaining on him. Maybe luck's on their side today and the Fundie's running out of fuel or he blew a shock.

And then his spirits drop as suddenly as they picked up. About a mile beyond the rider, the flatlands give way to a sudden jut of rocky outcroppings and steeper hills. He peers through the binoculars to get a better look, then curses to himself. It's the kind of rough, rocky ground that slows a Humvee into low gear, but a motorbike, smaller and more agile, can zip through with little difficulty. The Fundie rider can lose them there easily, and he appears to know it, making a beeline for the rocky sanctuary. He's a minute away, Guzmán estimates, two at the most.

Guzmán flips the switch on the targeting system and finds the rider. He calls down to G.G., tells him to give Esteban the kill order, and then he opens fire.

The rider's at the extreme end of the .50-cal's range, and there's a lag of seconds between the fired shots and their faraway impact visible through the scope. His first volley isn't anywhere close. He squeezes off another, leading the target more this time, missing again. The rider, now clearly aware he's under fire, begins to zigzag his way across the plain. With the extra maneuvering, it'll take him longer to get to his destination, but he'll also be much harder to hit.

Esteban opens up, firing off a quick burst. His results are no better. He fires again, missing so badly Guzmán can't even see the impact through the scope.

"Isa," Guzmán shouts down, "get up here!"

Isabel and G.G. scramble over the front seat and G.G. slides behind the wheel. Guzmán lowers himself into the backseat, letting Isabel climb up and take his place behind the .50 cal.

"Fuck, that's a long way out," she shouts, then fires a quick burst. Binoculars pressed to his face, Guzmán sees the impact. *Damn close for a first try.*

Another burst from the .50-cal, and seconds later it's all over. Isabel's second shot hits the rider in the upper torso, and he flies off the bike as if he's been yanked by an invisible rope. Rider and machine tumble away from each other, kicking up a cloud of dust.

"God DAMN, that woman can shoot!" G.G. hollers. He honks the horn repeatedly in celebration.

Guzmán sighs in relief, then reaches back and pats Isabel's boot in appreciation. "Bien hecho," he compliments. "Nice shooting, Isa."

She looks down at him, smiles. "Coulda put me up here in the first place, boss."

He grins back, amused. Having just saved all their asses, the sharpshooter's more than earned the right to a bit of cheek. "I thought I'd miss a few times, make you look good," he jokes back, then taps his temple. "Fríamente calculado." Up front, G.G. erupts into laughter.

The two Humvees approach the fallen rider. They find him sprawled out, twenty feet away from his motorbike, its motor still running. Esteban hops down to the ground and approaches the motionless figure. After a quick examination, he looks up to Guzmán's Humvee and shakes his head.

Damn. They won't be getting any intel out of this one. But at least he didn't escape.

G.G. exits the truck and strides over to the motorbike. He picks it up and throws his leg over the seat. Revving the throttle, he inspects the engine critically, moving his head from one side to the other. He bounces up and down, testing the shocks. "No damage," he calls over to Guzmán. "Not a bad little machine."

The rocky outcropping lies a few hundred meters ahead. A warning signals from somewhere deep in Guzmán's gut.

"G.G., Esteban," he calls from the Humvee's window, "back into the trucks."

Isabel jerks in the turret, then falls down onto the backseat, her body limp as if she's suddenly fallen asleep. Guzmán sees the bullet hole where her eye was an instant before. The back of her head is gone. Blood and gore ooze across the seat from a grotesque exit wound.

Before he can shout out again to the others, a flash of bright light fills the corner of his vision, followed instantly by a deafening explosion. The world slows down and his truck lurches upwards and sideways, lifted off the ground as if punched by some giant fist. Outside the windshield, the ground and sky spin like clothes in a washing machine window. He tumbles weightless around the truck's cabin, limbs flailing, particles of broken glass floating around him. His shoulders and head slam against the truck's steel roof. There is no up or down, only the churning chaos of the cabin.

Finally the spinning stops. Outside, the ground rises up vertically. Guzmán blinks, then realizes the truck's come to rest on its side. There's a high-pitched ringing in his ears, and underneath it he hears a soft popping of gunfire and shouting voices. Woozy, he manages to raise himself into a sitting position. Glass shards fill the cabin. Isabel is gone. Thrown clear during the vehicle's roll, he guesses. His body aches like he's been beaten with a baseball bat. He's got to get out, he knows, but his body seems disconnected from his mind, ignoring the urgency and animal panic running through his head. He looks up, sees the steering wheel a couple feet above him. He reaches for it and slowly pulls himself up. The ringing subsides a bit and he crouches in the cabin, his feet on the grass where the passenger window used to be, his head just below the open driver's window. He removes his sidearm from its holster and readies himself to pop out and open fire.

"Drop it!" a voice behind him cries. "Drop it now!"

His mind still muddled and slow, he turns toward the voice. Something that feels like a punch strikes down hard on his forearm. He looks down and stares dumbly at his empty hand. It takes a moment for him to realize that someone's knocked his pistol out of his grip.

In the turret opening kneels a young Fundie soldier, his face covered in Bible verse tattoos. He points a rifle at Guzmán and glares, baring his teeth like an angry dog.

"Get out," he sneers, "you filthy heathen."

CHAPTER 17

Soledad has heard of holos, of course. She's even seen them in movies and shows bootlegged across the border, but until now she's never witnessed the tech in person. Garcia the redhead stands in front of the far wall, the room lights dimmed, manipulating large, floating images with deft movements of his fingers, hands, and arms, swiping rapidly through picture after picture like someone might thumb through pages of a familiar book. Soledad sits at a table with Indigo; the two women watch the blur of images, captivated as much by the amazing visual technology as Garcia's proficiency in using it.

"I put together the best and latest imagery we've got from the western desert," he says, concentrating on his task. Images as tall as he is zoom past.

Swipe, swipe, swipe. More images whiz by. Then he stops. "Here we go," he announces, apparently finding what he was looking for.

He turns and looks at the Texans. "Do you have portable archives?"

Soledad and Indigo exchange looks. "No," Soledad answers, not even knowing what a portable archive is.

"Mem needles?" Garcia asks, lifting his eyebrows.

133

"We don't have this kind of tech back home," Indigo clarifies.

Garcia nods. "Okay, no problem. We can go old-fashioned and give you hard copies." He spreads his arms out wide and the high-altitude image quickly zooms into near-ground detail. The effect is like a sudden, high-speed fall, eliciting gasps from Soledad and the trader.

"Ah, sorry," Garcia apologizes. "I'll try not to move around so fast." He takes a step forward and points at a collection of buildings near the top of the image. "So this is Odessa right here." He lowers his index finger a couple feet. "And here's where they've got their vehicles."

Soledad leans forward, her eyes widening.

"Por Dios," Chavez blurts as he enters the room, his eyes widened at the floating image. "That looks like two hundred machines."

"Nearly three hundred," Garcia corrects. "And about the same amount in Midland." He zooms the image, this time more slowly, close enough now that Soledad can recognize individual vehicles. The image slowly pans over the fleet, and Soledad swallows at the collection of Humvees, motorcycles, and armored buses. She even sees a row of semitrucks with machine gun turrets.

"So what's the word?" Indigo asks Chavez, who left minutes earlier to check in with Guzmán and Dallas.

"Nothing new," Chavez grumbles, still fuming over whatever message he just decoded over the shortwave channel. He draws closer to the women and speaks quietly so the gringo can't overhear. "I tried to get through to him, but nothing. So I called Dallas. They haven't been able to reach him for hours."

"Christ," Indigo mutters, keeping her voice low. "He has no idea what he's running into."

If he's even still alive out there, Soledad thinks morbidly.

"He'll be careful," Chavez whispers, looking furtively over at Garcia. The hierba's effect is winding down, but it's still strong enough that Soledad can detect the tight thrum of anxiety in the old warrior's voice.

The trio turn their attention back to the holo. Soledad steps toward the hovering ghost of Odessa, her eyes narrowed. "Do you think Wright has enough?" she asks, turning back to Chavez. "Does that look like a big enough fleet to take Dallas?" The Americans didn't seem to think so and said as much, but they weren't wasteland warlords like old Chavez. If anyone could accurately assess their odds, it was Guzmán's right hand.

Chavez's perma-frown deepens, his brow furrows. "Hard to say. Depends on their weapons."

Then something near the edge of the image catches Soledad's eye. She steps closer. "Can you make that bigger?" she asks, pointing.

"Sure." Garcia twists and spreads his hands apart slowly, magician-like, centering and magnifying the picture. As he zooms in, the image pixelates, blurring for an instant, and then comes back into focus.

Soledad sees children.

There are dozens of them, their manacled hands and feet connected by long chains. She shivers, remembering when she first found Steffa in Conroe, clasped in rusted iron chains just like these. The tender skin of the girl's wrists and ankles raw and bloody, her eyes dull and lifeless.

Garcia slowly lowers his arms and shakes his head in disgust. "Jesus," he mutters.

"Debt holders," Indigo says. "That's what he calls them."

"Slaves are slaves," Soledad asserts, her cheeks warming in anger, "no matter what name you give them."

"When we heard about this," Garcia says, "at first we didn't believe it."

"It's no lie," Chavez assures him.

"We know that now," Garcia answers. "Once we were sure, we leaked the images to the media, hoping it would sour the support he has here."

"And let me guess," Indigo says, "they didn't believe it."

Garcia looks at her, nods. "Right. They thought it was all fake. Stories invented by his enemies. The blew it off as state propaganda and doctored photos."

"People believe what they want to believe," Soledad observes, "truth be damned." And doesn't she know it? She's read plenty of zealots in her time, and their minds work in strange and unsettling ways—whether it's a mouth-foaming Fundie or Guzmán's most hardcore loyalist. Perhaps better than anyone, she knows how a zealot's mind, rigid and intractable, has a seemingly limitless capacity to deny reality, even when the chained and manacled reality is shoved right in their faces.

Garcia swipes the image away, exhales in disgust. "If it were up to me, I'd..." His voice trails off. "But it's not up to me, I guess."

He makes a small flourish of his hand, and the holo projection fades away. The lights come back up, bringing the American's dejected expression into full illumination. "How can anyone follow a man like that?" he asks, the question directed to no one in particular. "I don't get it."

"The desperate want hope more than anything," Chavez says, his voice uncharacteristically reflective, "and that's what he's selling."

"The desperate I can understand," Garcia says. "When you're starving or scared for your life, you'll clutch onto anything. But what I can't see is how people *over here* can buy into it. He's got so many advocates here, so many people pulling for him. I just don't get it."

Soledad gets it. There's a zealot lurking inside some people, waiting to be cultivated by some charismatic speaker or flamed into existence by some personal tragedy. She's seen fanatics from every walk of life, from every point on the spectrum of wealth and privilege. A zealot knows no geography or class. Fanaticism is like a...*predisposition* that some have, carried deep within like a bad gene for cancer. She offers Garcia none of this insight, though, since it's a wisdom gleaned from her special way of seeing. Trying to explain such a thing to a non-reader would be like trying to explain math to a housefly.

"We have to get back," Chavez announces, stirring Soledad from her thoughts.

Somberly, she nods her head. How things have changed in such a short time.

Was she silly to think it wouldn't eventually come to this? That the days of blood and bullets were a thing of the past? Was she a kind of zealot of her own, willfully ignoring the reality of don Flaco's childlike insolence, his conspicuousness shortcomings?

She should have known better, dammit. She of all people should have known better. Should have seen all this coming.

Where is Guzmán right now? she wonders. Is he alive, barreling westward, standing tall and defiant in a Humvee's turret? Or is he dead already, lying sprawled out on the dusty floor of the plains?

And does it matter to her? There was a time when it would have, but now she's not so sure.

CHAPTER 18

In the falling light of sunset, a sullen Guzmán sits inside a steel cage mounted in the bed of a pickup truck, his hands tied behind his back, his wounded shoulder aching. Esteban, the other captured member of the squad, sits across from him, hands also bound, staring dully at his own boots. The truck, a rusted-out Chevy, moves quietly through the darkness, surrounded by a couple dozen vehicles: motorbikes, high-riding sedans with oversized suspension and tires, and more trucks. Some of the vehicles' bodies display names and numbers of Bible verses in large, crudely painted characters: John 3:16, First Peter (spelled Ferst) 5:8, Romans 3:23. The tribal markings of their Fundie clan.

The caravan rolls steadily westward, toward the orange globe of the setting sun. With the vehicles' headlights turned off, the near-dark gives their surroundings an eerie haziness. Guzmán can see through the cab window that the truck's driver is already wearing a set of night vision goggles, as are the motorbike riders and other drivers. New models, he notes. When they tied him and Esteban up and threw them into the cage, he noticed other pieces of equipment—body armor, helmets, rifles—all of them unusually modern and unused-looking. Where would Fundies get such things?

"They're going to kill us," Esteban says fatalistically without looking up.

"Probably." Guzmán watches Esteban. He looks younger now without his big gun, without his squad mates. A kid, really. A scared kid.

Guzmán's anger brews at a building simmer. What the hell happened to him? When did his cunning abandon him? He'd been nearly shot to pieces in an ambush, barely making it out alive. And then a handful of hours later, because he'd been too rusty, too long removed from the battlefield, he'd lost almost his entire squad, falling into a trap he should have seen from miles away.

His soldiers sacrificed. Mamá unavenged. He clenches his teeth, furious.

* * *

In the dim distance, a distant pattern of white and yellow pinpoints of light arrange themselves into a familiar pattern. Odessa is their destination, Guzmán realizes, recognizing the cityscape's fingerprint. He takes a deep breath of the dry desert air. Odessa. Oh, what glorious days he had here! He was the conquering revolutionary, taking town after town like a West Texas Genghis Khan wearing bullet bandoliers. It was here in Odessa where he consolidated his dominion over the vast natural gas fields of the western desert, those enormous basins of wealth buried far under the parched earth. The future seemed wide open, ripe with possibilities.

Como cambian las cosas. How times have changed, as the gringos say.

The convoy slows as they approach town. Guzmán hears the woman in the passenger seat call over the radio, indistinct words and phrases interspersed with pops and crackling static. The driver removes his goggles and finally turns on the truck's headlights. The other vehicles follow suit, illuminating the path forward. Guzmán's lower back aches from the awkward sitting position. His rear, bruised from miles jarring against the cage's unforgiving steel floor, feels like he's been riding a horse bareback for two straight days. The exposed skin of his face, neck, and arms is covered with a sticky coating of mingled sweat and dust. This is not exactly how he imagined his return to Odessa.

As they pull into town, a crowd has already gathered, alerted by the radio calls. "Por Dios," Esteban gasps as he sees the assembled throng. "What's that?"

A mob of hundreds packs Main Street, teeming in the hazy yellow glow of the few working streetlamps. Even at a quarter mile's distance, Guzmán can feel the horde's restless, violent energy.

"That's our welcoming committee," he answers.

The truck creeps closer to the crowd, now a couple blocks away. The rest of the convoy drifts away into side streets, leaving the Chevy with its caged cargo as the street's solitary vehicle. They're close enough now that Guzmán can see the women with their long twin braids, the men with their tattooed limbs. From every face peers a pair of wild, bloodthirsty eyes. That maniac Fundie stare, hungry and feral, that they all seem to have. He recalls the phrase Reader Soledad always used to describe it. *The zealot face.*

At the front of the crowd a large woman paces back and forth, shouting through a bullhorn. She seems to be holding back the mob with nothing more than her force of will, some preternatural stubbornness the crowd, even in its excited state, doesn't dare to challenge.

"Do NOT harm the driver or his passenger in the cab," she shouts, then repeats the words a second time, louder. "They are our brother and sister in Christ. They are NOT to be subject to our sacred wrath. Do you understand, brothers and sisters?" In response, a vicious cheer rises up from hundreds of voices.

The truck rolls to an ominous stop. The woman with the bullhorn cries, "BLESSED BE THE FAITHFUL!" and darts out of the way like a starter in a motorbike race. Then the crowd surges forward like a dam giving way and rushes the truck. Guzmán leans close to Esteban, looks him squarely in the eyes. "Try to keep your head down, joven."

Fundies swarm the vehicle. Guzmán and the young soldier scramble to the center of the cage, pressing their backs together, away from the frantic thrust of grabbing hands and clenched fists. Writhing, mad faces surround them, shouting and spitting on them.

"Demon seed!"

"Infidels!"

An outstretched arm manages to grab a handful of Esteban's long hair and yanks the soldier off balance. He tumbles sideways, rolling up against the cage's bars, where he's immediately pinned down by a dozen clutching hands. The youth shrieks as they claw at his face and neck and eyes, fingernails tearing cuts deep into his skin and fists yanking out handfuls of hair. Guzmán kicks at the Fundies, trying to fend them off, a tactic that only inflames their fury. Lying awkwardly on his side, hands bound behind him, Guzmán has no leverage, kicking uselessly as they rip Esteban to shreds. The soldier's face is a mess of blood and matted hair. Enraged, Guzmán rises to his knees and throws himself against the bars, shoulder-first. The cage lurches, nearly toppling out of the truck bed. Instinctively, the Fundies back away for an instant, long enough for Guzmán to nudge Esteban, dazed and bloody but still conscious, back to the center of the cage, out of reach.

They sit there for another minute, although it feels like much longer, back to back as the mob pelts them with small rocks, spits on them, and hurls handfuls dirt and dog shit at them. Then, finally, the press of bodies begins to dissipate and fall away. The woman with the bullhorn, standing nearby, is calling them off.

"Blessed be, brothers and sisters," she blares, pacing around the truck in long strides. "Blessed be. Breathe now, children, breathe. Let the heathens be. Let them be for now."

Some back away immediately, heeding the woman's words. Others, too worked up to stop, have to be pried away from the cage bars. Finally, the attack stops.

The truck begins to inch forward again. The crowd reluctantly parts, allowing them to pass. Eyes of mad men and women follow them as they slowly pass by, the surly gazes of attack dogs called off by their owner before they could make the kill.

"¿Cómo vas, joven?" Guzmán asks, turning toward the youth.

At first Esteban doesn't answer. After a moment he moans, "I can't see out one eye." He spits blood from his mouth. "Animales," he whimpers, his voice trembling. "Son animales."

The crowd now behind them, the truck moves along the dark, suddenly quiet street. From the alleyways a pack of motorbikes appears, forming a ring around them. Their small engines putter gently as they escort the caged prisoners, the riders' faces stony and grim.

"Where are you taking us?" Guzmán calls to the driver, who doesn't answer.

Crumbling storefronts and long-forgotten shops pass by, their roofs and facades so broken and collapsed they're hardly recognizable as structures, appearing more like heaps of debris lining the streets. A haphazard arrangement of hanging lights crisscrosses overhead, painting the empty downtown with the pale yellow glow of low-wattage incandescence.

When they turn a corner, Guzmán finally sees what he's been expecting, what he's been dreading: a gallows. Four bodies hang from thick ropes, their heads hooded, necks bent sharply at unnatural angles. The dead have signs affixed to their chests, little rectangles of plywood, all with the same word scrawled on them: *FLAQUISTA*.

A block later they reach a plaza centered on an enormous mesquite tree, its wide canopy reaching out twice the width of its height. From its thick branches hang a dozen more hooded bodies, also adorned with signs proclaiming their loyalty to Guzmán. The truck makes an unhurried loop around the plaza's perimeter, as if the driver wants to make sure the prisoners get a good, long look. Guzmán seethes, clenching his jaw so tight it hurts his teeth, but he refuses to react openly, refuses to give their sadistic driver any satisfaction.

Brakes squeaking, the truck and its motorcade come to a stop. Across the street Guzmán recognizes the old county courthouse, a squat building with a windowless facade of honeycombed concrete. He'd once used the place as his base of operations. The driver exits the truck, hurries across the street, and disappears inside. The woman in the passenger seat scowls at them through the cabin window.

"What's going on?" Esteban slurs through swollen lips.

Guzmán thinks he knows, but he stays quiet. The poor kid's frightened enough already.

A moment later, the answer comes. Two guards standing sentry at the top of the steps pull open the front doors, revealing the broad silhouette of a large man in a wide-brimmed hat. The shadow stands motionless in the doorway for a moment, like a boxer exiting his dressing room and waiting for the cue of his announced name before making his way to the ring.

Finally the man exits the building, slowly descending the steps with casual ease.

"Puta madre," Esteban gasps. "That's him, isn't it?"

Guzmán, mesmerized, doesn't reply. The man in the white linen suit moves toward them. Halfway to the truck, he pauses under a wire of hanging lights, giving Guzmán his first clear view of the preacher's face.

He's so old. So much older than the monster of Guzmán's memory. Sagging jowls, sunken eyes, the body bulkier, moving in space with the stiff, deliberate slowness of advancing age. Older, fatter, but still him, still Reverend Wright.

The preacher sees Guzmán and smiles, his face splitting wide in the malevolent grin from Guzmán's nightmares. The smile that hovers like a ghost over his memories of the day the Fundies burned down his home, sending Ernesto and his mamá fleeing from Houston. The day everything changed, the day his mother began her slow, torturous death spiral.

Ernesto Guzmán has never been a religious man. As a boy he slept through most Masses, never seeing the point in believing in Mary and the saints and some invisible man up in the sky. As an adult fascinated by history, he studied the Church and its origins, and concluded it was the greatest sham ever concocted by humankind. In its time, the Church had either endorsed or turned a conveniently blind eye to corruption, slavery, genocide, mass starvation, and misogyny. The Church had destroyed entire civilizations, robbed the Americas of its gold to embellish the walls and ceilings of huge, ostentatious basilicas in Spain and France and Portugal. The Church had been a boot pressed to the throat of humanity for eons, its authority derived from the faulty intellect of the average ignorant mind, its god nothing more than a ghost story told to gullible children.

But in this frozen moment, as he stares at the reverend's devilish leer, Guzmán comes as close as he ever has to a religious experience. If there really were such a thing as true evil, as the actual manifestation of all things unholy, then he's looking at its smiling face right now. He feels a coldness inside, as if some enormous hand made of ice has reached into him and grabbed hold of his insides.

Guzmán watches numbly as the reverend approaches and pulls a pistol from his jacket.

"Don Fla—" Esteban cries out, his words cut off by the gunshot to his head. The soldier reels backwards and goes limp, his body collapsing like a puppet whose strings have been cut. Blood and gore from the exit wound spill across the cage floor.

A mad rage overwhelms Guzmán. "¡HIJO DE PUTA!" he roars at the preacher, slamming his shoulder into the bars, tipping the cage again. "¡TE VOY A MATAR! I'M GOING TO KILL YOU!"

Unlike the Fundies from earlier, the reverend doesn't flinch. He remains as cool and untroubled as if Guzmán had just offered him a glass of lemonade, rather than his own painful extinction. The preacher stares at Guzmán with an expression that's both pleased and detached, like a painter pausing to assess his canvas, satisfied with his most recent brushstrokes.

Guzmán slams into the cage bars over and over, shouting curses at Wright. The truck rocks back and forth. Eventually, the pain in his shoulder is too much to bear and he stops, falling onto his rear, panting, his heart thudding heavily in his chest.

"Feel better?" Wright asks.

Out of breath and seething, Guzmán doesn't answer.

"I'm sure you do," Wright answers for him. "Keeping all those emotions bottled up is bad for your health."

The preacher steps closer, regarding Guzmán critically. "I didn't believe them when they told me over the radio that they'd captured the mighty Ernesto Guzmán. I thought for sure they were mistaken. Young soldiers get overly excited sometimes, as I'm sure you're aware." He spreads his hands wide. "But here you are, delivered to my doorstep like a present on Christmas morning. God is indeed favoring the faithful on this night, don Flaco."

"Blessed be the faithful," one of the motorbike riders calls over. The others echo him, a hellish chorus. Wright acknowledges them with a small nod of his head, politely grasping the brim of his hat between his thumb and forefinger.

Guzmán's breathing slows enough for him to speak. "You going to shoot me now?"

"Lord, no!" Wright chuckles. "What a waste that would be." He cocks his head to one side. "Do you know the story of Elijah and the priests of Baal?"

Guzmán glares at the preacher, saying nothing, Esteban's lifeless body lying beside him.

"The prophet Elijah," Wright says, "is my favorite Old Testament showman. He lived in Israel, and at that particular time in Israel there were a great many wicked people following the wrong god, not unlike the current situation in our beloved Texas." He punctuates the sentence with a wink. "This false god was named Baal, and one day Elijah challenged Baal's priests to a contest. We'll both build altars, he said, sacrifice bulls on them—a wasteful custom of those ancient times—and the god that answers with fire from the heavens wins. It was going to be a good old-fashioned showdown, don Flaco. Your god versus mine.

"So they gathered up on a mountain in front of scores of people, and Elijah—natural-born showman that he was—let the priests of Baal go first. The wicked men then proceeded to construct an altar, sacrifice a bull, and pray to their idol of Baal. But no fire lit up on the altar. Not even a single spark or wisp of smoke could be seen.

"Now, Elijah could have let them off the hook right then and there, but he didn't. Instead, he mocked and teased them, telling them their god must be asleep or indisposed. Maybe they should pray louder. Well, that must have set them off, because then they started stomping their feet and jumping up and down, even cutting their own flesh to get Baal's attention. They spent days trying, exhausting themselves in the effort. But of course nothing happened.

"And then came Elijah's turn. Now, he might have just built his altar, sacrificed his bull, and commenced to praying, but merely winning the showdown wasn't enough for Elijah. He wanted a victory for the ages. He wanted the crowd to see something they'd never forget. So after he put together his altar and slaughtered his bull, he had his people *pour water* on his sacrifice. Can you fathom such a thing, don Flaco? He had them *douse it soaking wet*. And the good Lord—in appreciation of such a fine piece of showmanship—sent fire from the heavens and burned up that sopping wet altar just like that." Wright snaps his fingers emphatically on the last word.

Wright looks away from Guzmán, his expression ponderous. "After that day, I imagine Elijah could do no wrong. After seeing such a sight, his people would have walked off a cliff for him, praising his name all the while."

The preacher again fixes his gaze on Guzmán. "Yes," he says, "old Elijah knew exactly how to make the most of an opportunity." He puts the pistol back into his jacket, the devilish grin returning. "And let me tell you something, don Flaco, so do I."

CHAPTER 19

The elevator doors open to an access tunnel. A short stairway leads to the roof.

A cool breeze greets Soledad and her two fellow Texans as they exit the stairwell, accompanied by Roman Kennedy and the redhead Garcia. A quadrotor sits on a landing pad a short distance away, its propellers already spinning at a low-rev idle. General Bennett's waiting for them on the rooftop, looking prim in her sharply creased uniform, her hands clasped behind her back and wearing an uncomfortable smile on her face.

She motions toward the squat-bodied aircraft. "You said you wanted to get back quickly. This'll get you there faster than a chopper."

"Thank you," Chavez says.

"And this one's got a pilot on board," Kennedy adds.

Chavez nods politely, acknowledging the Americans' thoughtfulness. "Again, muchas gracias." Over his shoulder, he carries a satchel stuffed with hard copy photographs. The going-away present of American aerial intel.

Hands are shaken all around. The Americans wish them good luck. Sincerely, it seems to Soledad, though the hierba has long since worn off. Still, the wistfulness of their best wishes and the forced smiles on their faces strike her as the same kind of send-off she saw Guzmán give once, when he assigned a favorite soldier to a mission where the odds of survival were next to none.

Kennedy grips Soledad's hand firmly. "Please give don Flaco our best."

Then Garcia approaches and hands a satphone to Indigo. She looks at the small black device curiously. "What's this for?"

"It's a direct line to my office," Kennedy explains to the trio. "If things start going the wrong way and you need to get out, call us on that. We can have a jet down there in less than an hour. Refugee status can be arranged for you and your families." He takes a deep breath. "I hope it doesn't come to that."

The thrum of the aircraft's rotors grows louder. Soledad's hair begins to whip around in the tornado of the quad's propwash.

The Texans cross the roof and climb aboard the aircraft, disappearing behind the cabin's sliding door. The rotors spin faster and the quad's landing gear lifts off the rooftop. The aircraft gains altitude and turns its nose southward.

*   *   *

The sun touches the western horizon as the quadrotor shuttles the three Texans home. Floating above the vast North Texas plains, the aircraft's a solitary bee buzzing over a thousand-acre field. The Blackland Prairie, Soledad thinks, looking out the window. That's what her father told her this part of Texas was called, so many years ago. A long north-south ecosystem of tall grasses and cedar elms and pecan trees and oaks. Dark, fertile soil. Good for farming. This is where bison had once grazed, Papi told her, and where the Comanche had once hunted them.

Their family lived in the area for a bit over two years while Papi did his survey work for the Bullocks, measuring the supply of natural gas in dozens of small basins between Dallas and the Oklahoma border. Soledad had been around twelve or thirteen at the time, and she'd liked it best of all the places they'd lived in their nomadic existence. Unlike so many other parts of Texas, this place had four real seasons. Summer was sweaty hot and autumn brought beautiful golden colors to the trees. And they even had snow one winter, though it had been a light covering that only lasted a day. When spring came around, countless bluebonnets and Indian paintbrush bloomed, transforming the countryside with miles-long swaths of vibrant reds and lavenders. She preferred North Texas to the arid west, and she far preferred it to the sticky, humid south.

"We should have told them about don Flaco." Indigo's voice through her earphones.

Chavez glares at the trader from his seat and points a furtive thumb toward the cockpit, where the pilot can hear every word they say over his own headset.

Indigo removes her earphones and wraps her hand around the small connected microphone so it can't pick up her voice. She motions for Chavez to do the same. Still glaring, he follows suit, as does Soledad. The quad's rotors fill the cabin with a deafening whine as the Texans lean in close to one another.

"They could have sent out drones to look for him," Indigo shouts, her words barely audible over the thunderous din.

"They could have sent out drones to take him out," Chavez counters.

"Come on!" Indigo scoffs. She tilts her head toward Soledad. "She didn't pick up anything but goodwill from them. They didn't have to tell us so much, you know. They were trying to build trust back there."

"Well, I don't trust gringos," Chavez insists. "At least not so soon." He leans back in his chair, placing his headset back with an air of finality that tells Soledad the conversation is over.

Later, the three Texans watch in silence as the American aircraft lifts from the rooftop of City Hall for its return journey to the States. It hovers for a brief moment above the Dallas skyline and then turns northward, floating away into the failing light of early evening.

Immense structures of steel and glass tower around Soledad. Inside them live thousands of flaquista soldiers, well-armed and—even with their all their frustrations of late—still loyal to the cause, still willing to lay down their lives to keep don Flaco safe, to keep her safe. Before today, she considered Dallas a kind of fortress, a safe, impenetrable citadel protecting her and little Steffa.

But now, standing there in the chilly evening air, she wonders if she'll ever feel safe again.

CHAPTER 20

"Shhhh," Magnolia shushes, her forefinger tapping her lips, as she opens the door for Soledad. "The baby just went to sleep."

Soledad nods, padding through the doorway of her condo.

"You're back early," Magnolia says, keeping her voice low. "Did everything go all right?"

"Everything went fine," Soledad replies, too tired to go into the details. "Can I see her?"

Magnolia smiles, touches Soledad's arm. "Of course you can, dear."

They find Steffa sprawled out on her bed, barefoot but otherwise still fully clothed, her face hidden by a tangled bird's nest of hair. Every few moments the girl makes soft babbles as she exhales. Baby sounds, Magnolia calls them. Soledad stands and watches the dozing child, wishing she could crawl under the blankets next to her, sleep peacefully, and dream away the whirlwind of the past couple days.

"Lord," Magnolia whispers, "what are we going to do with that child's hair?"

Soledad smiles. "I can't talk her into cutting it."

"And I can't talk her into brushing it."

There's a soft rapping at the front door. Soledad sighs. *Now what?* A moment later, she spies Indigo through the peephole.

"I'm tired," she tells the trader through the door. "Come back in the morning."

"Open up," Indigo urges. "Come on, Sol."

Inwardly cursing herself, Soledad regrets answering at all. She should have just stayed quiet, let Indigo assume they were already in bed.

"Soledad, it's serious," the trader pleads.

"So tell me," Soledad answers, the locked door still between them.

"Jesus Christ, Sol," Indigo snaps.

A moment of indecisive silence passes, finally broken by Soledad's resigned grunt and the swish-clack of half a dozen locks being turned.

Indigo strides through the doorway, carrying a small burlap bag. "The girl awake?"

"No."

Magnolia appears in the hallway, greeting Indigo with the same shushing she gave Soledad minutes earlier.

The trader holds up the bag. "Candied oranges slices. Her favorite."

Magnolia approaches. "I'll give them to her." She takes the bag, eyeing the trader with her usual disdain. Magnolia has confided in Soledad more than once that she doesn't care for traders. They'd sell their own mothers if there was a pellet in it for them, she said.

"I'll be going now," Magnolia says, "unless you need anything else."

Soledad swallows, saying nothing.

"Or I can stay if that would be easier for you," Magnolia adds, seeming to pick up on the reader's uncertainty.

"It's not too much trouble?" Soledad asks.

"Of course it's not, dear."

Soledad feels the tension ease in her neck and shoulders. Everything always seems to run smoother when Magnolia is around. A sudden gratefulness wells up in her, a thankfulness for this gray-haired angel who has brought so much more than a tidy kitchen and a reliable caregiver into their lives. She's somehow managed to create a loving home in their overprotected, cordoned-off existence. Their condo has become, under Magnolia's tender care, a peaceful port in the relentless storm of their world.

"Thank you, Magnolia."

The nanny bids her good night and shuffles off to the spare bedroom.

Soledad turns to the trader. "All right, so tell me."

"Drink," Indigo mutters, shouldering past Soledad toward the kitchen.

Soledad shrugs. "Help yourself."

Removing two shot glasses and a bottle of mescal from a cabinet, Indigo makes her way to the living room and plops tiredly down on the sofa. Soledad follows, sitting opposite the trader, who's already pouring herself a drink.

Indigo downs her drink in a single swallow, then pours herself another. "Can I pour you one?"

"Why are you here, Indigo?"

The trader's glass pauses on its way to her mouth. "Guzmán's party was ambushed."

Soledad feels a twitch in her stomach, though she can't claim to be surprised. "Where?"

"Somewhere around Abilene," Indigo answers. "They're not exactly sure. One of the soldiers got away on a bike, showed up back here an hour ago. G.G., I think they called the kid. Know him?"

Soledad shakes her head.

"The kid says a group of Fundies came out of nowhere and hit 'em hard. He thinks he might be the only one who made it out, but he's not sure."

"Maybe he's full of shit," Soledad offers grimly. "Maybe he came to his senses and abandoned the mission when no one was looking."

"Could be," Indigo tips her head, "but his story lines up with when the shortwave operators said they lost contact with the convoy. And I just got back from talking to him. He didn't strike me as the cut-and-run type. Still, you never know."

"Is that why you're here?" Soledad asks. "You want me to read him? See if he's lying?"

"It wouldn't make a difference if he was lying or not," the trader replies. She takes a sip of mescal and lays her head back on the cushion, gazes at the ceiling. "Chavez was already fit to be tied when he found out the convoy was incommunicado. Then when that rider showed up with his story about a Fundie ambush, that pushed the old bear over the edge. He's in all-out war mode. Got every last soldier in the city gearing up to head west."

"When?"

Indigo passes her glass to Soledad. "Yesterday, if he could manage it," the trader says, "but I reckon it'll be sometime around dawn."

Soledad drinks. The alcohol, a gift from don Flaco, warms her insides as it goes down. She hands the glass back to Indigo. "What do you think's going to happen?"

Indigo tosses back the last drops, exhales. "What was bound to happen, I suppose, only sooner than I expected." She reaches for the bottle and fills both glasses. Soledad takes her glass, standing and moving to the window.

"Do you think he's still alive out there somewhere?"

"I don't know," the trader answers.

Soledad absently fingers the Virgin pendant. "How do you think this will all turn out?"

Indigo purses her lips and frowns as if she's been contemplating this very question for some time, but still unsure of the answer. "It's a coin toss," she finally utters.

Soledad shakes her head, gazing out over the darkened cityscape. "I'm not so sure," she says, her voice falling.

"What makes you say that?"

"The Americans picked their horse in this race. That's what dropping the blockade was all about. Check the history books, Trader Indigo. When the gringos back someone, they usually win." Soledad sighs. "The preacher's got too much momentum on his side. Too many gringos are pulling for him now."

"Did you *see* that, in someone's head, when we were in the States?" Indigo asks, referring to Soledad's special talent.

"No, it's not that. It's just a gut feeling. Like when you know you're on the losing team, even before the game begins."

Soledad crosses the room, sits back down. Indigo has taken out the satphone, fiddling with the little black rectangle as she takes another drink. "Christ," the trader says, "all that tech they have and they can't give us even the smallest bit of help. What Chavez couldn't do with just a couple working gunbirds."

Soledad eyes the device in the trader's hand, recalling the Americans' offer of amnesty. The decision comes to her quickly, reflexively. She reaches her hand out, palm up.

"Indigo, pass me the phone. I need to call the gringos."

CHAPTER 21

Soledad ends the call and sets the satphone on the table. The trader stands across from her, arms crossed expectantly.

"Well?" Indigo asks.

"The jet will be here in the morning," Soledad answers, "out at the old airport." Once she got through to Garcia, the arrangements were made quickly. They'd start the paperwork for her refugee status right away, he assured her. She collapses onto the sofa, letting out a huge breath. A wave of emotion comes over her, a mixture of so many contradictory feelings she couldn't name them if she tried.

"That didn't take long," Indigo says.

Soledad nods. "Maybe they expected us to ask for a ticket out."

"Or maybe they felt guilty for screwing us," Indigo scoffs, reaching for the bottle of mescal. She fills their glasses and picks up her own, but doesn't take a drink. She studies Soledad's face as if searching for an answer to a riddle. "So you're leaving? Just like that?"

"Yeah."

"You know," Indigo remarks, "six months ago you talked me into sticking around here and helping out."

Soledad fidgets, her relief dissipating. She ought to have some sensible answer—something about practicality and survival and taking care of Steffa and besides don Flaco went nuts and is probably dead—but she can't bring herself to respond. Instead, she awkwardly reaches for her glass.

"Feels like a lot longer than six months," she finally answers, then takes a drink.

Indigo sits at the opposite end of the sofa. "I can't believe you're going to cut and run like this." She shakes her head, disappointed. "You've seen up close what that monster of a preacher is all about. And now you're just gonna bail out?"

"Indie, don't," Soledad sighs. "I'm too worn out for a lecture."

"Chavez might actually pull it off, you know. He knows that desert like the back of his hand. I wouldn't bet against him."

Soledad shrugs. "Chavez wins, the preacher wins. I'm leaving no matter what."

The admission strikes Indigo speechless, her face dropping. "Say again?"

Soledad stares down at the tabletop. "Maybe it's wrong of me, Indigo. Maybe it is. I don't know what I thought I owed Guzmán at one time, but whatever it was, it's not there anymore." She touches the Virgin pendant lightly. "Maybe whatever I owed wasn't even to him."

"You're tired, Sol. You need some rest."

"Yeah," Soledad agrees, "I'm tired. Tired of this gilded cage, tired of being the linchpin of an entire movement, tired of watching him piss it all away, day after day, week after week. I didn't want any of this, Indie. I never did."

They sit gazing out the window, an awkward, heavy silence between them. Finally, Soledad says, "Why don't you come with us?"

The trader's poker face doesn't flinch. "No, thanks."

"Why not?"

"I've got my reasons."

Soledad sets down her glass. "A trade concession isn't worth risking your life over."

"That entirely depends on the income level," Indigo replies, downing her drink. "And it ain't just about that."

Soledad grunts. "So you're telling me you're a flaquista to the marrow now?"

"And what if I am?"

"Don't make me get the hierba out," Soledad warns.

Indigo chuckles, breaking the silence. "Well, I wouldn't say to the marrow. But anyone with a half a brain can pick the good guys from the bad guys in this movie." The trader leans forward, refills her glass, tops off Soledad's. "And besides," she adds, but then stops, seeming to lose herself in thought.

A change comes over the trader's expression, a kind of sadness. "Besides what?" Soledad prompts.

The trader exhales, absently rotating the glass with her fingertips. "Do you remember Prayer Donovan?"

Prayer Donovan? It's an odd, out-of-nowhere question. Of course Soledad remembers Prayer Donovan. She'll never forget the name or the man, the turncoat Fundie who helped her get out of Conroe. At the time, Soledad hadn't known it was Donovan, the legendary warrior known and feared throughout the Republic. Only later did she piece together the identity of the stranger who'd come to her aid. Donovan had—for reasons she'd never come to understand—saved Soledad's life that terrible night in Conroe. And had he not intervened on her behalf, she surely would have been among the hundreds who'd died in the horrific firefight.

"Of course I remember him," she answers. "Why?"

"I watched him die," Indigo murmurs. "Did I ever tell you that?"

Soledad shivers. "No, you didn't."

Indigo takes a deep breath before going on, as if giving voice to such a heavy memory requires a special effort. "At the end he...confided things. Confessed things to me. Regrets and such." She swallows hard. The poker face is gone, broken apart by the memory. In all the months she's known the trader, until this moment Soledad has never heard Indigo's voice betray the slightest wobble, never seen her lose tight control of her emotions.

The trader knocks back half of her drink and wipes her mouth with the back of her hand. "I don't want to go out like that, knowing I haven't done anything for anyone except myself, knowing I spent the better part of my years on the wrong side of things. That's why I stayed in Dallas six months ago, and that's why I'm not going anywhere now." She looks over at Soledad. "But that's me. You gotta do what's right for you, I guess."

Soledad turns away from the trader's steady gaze and the twinge of guilt it induces. "You going to hate me for deserting?"

"Nah," Indigo responds. "I'd rather you stay, but part of me gets it. You've been carrying a weight around I can't understand. I don't think anybody can unless they live in that fishbowl themselves. And you got that little girl to think about, besides."

For the first time, Soledad sees a vulnerability, a tenderness in Indigo's face she always assumed didn't exist. Even the times she had the benefit of hierba-assisted insight, she never detected the depth of emotion she senses at this moment—as much in herself as the woman next to her. A sudden, painful realization hits her: these may very well be their last moments together.

Soledad moves closer. She reaches for Indigo's glass, takes it, and places it on the table. "I'll miss you."

"I wonder," Indigo answers, though not as an insult, her tone more thoughtful than biting.

"Don't wonder." Soledad moves closer still, placing her hand on Indigo's thigh, giving in to a longing she doesn't quite understand. Has this feeling been there all along? Buried or maybe denied? She isn't sure, and at this moment, with the excited flutter of her insides, she doesn't want to think about it. She only wants to act upon it, this whatever-it-is between them, in these final hours before their worlds split apart.

Indigo leans toward Soledad, their faces nearly touching. "We could have done this sooner, you know." She places her hand on top of Soledad's, squeezing gently.

"I know," Soledad admits, desire welling up inside her, overtaking her. She takes the trader's face into her hands. "So let's make up for lost time." She presses her mouth to Indigo's, their bodies coming together.

CHAPTER 22

Guzmán sits on the cold concrete floor of a tiny jail cell, shoeless and stripped of his body armor, bared to his cotton undershirt and blood-smeared camouflage pants. An hour ago—or maybe a couple hours—they brought him water, but there's been no food. His stomach cramps with hunger and his shoulder aches with a steady throb.

He leans back against the wall, wrists still bound behind him, staring blankly at the rusted iron bars. It was in this very same county courthouse in Odessa that he planned out his conquest of Texas. Odessa had been a key piece in the big game, an opponent's queen captured early in a chess match. Taking the town cemented his control of West Texas, and more importantly, his exclusive dominion over the invaluable millions of cubic meters of natural gas underneath the parched ground. It was here, in this small dusty city, where he first believed he could actually break the heavy chains of Dallasite hegemony, where the hyperbolic rhetoric of his speeches to cheering crowds converged with the possible. Of course, back then the accommodations were much more to his liking. He set up shop in the spacious top-floor office, a space that once belonged to a long line of judges or county commissioners or other high-ranking officials.

In that office overlooking the city and the desert beyond, he laid out maps and debated strategy with Chavez and his military advisers. And afterward, when he was alone, he read history books until well past midnight—a passion that had begun in his teenage years— keen to learn what he could from the great men and women of the past. The Mexican revolutionaries—Zapata, Morelos, Villa—made for great reading. Wonderful stories of adventure and betrayal and daring, certainly entertaining—but offering little in the way of practical advice for a would-be conqueror. Most of his cultural forebears had been shortsighted and rash men. Benito Juarez, a brilliant politician and statesman and perhaps Guzmán's favorite figure from the period, had been one of the exceptions.

But it was the Roman Empire, not his Mexican predecessors, that intrigued him most of all, and he devoured every text he could find on the subject, rereading many of them multiple times. Octavius, the first emperor, who later became known as Caesar Augustus, fascinated Guzmán. Astute and cunning, Augustus was both a military success—his troops had conquered Egypt, among many other victories—and a shrewd political opportunist, managing to consolidate his power during a turbulent period when multiple factions warred for control of the empire. And once Augustus attained supreme, virtually unchecked power, he proved to be a genius administrator as well, instituting reforms and reorganizing the Roman state apparatus, laying the foundation for an empire that would endure a thousand years. By most accounts, Augustus had been a wise and prudent ruler.

Guzmán aspired to be an Augustus, to be the first Caesar of Texas. An enlightened leader of the people, a visionary transforming a blighted land into something greater than it had ever been before. A man for the history books, worthy to have his name mentioned in the same pages as Lincoln and Mao and Churchill.

Had Augustus ever been as distracted as he had? Had he ever let his passions get the better of him? Had he ever been so possessed by hate or vengeance or wrath—even for a short while—that he'd forgotten his larger destiny? Or had he been able to control himself, to rise above his baser nature, and never falter? Maybe they'd simply left those stories out of the history books. Or maybe he *had* been exceptional, the rare sort who could rise above the pettiness of his own urges, and that's what made all the difference. Maybe that was what separated the great ones from the rabble.

His death must be close, he chides himself. Only a dying man would have such thoughts, such torturous self-examinations.

Two cheerless guards stand outside his cage, watching over him, AKs in hand. Every square inch of their exposed skin is covered with ink, elaborate drawings of Old Testament wars, whole paragraphs of Bible passages. A third Fundie now appears in a doorway, an older man who looks well into his sixties. He approaches the cell and kneels down. His hair is all white, thin and wispy on top. The man smiles at Guzmán and asks him to turn around so he can untie his hands. After he removes the bonds, the man reaches through the bars, holding out the pipe and tobacco bag they'd taken off Guzmán earlier.

"Thought you might like a bowlful before we leave." The old man's eyes are kind, even sympathetic. His Bible verse tattoos, faded and illegible, cover his wrinkled, sun-worn forearms.

Rubbing his sore wrists, Guzmán takes the pipe and bag. He chuckles darkly. "Last smoke for the condemned?"

The old man smiles, but doesn't answer.

Guzmán opens the bag under his nose and inhales deeply. His veracruzano tobacco. He'll miss everything about it: the sweet taste in his mouth; the soft crackle when he inhales; the lovely blue smoke wafting upwards; the clean smell of roasted leaves. The aroma of contentedness, of quiet reflection, of better times.

He smokes quietly in his cell for some minutes, then takes a long final draw. The leaves glow orange and warm, quietly popping and giving up the last of their smoke, then die out and become ash. The bowl finished, Guzmán automatically starts to tap it out, then realizes the uselessness of doing so and instead simply lays it on the floor. He stands and tells the old man he's ready.

The man has him turn around, then reties his wrists. "Godspeed, don Flaco," the old Fundie tells him, then leaves.

The guards unlock the cell door and escort Guzmán outside into the crisp night air. Without speaking they return him to the cage atop the truck, where Esteban's body has been removed but the smeared mess of his death remains. They silently lock him inside and moments later they're driving through town, its streets empty and eerily silent.

Guzmán hears what sounds like the distant buzz of a crowd. He swallows, remembering the preacher's words about taking advantage of an opportunity. At the end of Main Street, he finally spies the source of the noise, an old football stadium at the edge of town. Their destination, he assumes. As they approach the arena—by far the largest structure in town, still impressive even with its crumbling concrete and run-down appearance—they're joined by a group of riders on motorbikes, flanking the truck on both sides. They drive on with the grim, unhurried pace of a funeral procession.

The truck stops in front of the stadium entrance, a large arch of fractured, jagged-edged cement that seems a gaping mouth with broken teeth. Beyond it, Guzmán sees silhouettes and half-illuminated figures scurrying back and forth, lit by the same orange glow that flickers above the stadium like the incandescent crown of a candle's flame.

The truck and motorbike engines shut off, and as their noise dies, he hears the amplified modulation of a bullhorn coming from somewhere inside the stadium. He can't make out the words, but the voice unmistakably belongs to the preacher.

His two minders open the cage and escort him toward the entrance with a firm grip on either arm. He doesn't resist, passing through the huge arch with his chin high, chest out, and a defiant scowl on this face. Though his insides snake around like mad and his heart thuds wildly in his chest, he's determined he won't falter in his final moments. The last look they'll get of Ernesto Guzmán won't be that of a frightened coward or a crying fool begging for mercy. He refuses to give them the cowardly death they're hoping to see.

As they pass through the entrance, a crowd immediately swarms him and his captors, shouting and taunting him. Shadowy faces in the unsteady light, eyes wide with anger, teeth bared like feral dogs.

"HEATHEN!"

"INFIDEL!"

Some shriek in tongues, their eyes rolled back into their heads, spitting out gibberish as they wave their arms frantically overhead. Others laugh and mock him, telling him to smoke a turd in Hell, to say hi to Satan.

Guzmán keeps his unflinching gaze forward as they creep forward through the deafening throng. The press of bodies grows larger and closer, though his minders are able to keep them off with outstretched arms. Make way, make way, they shout to the horde, their progress slowed as the crowd swells into the hundreds.

Finally, they emerge from the concourse onto the wide expanse of trampled overgrowth that was once a playing field. A deafening roar of jeers greets don Flaco's arrival. Thousands of Fundies pack the arena's enormous bowl. The sheer magnitude of hate and bloodlust feels like a wave crashing down on Guzmán's head, sending a sharp shiver down his back. His mouth dry, pulse racing, he manages to maintain the outward appearance of the stoic rebel.

Scattered around the arena's weed-choked ground are several thick poles standing ten meters tall, their tops ablaze with enormous fires. Torch poles, reminding him of similar ones at the Fundie camp he raided in Conroe. In the middle of the field there's a wooden platform. At first glance Guzmán mistakes the structure for a gallows, but then he realizes it's simply a sort of stage, in the center of which stands Reverend Wright. The preacher is costumed in his trademark white linen suit and wide-brimmed hat; he has a bullhorn pressed to his mouth as he motions toward Guzmán with a grand sweep of his hand. Whatever he's saying is lost in the crowd noise, but his movements remind Guzmán of a ring announcer's exaggerated drama, introducing a fighter in a boxing match.

His handlers jostle Guzmán forward, toward the center of the arena. Beyond the platform, there's another structure of some kind, but Guzmán can't quite make it out from his vantage point. As they approach the stage, the preacher shouts into the bullhorn, the words rendered completely unintelligible by the thunderous roar of the packed stadium. Eventually, Wright gives up and lowers the bullhorn, letting it dangle at his side. Jostled up the steps onto the stage, Guzmán notices the wide grin on the preacher's face.

The reverend ambles over to his prisoner, leans close to him, and with the unabated thunder of thousands nearly drowning out his words, shouts into Guzmán's ear. "Listen to that, don Flaco. I've never heard such a roar in my life. Congratulations!"

Standing there shoeless with his hands bound behind him and his mind racing, it takes a moment for Guzmán to understand. But then as the satisfaction in the preacher's face sinks in, Guzmán realizes he's being paid a compliment of the highest order, delivered with the utmost sincerity. Look at this thing you and I have created, Wright's gaze seems to say. Let's take a moment to revel in our success, shall we?

Now atop the stage, Guzmán can see the other structure clearly. It looks like an oversized boxing ring: a raised platform with ropes running around the perimeter. What will they do to him there, he wonders. Torture a confession from him? Force him to convert? Lop his head off with a machete?

It takes a full minute for the crowd noise to die down enough for Wright to speak. Finally, he raises the bullhorn to his mouth again.

"Brother and sisters," he cries, "the Lord has delivered unto us a sinner, a heretic who needs no introduction. I shall not poison the air of this blessed evening by uttering his name." The crowd roars its approval.

"Never has our beloved Texas known such treachery and transgression, my friends. This man has killed, he has raped, he has pillaged our towns and cities. He has stolen our lands and corrupted our people." Wright's voice rises and falls hypnotically, and he pauses dramatically between each phrase. Guzmán has always heard about Wright's fiery speeches and the preacher's skill at manipulating the masses. Now with his own eyes he sees none of those stories were exaggerations. The cadence and power of Wright's words are relentless, ocean waves pounding the beach of his audience's attention. The preacher pricks them, goads them, his voice rising up in dramatic crescendos, then falling with somber gravity.

"...and tonight, brothers and sisters," the reverend blares, his words lengthening, vowels expanding, "he will feel the wrath of our Lord and savior. We shall teach it to him!"

A sea of arms waves wildly from the stands. The reverend yells into the bullhorn, his face red, the veins in his neck straining with the effort to keep his voice above the roaring congregation.

"Brothers and sisters, I give you ZARA MULCAHY!"
As he shouts the name, he motions toward the edge of the
arena, where a phalanx of Fundies in soldier fatigues
emerges from an entryway. At the front is an enormous
woman, tall and thick-limbed and clad in body armor. Her
hair is arranged into two long braids that dangle to her
waist. She walks briskly, with purpose, brandishing a
baseball bat in one hand, an ax in the other. Halfway
across the arena, she pauses and lifts the ax high over her
head, turning to acknowledge the crowd. The stadium
erupts into a thunder of cheers that Guzmán can feel in his
bones.

Zara. He's heard the name from time to time over the
years. One of Wright's inner circlers, a fighter whose
reputation rivals that of his own late Lela's. He looks at the
ax she's wielding and swallows. Will she be his
executioner? Is that what the preacher has planned for
him?

The woman marches forward, the tip of her retinue's
spear, over to the roped-off platform, then climbs up onto
it. She raises her arms, bat and ax held aloft, bait dangled
that earns her more cheers and applause. Guzmán's
handlers lead him down the stage stairs and steer him
across the field toward the ring. The woman glares at him
as he approaches, impatiently knocking her bat and the
butt of her ax together. Whatever's about to happen, she's
anxious to get on with it.

They shove him up a stairway at the edge of the
platform. One of his minders pulls up on the ropes,
creating an opening to step into the ring, and Guzmán is
shoved through the ropes. His hands still tied behind him,
Guzmán tumbles headlong onto the plywood floor to the
jeers of thousands, ending up on his back. Awkwardly, he
rises to his feet. The Fundie Zara glowers at him from
across the ring, her eyes wide and wild. *A zealot's stare.*

The Fundies who entered the arena with Zara now
crowd around the platform's base, fists raised, calling up to

her.

"You can take him!"

"Send that demon back to hell!"

Are they supposed to fight? Is that what this is? They want him to fight this Zara woman? Yes, that must be it, remembering Wright's gleeful retelling of the story of Elijah, the value of a public spectacle. He whirls around to his two handlers. "You going to untie me at least?"

They answer him with a grin, then turn and go back down the stairs.

Perfecto.

"Two enter the ring," Wright cries through the bullhorn, "but only the righteous will leave alive. May the Lord guide your hands, Sister Zara!"

At the side of the ring—and now he can only think of it as a ring, as a place for fighting—he spots the old man who returned his tobacco to him. The man holds a ball peen hammer in one hand, a circular bell hanging from a rope in the other. He grins up at Guzmán and strikes the bell.

The crowd roars as the warrior Zara, her ax and bat raised, screams a war cry and rushes toward him.

CHAPTER 23

Guzmán dodges, but not fast enough, and the Fundie soldier Zara lands a hard blow of the bat squarely on his injured shoulder. The crowd cheers the first landed shot, a noise Guzmán hardly notices as a wave of white pain surges through his body. He staggers away from the woman, crashing into the turnbuckle. Grinding his teeth against the pain, he turns as she rushes him again, ax raised high. He darts to the side, the ax head narrowly missing him.

He moves to the opposite side of the ring, half-stumbling, weakened by a day without food. With his hands bound behind him, he's forced to lean awkwardly forward, making it difficult to keep his balance.

Zara charges again, straight forward, madness in her eyes. This time Guzmán's ready, and he manages to spin away without getting hit. The Fundie soldier's momentum sends her bouncing off the ropes and she nearly loses her footing. She turns to Guzmán, breathing heavily, her face twisted into a wolf's snarl. She moves forward and begins to stalk him around the ring.

His shoulder throbbing, Guzmán pivots away, his eyes locked on Zara's feet as she moves. She's strong and formidable, but she's flat-footed and clumsy, he notes, sizing up her awkward shuffle. She rushes him again. He attempts to slide sideways out of the upraised ax's range, but then feels his back against the corner buckle. As the Fundie swings the ax wildly downward, he tries to lunge away, but the sharp edge catches him with a glancing blow to the head.

The arena erupts into cheers as he falls to the plywood floor and rolls away. He quickly bounces up to his knees, feeling a warm rivulet of blood flowing down his forehead from a pulsing wound somewhere on top of his skull. *Scalp wound*, he thinks, angry at himself for getting caught in the corner. It's going to bleed like crazy. He rises to his feet, blood streaming down his nose, chin, and chest. Zara stands across the ring, sneering and heaving in large, gulping breaths.

Again, Zara charges, but this time he's ready. He moves away neatly and untouched, a matador to the Fundie's bull. They circle each other around the ring, their features glowing orange in the torchlight. Guzmán watches Zara's movements carefully, her heavy breathing.

She's nearly gassed already, he notes. The Fundie's steps fall in heavy, awkward clops; her rib cage expands and compresses with large, heaving breaths. She's a tough fighter, but she's all rage with little technique. He's seen scores of boxers—usually the toughest ones with cast-iron jaws—fight the same way. All cojones, no brains. A strategy begins to take shape in his mind.

He shifts his weight to the balls of his feet and shuffles around her. When his opponent gets close, he quickly changes direction, circling out of range. Frustrated, she swings wildly with the ax and misses badly. A moment later she tries with the bat, missing again. After a minute of failed swings, the crowd becomes agitated. Boos rain down upon Guzmán.

"Stop running, coward!" someone hollers from behind him.

"Stand and fight, yellow belly!"

He shuffles away from her, dodging swing after swing. Her fatigue grows, and she loses what little technique she possessed, telegraphing each move with her eyes, holding her gaze on her target for a moment before she strikes. He begins to see her attempted blows even before they come, evading them easily. A strange euphoria begins to grow inside him. If these are to be his final moments, he's going to enjoy them to the fullest. *Fuck, yes, you crazies. I'll give you a good show.*

He begins to taunt the Fundie.

"What's the matter, woman?" he calls to her, flashing her a bloody grin. "You too slow to hit a wounded old buffalo with his hands tied?"

The Fundie shrieks, her eyes bulging in rage. She bursts forward, arms flailing. Guzmán sidesteps her clumsy charge, spitting blood at her as she stumbles past. He dances away, laughing. "Why don't you pray for some speed," he mocks. "You're slower than a grandfather's morning shit!"

Zara seethes, her irate face covered with a speckling of his blood. Angrily, she wipes her face with her sleeve. The crowd noise rises to a deafening roar. The Fundie raises her arms overhead and pleads to the sky, babbling in tongues.

Guzmán spots Reverend Wright at the side of the ring, the preacher's white linen suit gleaming like a beacon. Wright pounds the ring floor with his palm like an angry trainer, shouting up at Zara along with the crowd, urging her on. The sight of Wright incensed and howling puts fresh fire into Guzmán's blood. He shuffles around Zara, suddenly light on his feet.

"Pray louder!" he teases. "I don't think He hears you!"

Guzmán looks over at Wright. "Maybe your god's asleep!" he cries. Wright stares at him dumbfounded, a hamstrung Elijah.

¡Eso! Guzmán grins at the reaction. That one was a nice

kick to the balls.

Distracted by the preacher, he takes a hard blow to the side of his neck from the bat. He whirls away from the contact, cursing himself for taking his eye off the Fundie woman.

His neck smarting, he returns to his shuffle, keeping his distance. Blood drips down into his eyes, blurring his vision. He blinks forcefully, but it doesn't help. He's nearly blind in one eye. The bleeding continues unabated as he moves cautiously around the ring. Soon, he knows, he'll tire from the blood loss. But even so, he's going to enjoy these last moments as much as he can, and if he can take down one last Fundie in the process, all the better.

His dance finds its rhythm again, and he moves light and quick on the balls of his feet. The Fundie Zara misses over and over. She tires, her wild swings nowhere close to their intended target.

"Hey, preacher!" Guzmán calls, though this time he doesn't look over. "I think you fucked this one too hard last night. You wore her out!" He laughs maniacally, and through his blood-blurred vision he risks a quick peek at Wright at the edge of the ring, finding the preacher's face contorted with rage.

Oh, what a feeling! He'll never get his revenge, but right now he's besting the treacherous old bastard, and it's tastier than a fine steak, more satisfying than a perfect lover.

Zara's attack slows; she plods heavily forward. She no longer brandishes the weapons high and threatening, instead holding them low at her sides, as if they've suddenly tripled in weight. She's ready, tired and confused like a bleeding bull in the last tercio of a corrida. If only had his hands free, what work he could do on her with his fists.

He pivots and finally moves to offense, kicking her on the thigh hard with his shin bone. The hit lands with a meaty thud and stops Zara in her tracks. The crowd gasps.

The Fundie woman grimaces, baring her teeth. After a moment's hesitation she moves forward again, stalking Guzmán around the ring. He gives her a second kick, a harder one this time, on the same spot, and her leg gives out. She drops briefly to a knee, then gets back up. With a noticeable limp, she continues forward, wincing with each step.

Guzmán lands another kick, then another, torturing her with accurate, sharp strikes. The crowd anxiously shouts and urges her on, but she's moving too slowly now. She can't even get close enough to swing at her target.

"Should I show her mercy?" Guzmán shouts over to Wright.

Kick.

"Some *Christian* mercy?" he teases.

Kick.

Reverend Wright stares at him, the preacher's face twisted in a mask of fury, eyes aflame with rage. Guzmán flashes back to that fateful night, when Wright's face was lit up by another roaring fire. The joy of the moment, of his domination over the Fundie woman, drains from him in an instant. Overwhelmed with rekindled vengeance, he rushes the preacher in a furious scramble.

A surprised cry rises from the crowd as Guzmán kicks through the ropes at Wright. The blow hits nothing but air. The reverend's bodyguards, watchful and alert, have already yanked Wright backwards and safely away from the edge of the ring. Guzmán spits blood in the reverend's direction and places his foot on the middle rope, preparing to hurl himself out of the ring and onto the preacher. Before he can leap, a shriek comes from behind him, and he turns to see Zara rushing forward, ax and bat overhead, in a sudden burst of mad energy. He turns, sidesteps her, and lands a powerful kick to her midsection before she can strike.

The blow stops her cold. She collapses to the ring floor, her weapons falling from her hands. A shocked hush falls over the crowd. She writhes on the dirty mat, arms clutching her belly and mouth gaping open, the wind knocked from her lungs by Guzmán's well-placed kick.

"How's this for Christian mercy, preacher?" Guzmán cries, bringing his heel down onto her face. "The same mercy you showed Mamá." He stomps again, this time crushing her nose and knocking her unconscious. Her arms and legs go limp, and she lies rag-doll helpless, blood streaming from her nostrils. The stunned crowd looks on, aghast as Guzmán slams his boot into her cheek.

"The same mercy you showed my Lela!" he shouts, stamping down on her neck this time, using all his weight, feeling her windpipe crush like a bag of seeds under his heel. Possessed, he slams his foot down on her neck again and again, even after he knows she's well past dead. Finally, Wright's bodyguards scramble up into the ring and tackle him, stopping the attack.

Chaos bursts into bloom all around them. Fundies storm the ring from all sides, intent on tearing the infidel apart. Hands pull at his hair and scratch him, but Wright's bodyguards manage to keep the mob at bay until the preacher can climb into the ring with his bullhorn.

"Brothers and sisters, please!" his amplified voice blares as he waves his arm frantically. "Leave the infidel to me," he pleads. "Leave him to me!"

With no small effort he eventually gains control of the frenzied crowd, imploring his followers to leave the ring. Slowly, the ring empties, leaving just Wright, half a dozen of his personal security team, Guzmán, and the dead Fundie's body. Guzmán, woozy and held tightly by a Fundie at each arm, feels as if he's been run over by a truck. His ears ring and his ribs ache from blows the bodyguards couldn't stop. One of his eyes is swollen shut.

Wright paces back and forth along the ring ropes, shouting to the crowd. "We will not seek retribution on this night, brothers and sisters! Such vain and selfish motives would not honor our fallen warrior!"

He strides over to the body, kneels down and gently grasps her lifeless hand. Squeezing his eyes shut, he mutters a prayer, then stands again, ruefully shaking his head. The crowd, still churning and restless, watches his every move. He turns to face them, his brows lifted, eyes round in despair. He removes his hat very slowly, a theatrical flourish that stretches out the moment's drama. Silence gradually comes over the arena as he stands there gravely, waiting patiently for quiet. He's in total control now, a virtuoso actor before a rapt audience, performing the role he was born to play.

Wright leaves the bullhorn at his side, letting his followers hear the depths of his melancholy, unmasked and unamplified. "No, my brethren, this is not what she would have wanted. And this is not what the Lord wants, either. We shall not sully ourselves with lustful revenge on this night."

Then he takes another long pause. Guzmán watches, still dizzy, as the crowd begins to churn uneasily, anxious to hear the cursed heathen's fate. Wright lets them simmer for several moments, then brings the bullhorn back to his mouth.

"The Lord's justice must follow our traditions, our sacred ways. And it shall. So tonight, go home to your families and loved ones. Kiss your children good night and say your prayers."

His voice then rises from its somber monotone into a sudden joyful cry. "And return here tomorrow, my friends, with as many throwing stones as you can carry!"

Thousands of voices rise up in a cheer so loud Wright has to scream into the bullhorn to be heard. "And we'll show this infidel the wrath of the righteous!"

CHAPTER 24

"Why is Indigo in your bed?"

Soledad blinks and squints, realizes through her haze that Steffa is standing next to her. The room's still dark, though with the first light of dawn coming through the blinds Soledad can just make out the confused curiosity on the girl's face. She follows the girl's gaze, looking over at Indigo, still asleep and snoring, her back turned to them.

"She snores," Steffa whispers, giggling.

Soledad sits up and clears her throat, the sheets bunching up around her waist, revealing her naked torso. The Virgin pendant hangs from her neck.

"My necklace!" the girl blurts.

"Shhhhh!" Soledad scolds, putting her finger to her lips. "You're going to wake her up." Soledad rubs her temple, takes a deep breath. Her head throbs with a mild hangover.

"Here," Soledad whispers, "let me give it back to you." She starts to pull the necklace up over her head, but the girl lays her hand on top of the pendant, keeping it in place.

"It's okay," Steffa says. "You can wear it."

Soledad manages a smile. "Thank you, bumblebee."

"Why are you naked?" Steffa asks, staring at Soledad's breasts. "Where's your t-shirt? Is Indigo naked, too?"

Way too early for these questions. Suddenly self-conscious, Soledad pulls the sheets up over her chest. The bed smells like sex and sweat. "Why don't you get breakfast started?"

The girl's eyes widen. "I can cook the eggs?"

Bait taken, Soledad notes. "Only if you promise to be careful with the stove," she whispers.

"I will," the child says eagerly.

Soledad leans close to the girl. "I think Indigo likes hers scrambled. You remember how to do that?"

The girl nods enthusiastically, then pads out of the room, closing the door behind her. A moment later, Soledad hears the clinks and clanks of cookware coming from the kitchen.

"You let that child cook?" Indigo asks, still turned away. "With fire?"

"Jesus," Soledad curses, "were you awake all this time?"

Indigo props herself up onto her elbows and yawns. "Why are you *naked*, Sol?" she mimics, then laughs. "Wish I coulda seen your face on that one."

"Not funny." Soledad massages her temples. "God, my head."

"Hangover?" Indigo asks.

"A little one," Soledad replies.

Indigo lifts her chin. "So you gonna blame the mescal?"

"What do you mean?" Soledad says, though in the next moment she realizes exactly what Indigo means. "No," she answers, then immediately wonders the same thing about Indigo. "You?"

Indigo shakes her head. "Lord, no." She sits up and kisses Soledad on the mouth. It's a long, lingering kiss. It feels like a goodbye kiss.

Indigo slides off the bed and fumbles around the floor. "Where'd I leave my clothes?"

Soft tinkling sounds of plates and silverware come

from the kitchen. Indigo finds her pants and pulls them on.

The light from the window reflects off the Virgin pendant, catching Indigo's eye. She nods at it, changing the subject. "You gonna start going to Mass now?"

Soledad absently runs a finger over the folds of Mary's dress. "It's not mine," she says. "Well," she corrects herself, "it's mine now. Someone gave it to me."

Indigo notes the sudden faraway look. "Lela?" she guesses.

As it always does, her name unleashes a painful tumble of emotions: the sadness of her loss, the horror of her death. Soledad swallows and changes the subject. "Let's get some breakfast."

*   *   *

"So you made these all by yourself, huh?" Indigo takes another bite of her dry, woefully overcooked eggs. She chews, gamely smiles at Steffa. "Mmmmm."

Still holding the spatula, the girl stands beside the table with a proud smile on her face. Soledad tries not to laugh as she fakes her way through her own disaster, a rubbery cheese omelet with a brown outer crust. "Crunchy," Soledad compliments, "I like it."

Soledad washes down another dreadful mouthful with a large gulp of coffee. There are no eggs on Steffa's plate, she notes, only a pair of toasted bread slices. She wonders for a moment if the girl knows how poor a cook she really is, if that proud smile of hers is as much a fake as Soledad's own.

"I have a surprise for you," Soledad tells the girl. "We're going on a trip."

Always suspicious of the unexpected, Steffa narrows her eyes. "Trip to where?"

"We're going to the States," Soledad replies. When Steffa doesn't react, she adds, "In an airplane."

Surprised, the girl's mouth forms a silent *wow*. "Really? A real airplane up in the air?"

"Yes, ma'am, a real airplane."

"Is Magnolia coming, too?"

"Sure, if she wants to."

"But what if it crashes?" the girl asks, her face suddenly knotting with worry.

Soledad reaches out and gives the girl's shoulder a reassuring squeeze. "It won't, bumblebee. It's a good plane, an *American* plane."

"Is Indigo coming?" Steffa asks, her eyebrows lifted optimistically.

Though she might have expected the question, Soledad finds herself without an easy reply. She and Indigo exchange a look, urging each other with their eyes to break the awkward silence with an answer. Thankfully, Magnolia enters the kitchen from the hallway, interrupting the girl's interrogation.

"Have you heard? Have you heard?" the woman blurts, holding a small shortwave radio and fumbling with the dials. She looks as if she just rolled out of bed, dressed in the old, frayed robe she keeps in the guest closet for her occasional overnight stays. Her thick hair hangs down her back in an unkempt tangle of white and gray. She moves to the kitchen table and—after a quick, dubious look thrown in Indigo's direction—places the radio on the tabletop.

"Heard what?" Soledad asks.

"Magnolia!" Steffa cries. "Can I cook you some eggs?"

As Magnolia fiddles with the radio, her brow furrowed in concentration, she brushes the child's cheek with the back of her hand. "No, thank you, my dear." After a moment, she seems to find the right channel and the radio crackles with static as she increases the volume.

Soledad stiffens as Reverend Wright's voice comes through the small speaker. "…By the breath of God they perish, and by the blast of His anger they come to an end."

"What is this?" Indigo asks.

"Shhh!" Magnolia shushes. "They've got don Flaco."

"Don Flaco?" Soledad cries.

Indigo drops her fork.

"...and he that blasphemeth the name of the Lord shall surely be put to death, and all the congregation shall certainly stone him." A sound follows that Soledad at first mistakes for static, but then she realizes it's a cheering crowd, celebrating the announcement of a death sentence.

*   *   *

Soledad and Indigo stand nearby as Chavez leans into the Humvee's rear storage compartment, rushing through a final check of firearms and ammunition. A soldier wearing battle gear hurries over.

"Ready to roll in fifteen minutes, sir," the soldier announces.

Chavez, tired and irritable from his all-nighter pulling together every last soldier, vehicle, and weapons cache available to him, angrily slams the storage hatch closed and whirls around to face the soldier. "¡Puta madre, hombre!" he hollers, his expression livid. "*Another* fifteen minutes? No more delays, I want us out of here in FIVE! ¿Me entiendes?"

"Yes, sir," the soldier barks, then turns and sprints away.

All around them, the vehicle depot at the edge of the city is a madhouse of activity. Soldiers scurry back and forth, laden with weapons and boxes of ammunition. Shouted orders and revving engines fill the chilly morning air. In a grassy expanse beyond the city, hundreds of vehicles have been amassed into neat rows. Armored buses, semitrucks with multiple turrets, motorbikes, Humvees, Jeeps, pickup trucks of every make and model with huge knobby tires and wasteland-ready suspension, their bodies a meter and a half above the ground. More arrive in a constant stream from the city, forming an enormous rolling armada of guns and metal. Soledad finds herself awed. And terrified.

"Jesus, look at all that," Indigo exclaims, equally impressed. Then she raises her voice to a shout so Chavez can hear her above the bustling noise. "You're driving into a trap. You know that, right? The preacher going on the radio like that, bragging he's gonna stone don Flaco today. He's playing you, daring you to come out and fight."

Chavez frowns at her. "Me vale madre, mujer. Maybe it's a trap, and maybe it isn't." He spreads his hands out wide. "It doesn't matter. The gringos were right. We have to take out that preacher before he gets more help. We have to break their backs *now*."

He steps up onto the running board of the Humvee and urges the troops in a loud, booming cry. "¡Compadres, apúrense! ¡Hay que irnos de una vez, ya no hay tiempo!"

Soledad says nothing, watching him finish his preparations, feeling strangely separated from the hustle and clamor surrounding her. By the time Chavez makes it out west, she'll be long gone, having made her escape.

Chavez climbs into the Humvee and starts the motor. Soledad shifts her weight from one foot to another, unsure whether or not she should go wish him luck or bid him goodbye before he drives away. She doesn't move and then the moment passes. The Humvee rolls away, toward the growing cavalry of machines gathered on the flat, grassy prairie beyond the city.

She never got to tell don Flaco goodbye, either. Morbidly, she wonders how his end will come. Will he die as Lela did, buried neck deep in the ground, crushed by hate? She reaches up and rubs the Virgin pendant through her shirt, swallowing hard against the unexpected welling of tears.

"Come on, Indigo," she says. "I've got a plane to catch."

CHAPTER 25

Guzmán tosses another shovelful of dirt behind him. The hole he's standing in isn't even waist-deep yet and already the rough wooden handle has his hands painfully blistered. He looks up at the two guards watching over him, their shotguns at the ready.

"One of you have a pair of gloves, by chance?" he asks.

The guards glare at him, their heavily tattooed faces unflinching. Neither answers. Behind them, the sun rises large and bright over the eastern horizon, promising a hot desert morning.

"I didn't think so." He exhales and sits down on the edge of the hole, wiping sweat from his brow.

"No breaks," grunts one of his minders. When Guzmán doesn't move, the man rushes over and kicks his injured shoulder. A bolt of searing pain shoots through Guzmán's arm and he doubles over, clutching his shoulder and cursing the Fundie under his breath. "I said no breaks," the guard repeats, and with his uninjured arm Guzmán grabs the shovel and continues his work.

As he steps onto the shovel and thrusts the blade into the soft earth, he glances around at the arena floor. Empty and quiet, the stage and fighting ring removed, it seems a world away from the torchlit hell of the night before, when thousands packed the stands cheering for his death. It's peaceful, even agreeable, this place where he'll die, buried to the neck in the very hole he's standing in right now.

Digging his own grave. He's heard the gringo phrase many times. Reader Soledad often used the expression in reference to the endless parade of hustlers who came to bend a knee to him, to con don Flaco with some outlandish moneymaking scheme. Digging their own graves, one lie at a time. That's what she'd say. The gringos have so many colorful expressions like this in English, and this was one that he especially liked. And now, as fate would have it, he finds himself literally tasked with doing that very thing. He's even morbidly amused by it, missing none of the irony of his current chore.

He wonders what old Chavez might say if he could see his patrón right now. Ya te dije, he'd be saying, arms crossed, scolding him like a cross teacher at a slow-learning student. I told you so. And why didn't Guzmán listen to him? He's listened to him a hundred times before, and the old bear has never steered him wrong, not once. What finally broke inside him that he had to ignore Chavez's counsel and go speeding off across the plains?

Sorry, old Chavez. You were right. I was wrong. Tan fácil como eso. Easy as that.

He should have been more patient. He should have stayed in Dallas, should have played the long game better. He'd played it so well for so many years. But it only takes one mistake, one blunder to end it all. He remembers one of the first times he saw his late lieutenant Lela fight in a bare-knuckle boxing match. She lost round after round, getting beaten soundly by a monster of an opponent. Her face was swollen, blood streamed from her nose and mouth. She was a total mess, staggering badly, maybe one or two punches from being knocked out. And then, distracted and overconfident, her opponent dropped his guard for a moment, exposing his chin well within Lela's reach. She saw the opening immediately and pounced on him, landing a left hook that shattered his jaw and put him to sleep. Her opponent had fought the perfect fight, and up until the moment of that fateful left hook, he didn't even have a mark on his face. But one mistake was all it took.

Guzmán grunts, driving the shovel's blade into the ground. That's why he won't end up in the history books. That's why Ernesto Guzmán's picture won't sit beside Lincoln and Benito Juarez. Those men could control themselves until the fight was finished, never letting their guard down even for a moment. They never would have run off on a whim of anger, blind with revenge. Not like him. What a fool he's been. Now it's all over. *He's* all over. And if anyone remembers him at all in the years and decades ahead, they'll lump him in with the Zapatas and the Villas of history. They'll say El Flaco was just another shortsighted Mexican who could fight with the best of them, but never managed to master his own passions.

You always said I liked fighting too much, didn't you, Mamá?

Even when he'd been beaten, hopelessly outmatched by older children twice his size, coming home bruised and crying, he never seemed to learn the lesson Mamá hoped he would. All he could think about was how he'd get his revenge, how he'd pay back the older kid who'd beat him. Terco como una mula, Ernestito. Stubborn as a mule, she'd always say to him. Too stubborn, it turns out, to earn her the revenge she deserved.

Perdóname, Mamá.

Shamed, he brings his thoughts back to the present, to what might be happening back in Dallas. By now Chavez has sent out search parties to look for him, no doubt. Or maybe he's gearing up for an all-or-nothing battle to settle things once and for all. Guzmán pictures the old bear hunched over a map spread out like a tablecloth, barking orders. Poor old Chavez. Everything's in his hands now. He'll have to take care of Dallas and end that baby-slaving preacher on his own.

"You do good work for a one-armed digger," a voice behind him says. He turns to see Reverend Wright approaching, trailed by a bodyguard with a sniper rifle over one shoulder and a three-legged stool in his hands. The preacher looks like a backwoods farmer, dressed simply in a long-sleeved cotton undershirt and faded denim overalls. "I'd say you're about done with your chore," the preacher observes. He addresses the bodyguard, motioning to a spot on the ground near Guzmán's hole. "You can set it right there, Charlie. Thank you, son."

His escort places the stool on the dirt, then Wright dismisses him along with Guzmán's two minders. All three hesitate, exchanging nervous looks.

"I need a few moments alone with the condemned, friends," Wright clarifies. "I'd like to give him one last chance to redeem his wicked soul, to accept Jesus Christ into his heart now that the hour of his earthly death is near." The explanation strikes Guzmán as so absurd he nearly laughs out loud. The Fundie guards, however, seem to buy it entirely, and all three nod in grave understanding. The one named Charlie disarms Guzmán of his shovel and the trio retires to a shaded entryway, where they're far enough away to give the men their privacy, but still close enough to keep an eye on things.

Wright takes a seat on the stool, removing a bandanna from his pocket and wiping sweat from the top of his head. "Lord, already starting to heat up out here," he comments, with the casual intimacy of a man chatting with a longtime friend. "I'll never know how you could stand this heat for all those years out here."

"You get used to it," Guzmán replies, settling down onto the edge of the hole.

"Would you mind if I asked you something, don Flaco?" The reverend leans forward, hands on thighs, gazing at Guzmán with what appears to be sincere curiosity.

"Ándale. Go ahead."

"Why'd you do it?" Wright asks. "Why'd you risk your neck coming out here? I lost more than a bit of sleep last night pondering it, and I simply can't get my head around why you'd do such a thing."

"I wanted to kill you myself," Guzmán answers honestly. He wonders if he could dash across the five meters separating them and snap the preacher's neck before the bodyguards could react. He furtively glances over his shoulder and finds the disappointing answer. The Fundie named Charlie holds a sniper rifle at the ready, peering through the scope at Guzmán. He wouldn't make it two steps out of his hole if he moved to attack the reverend.

Wright nods thoughtfully. "Oh, I don't doubt that for a minute, but I'm not sure that answers my question." He narrows his eyes. "I bet old Chavez was fit to be tied when you told him you were coming out here. Tried to talk you out of it, I'd wager." When Guzmán doesn't answer, he adds, "Yes, well, I would have done the same. If I can be frank with you, this little jaunt of yours across the plains has not been your finest hour, don Flaco."

"Can I go back to digging?" Guzmán asks flatly.

Wright's face brightens and he clasps his hands together, pleased. "Ha! There's that humor I've always heard so much about." Still smiling, he shakes his head ruefully. "Oh, don Flaco, this world will surely be a lesser place without you in it. You've been quite the inspiration, let me tell you. Only with a rival as great as yourself could I have risen to such heights. I suppose I ought to thank you for the motivation."

Guzmán crosses his arms.

"You played the game so well for many years," Wright compliments. "And taking Dallas? Lord, what a bold move. That'll be your masterpiece, the great victory they'll remember you for." He leans forward conspiratorially, a knowing gleam in his eyes. "But we know you took it a bit prematurely, didn't you? You didn't have enough troops to leave behind to hold the western desert. Well, don't beat yourself up too much over it. It's a classic blunder—spreading one's forces too thin—and you're not the first to put ambition over logistics." He pauses for a moment. "And today, I'm counting on old Chavez to make the same mistake."

"What are you talking about?" Guzmán snaps.

"This morning I announced your execution over the shortwave," the preacher explains. "In a sinful, dark world such as ours, good news should be shared far and wide, don't you think?" Wright lifts his eyebrows and smiles at his own joke, waiting a moment for a reaction from Guzmán that never comes.

"Our scouts outside Dallas," the reverend goes on, "tell us he's sending what looks like every last soldier, gun, and vehicle this way. They'll be here soon. And what a sight it'll be, all that steel rolling across the desert. It's a shame you won't be around for it."

"They'll wipe you out," Guzmán sneers.

The preacher nods. "In a head-to-head fight, I'm sure they would." A satisfied smile spreads across his face. "But that's not how things will unfold today."

Guzmán stares. The old crook is toying with him, teasing him, and enjoying every minute of it. The sun creeps higher in the sky, burning off the last of the cool morning air.

"Listen," the reverend says, bringing his finger to his lips. "Can you hear that?" Somewhere beyond the stadium Guzmán hears a faint rumbling sound, like muffled thunder. "That's my fleet heading out now."

"You running back to Houston," Guzmán teases, "with your tail between your legs? Just like you did after Conroe?"

For a moment, Wright visibly bristles at the reference to his embarrassing defeat, but he recovers quickly. "Come now, don Flaco," Wright chides, "do you really think so little of me? You think I'm so foolish that I'd take all this land and then just turn around and give it right back? No, no, no, my dear friend. This is chess, not checkers. If I want to defeat your flaquista army, I have to get them out of their Dallas fortress first, don't I? And right now, it looks like we've taken care of that."

"And then what?" Guzmán asks, unable to resist.

"Once they're out in the daylight, fully exposed, we'll pick at them around the edges. Hit them in their weak spots." As an offhanded aside, he adds: "It never ceases to amaze me how many volunteer for martyrdom, don Flaco. I'm truly blessed to shepherd such an amazing flock."

Martyrdom. The word clarifies Wright's battle strategy. He plans to use suicide bombers. Trucks and motorbikes laden heavily with explosives, piloted by his most zealous faithful. It's a ploy Chavez won't be able to match. A ploy that—combined with his influx of new weapons—will likely give Wright the advantage. How many of his followers are joyfully awaiting their own deaths at this very moment? Dozens? Hundreds? What a twisted piece of work this man is. What a soulless, callous monster lurks behind those eyes.

"It's a strategy not unlike the one you used last night," Wright points out. "Kicking and moving, kicking and moving, until poor old Zara couldn't take any more. Yes, that was a fine fight plan, don Flaco. Well thought out and executed to perfection."

"You're taking a big risk," Guzmán warns. "Chavez has been fighting in this desert a long time."

"Agreed, he's a wily foe," Wright answers. "But then, I've got the Lord on my side."

He stands up and looks down at Guzmán, the facade of the affable farmer finally dropping away like a mask, revealing an unsettling, expressionless gaze. "I wanted you to know this before you met your end," he sneers. "I wanted you to know everything you fought for will be for naught in a matter of hours. I wanted you to know that when they finish stoning you to death, I'm going to have your head put in a box, and each day when I wake up, after I say my morning prayers, I'm going to make that box my toilet. Think on that during your last few hours."

Wright turns his back and walks away, disappearing into the shade of an exit tunnel. Guzmán's two minders return, one of them carrying the shovel, which he tosses on the ground next to the hole.

"Dig," he grunts.

CHAPTER 26

Soledad stands next to Indigo, watching as the small American jet makes its first pass over the deserted airport's ancient, pockmarked runway, the aircraft's sleek white fuselage brilliant in the clear, bright sky. In a parked Humvee a short distance behind them, Steffa sits with Magnolia and their driver, Nico. After a prolonged amount of hemming and hawing and handwringing, Magnolia finally decided to come along.

Steffa points skyward and leans half her body out the Humvee's lowered window. "It's our plane! Look, it's our plane!"

"It is," Soledad calls back to her. "Now you stay put until I say it's okay, just like we said, all right?"

"Awww," the girl responds, frowning as Magnolia gently guides her back into the vehicle.

"You'll see it soon enough," Soledad assures her, turning back around to watch the plane's descent. The jet approaches, floating slowly downward and then landing at the far end of the runway. Little bursts of white smoke puff out from the landing gear as rubber wheels touch down. A few moments later, it finally rolls to stop a short distance away. A door panel yawns open, and a folding staircase stretches outward until it touches the ground.

The bitter taste of hierba still coats Soledad's tongue as Garcia emerges from the aircraft. He ambles over to the two women, smiling. "Good morning," he greets. Behind him, two men in identical black business suits exit the jet but don't come over. Security, Soledad assumes.

"Morning," Soledad replies. "Welcome back to the airport." She motions over toward a large hangar. "That's where you saw your vintage drones, remember?"

Garcia chuckles. "Right. I hope I didn't offend you by saying that."

"Not at all," Soledad answers. "So you know a lot about drones?"

The redheaded American looks at her sideways. "Some."

Soledad furrows her brow, feeling the hierba's effect reaching its peak. "Thought you said you could take one of those Reapers apart blindfolded?"

"No," he corrects, his expression beginning to cloud over with uncertainty. "I said I could take it apart and put it back together in three hours."

Thrusting her awareness into someone else's mind while simultaneously making small talk is no easy thing. It's like solving a math problem while reciting a poem, hoping you have enough control over both actions that the equation comes out right and the poem doesn't come out as gibberish. It's even more difficult performing the feat stealthily enough that Garcia's conscious mind isn't aware of it. This is, she suddenly realizes, the first time she's ever attempted something so difficult, so demanding of her special talents.

She pushes in. Images and sounds and smells fly through her awareness. Memories of Garcia's past. She mentioned the drones to stir up specific recollections, and she can sense them now, flashing with the sudden brilliance of lightning strikes at midnight. Garcia working on the open carapace of a gunbird, expert hands working on the electronic innards, switching out parts with practiced precision. She can feel the smooth metal against his fingertips, smell the stale, metallic air of the hangar. It only takes a few moments more to find what she's looking for.

He knows how.

"Soledad? You okay?"

The trader's voice sounds far away, her words low and muffled. Then in the next moment Soledad snaps back to the hangar. Indigo's hand is on her, gently patting the back of her shoulder.

"Is she all right?" Garcia asks.

"She's fine," the trader answers.

Soledad swallows, steadying her lightheadedness with a deep breath through her nose. She turns around, looking toward the Humvee. Nico the driver sits behind the wheel, watching her with an intent, expectant stare. She gives him the prearranged signal, a casual wave of the hand, and he immediately barks orders into a hand radio.

From the nearest hangar, a large rolling door flies upward, metal rollers roaring in their tracks. Six Humvees burst out of the hangar one by one like fired bullets, speeding directly toward the jet.

Soledad puts a protective hand out for Indigo, forcing her backwards and away from Garcia.

"What the hell?" Indigo cries, nearly stumbling over.

The Humvees screech to a stop in front of the jet, blocking its path. Flaquista soldiers sporting black bandannas stand in turrets, the long barrels of their .50-caliber guns aimed menacingly at the aircraft. The twin security guards brandish handguns and throw confused, helpless looks over at Garcia.

"What the hell is going on here?" Garcia cries, his hands spread wide, his face a mask of disbelief.

"Tell the pilot to cut the engines," Soledad orders. She glances behind her, checking to make sure Nico has chauffeured Steffa and Magnolia safely away as she instructed. He has; the Humvee they arrived in is nowhere to be found.

Garcia looks at her as if she's gone crazy. "Have you gone completely—"

"Cut the engines, now!" Soledad produces a Glock from her vest, points it directly at the American.

"Sol," Indigo cries, "what are you doing?"

She looks over at Indigo. "Change of plans."

*　　*　　*

"You might have said something, you know," Indigo complains, still bristling. "Given me some kind of warning or something. Christ, woman, I nearly had a coronary back there."

Soledad and Indigo stand some distance away from Garcia, who's hunched over a gunbird's fuselage. The outer skin of the drone's bulbous head is missing, revealing tightly packed electronics and a small dish-shaped antenna. The American studies the innards like a doctor concentrating on a complex surgery. Armed flaquista soldiers hover nearby, watching him closely.

"Sorry, there just wasn't time," Soledad says. And there wasn't. She hatched the plan quickly back at the condo, left alone with her thoughts when Indigo went to the market to fetch some going-away candy for Steffa. She stuffed her mouth with hierba and called Nico over the hand radio. Amazingly, the driver was able to round up half a dozen Humvees and a handful of soldiers on short notice, part of a small contingent Chavez had left behind to keep the city secure. Pressed for time, they left for the airport with Magnolia and Steffa as soon as Indigo returned, candy bags in hand.

"I never had a minute alone with you to clue you in," Soledad explains.

A lot of things could have gone wrong with her plan. She might not have remembered Garcia's comments about his drone expertise from the other day, first of all. And then the Americans might have sent someone other than Garcia to pick her up. And most crucially, she might have looked into his head and seen nothing: that he didn't have the expertise to revive a drone or two they could send out west to help Chavez. But none of the things that could have gone wrong did go wrong. Still, she feels anything but optimistic about this long-shot idea of hers. So many things could *still* go wrong.

"You just blew your chance to get a refugee visa," Indigo observes. "Though I guess you know that."

Soledad nods. "I guess I did."

Garcia comes over, rubbing his palms together slowly, like a mechanic who's been working on a car engine. The American shrugs, his expression blank. "I can't get them airborne."

Soledad spots the lie immediately. Garcia's an easy read. Concealing a bluff clearly isn't his strong suit. If he were a poker player, he'd be the kind Indigo calls *easy money*.

Indigo turns to Soledad, lifts her eyebrows expectantly.

"Not even close," the reader confirms out loud, not bothering to use a surreptitious signal.

Indigo removes a Glock from her pants and steps forward, leveling it at the American's head. "Call me crazy," the trader says, "but for some reason I don't believe you."

CHAPTER 27

Chavez rides in the Humvee's passenger seat, pressing the palm of his hand to the roof to steady himself against the jolting high-speed run. His driver, a tall, lanky soldier called Chango—a nickname born of his large, monkey-like ears—focuses intently on the path ahead. Half a mile to their left the ancient thoroughfare of I-20 guides their way westward. Around the truck an enormous convoy of steel and guns speeds across the flat, featureless plains, vehicles of all shapes and sizes, a rolling wave of destructive power.

A handful of hours have passed since they left Dallas, and Chavez's own grim thoughts have pestered him the entire time. The Fundies know they're coming. There seems little doubt of that. They would have had scouts posted outside Dallas, watching his fleet leave the city, counting every vehicle down to the last motorbike and radioing the numbers back to their commanders. And they're surely tracking them this very moment, following at a safe distance, updating his location at regular intervals. The flaquista attack, when it finally comes, will be anything but a surprise.

A knot of anxiety in Chavez's gut ties itself tighter as he studies the Americans' photos and intel yet again. He rifles through the stack of papers on his lap—a task made close to impossible for all the truck's jostling—looking for anything that might give him an advantage. He goes through every sheet, but still he's unable to come up with anything helpful. The preacher's got more vehicles than he does. He can see that clearly enough in the drone images. And if he's got more vehicles, he's got more firepower as well.

Por Dios. It's the kind of engagement he's always tried to avoid. The all-or-nothing gambit, the winner-take-all bet in the last hand of a card game.

But what choice does he have? Time has run out of them. Time has run out on his jefe.

He morbidly pictures what might be happening at this very moment to his patrón, to the man he's fought with for the last two decades. The man he's eaten nearly every meal with over those years. The man he's put his faith in, who's proven himself worthy of it over and over again. As a street orphan, Chavez never knew his blood family. He's never married, never had a son of his own, but if he had...

Or perhaps it's already happened, Chavez suddenly thinks, his throat tightening reflexively at the thought. He clenches his jaw, pushing horrible images from his mind.

"Faster, Chango," he demands.

"Sí, jefe," the driver replies.

Chavez leans forward and—for the fourth time in the last hour—taps the small display on the dashboard, bringing up a map of West Texas. Bobbing around in his seat, he concentrates on the display as he manipulates it with his fingertips, scanning the terrain, moving the map back and forth, zooming it in and out obsessively.

But like the papers now falling from his lap to the floorboard, the display reveals nothing to him, offering him no advantage to exploit, no play he can make.

He keeps searching, his eyes straining, his veteran warrior's mind searching for a strategy, as if it's hidden somewhere on the dashboard map, waiting for him to find it.

Under a blazing sun, the convoy of thundering engines pushes ever westward.

CHAPTER 28

"You didn't have to stick a gun to my head," Garcia whines, lying on his back with his arms thrust upward, elbow-deep inside the gunbird's body. "I might have helped you anyway, you know. That baby-slaving bastard's got it coming as far as I'm concerned."

Indigo and Soledad sit on aluminum stools, watching him. The inside of the hangar grows warmer; the growing dampness under Soledad's arms is an uncomfortable reminder of the passing time. How long has the gringo been at it? Soledad wonders. An hour? More? She's lost all sense of time. A quarter hour seems to pass in the blink of an eye.

"Thought you needed some extra motivation," Indigo replies, the Glock still in her hand, an unsubtle threat resting on her thigh.

Garcia motions to the scattered pile of tools and electronics next to him. "I didn't know you had the proper gear on hand. You might have shown all of this first."

"Less talk, more work," Indigo snaps.

"Are all Texans this rude?"

"Are all gringos this chatty?"

Soledad gets up from the stool and paces about

impatiently. "How long?" she asks again.

"Look," Garcia answers, crawling out from under the drone and rising up to his knees, "I told you before. You got a bunch of customized shit inside this thing that's there to talk with the Dallas AIs. And it doesn't look anything like what we have in the States. We're talking *antique* tech here, so it's a bit like working on something from a flight museum. Half of what I'm doing is guesswork."

He wipes sweat from his forehead. "Then, assuming I don't cut some vital wire or remove a board that I should've left in place"—he motions to the pile of gear—"I've still got to piece together a manual remote from all this. After that, we have to run a test flight, if by some miracle we even get that far. All this before we can even think about sending a bird out west. Got it?"

Their attention is diverted to the hangar's entrance, where a pickup truck with broken taillights backs up and stops a short distance away. The driver exits and lowers the tailgate, revealing a cache of missiles lying across the bed. He smiles at them proudly.

"Nice work," Indigo calls over to him. Then she turns back to Garcia. "Back to the salt mines, compadre."

Garcia returns to his task, and Indigo strides over to the truck to inspect the munitions. Soledad approaches Garcia, kneeling down close enough to speak to him without being overheard.

"Hey," she says, her voice low. "I need a favor."

He sighs, keeping his eyes on his work. "Sure, why not? Toss another one to the pile. What can I do for you? Build an H-bomb maybe?"

"Can you take my daughter and her caretaker out of here?"

Garcia's hands stop their work. He cranes his neck and looks at her as if she's just told him a joke he doesn't understand. "You're serious?"

"Yes."

The American snorts. "Lady, if I don't get these birds flying soon, your friend over there is going to make sure I don't go home or anywhere else, ever. So even if I wanted to pack up a couple refugees, the odds of that happening don't look terribly great."

Soledad swallows, looks earnestly into his eyes. "Listen, you're not going to die here today, no matter what happens. Even if you can't get those gunbirds working. The gun to your head, the threats, it's all bullshit. Chavez is racing across the wastelands right now with damn near every soldier and vehicle we have. We're desperate to help any way we can. And we didn't see any other way."

The redheaded American stares at her for a long moment. The hierba's effect has ebbed, and although she can clearly sense his wariness, his skepticism, she can't tell if anything she's saying is making a dent in the solid wall of his doubt. "Why are you telling me this?"

"Because something tells me I can trust you." It's not technically a lie, but it's nowhere near the whole truth. The truth would take far longer to explain, and she doesn't have time. There's no time to tell him what she is and what she can do. No time to explain that when she was inside his head she saw something, a thing she couldn't name if she had to. Something she first sensed in Dallas when he reacted to the children in chains in the holo images. Something that told her his sense of right and wrong transcended politics and borders and even the orders of his superiors. She's seen the shape of his soul.

"Please," she pleads. "I couldn't bear it if something bad were to happen to them."

Green eyes stare back at her. Behind them she senses something change, like a lock slowly sliding open. The American nods. "All right."

Not lying.

A wave of relief washes over Soledad. If everything else goes to hell and their world breaks apart, at least Steffa and Magnolia will be safe. "Thank you."

"Sure," Garcia says. He picks up a rag and wipes his hands with it. "Now let me try to get this thing working. The clock's ticking."

CHAPTER 29

Is his jefe dead already? As the hours pass and his fleet races headlong across the Republic, the question buzzes madly about Chavez's mind like a fly trapped in a glass bottle.

He distracts himself with the details of leadership, barking a constant stream of orders over the hand radio. Tightening up formations. Checking in with the squad leaders. Miles ahead of them, the scouts on motorbikes haven't seen anything yet. But they will soon. Already he sees the flat tops of plateaus cutting across the horizon. The air is dry and dusty, and the greens and yellows of the central plains have given way to the dull grays and browns of the west. Abandoned oil derricks from the previous era begin to appear, rusted out and standing in the scrub brush like huge steel birds with large heads. They're getting close.

Maybe he's gone already.

Stop dwelling on it, you old fool. If he's gone, you can't do a damned thing about it, can you? If he's gone, he went to his grave hoping you'd do exactly what you're doing now. Your jefe isn't (wasn't?) a perfect man, not by far. He's vain and ill-tempered and he debauches far too much, but he always knew what he was doing was right, that his cause was a just one. How many times have you seen him abuse his power, in all the years you've known him? None. How many times have you seen him tolerate those who abused theirs? None. He had his flaws, but Ernesto Guzmán is (was?) a good man in a bad world. And his movement was a good one. It broke chains of oppression, it fed the hungry, it protected the vulnerable.

So if his jefe's dead, then so be it. He'll save his tears and his mourning for later. Right now he needs to do everything he can to keep don Flaco's movement from dying with him.

The hand radio hooked to his belt crackles to life, static mixed with an excited voice coming through the speaker. He unhooks it and puts the mic close to his mouth. "Come again," he shouts, moving the volume dial to its loudest position. The landscape speeds past and the Humvee's shocks creak and groan as he bounces around in his seat. The voice repeats the coded message, an update from one of the scouts on motorbike.

Chavez listens, then lifts his binocular to his face.

"Did they spot something?" Chango the driver asks.

Chavez doesn't answer, peering through the lenses. A smudge of brown haze stretches across the horizon, the telltale dust cloud kicked up by an enormous number of vehicles. A jolt of adrenaline shoots through his body.

"There they are."

"Oh, Jesus," Chango exclaims. "I can't believe it."

Lowering his binoculars, Chavez looks over at the driver. "Can't believe it? Did you think we were going to miss an army that big, joven?"

"No, sir," the driver replies. "That's not what I meant. Look over there." Chango motions out the window, toward the south.

Chavez leans forward and peers southward. Some miles away, the border between sky and ground has disappeared, as if an immense rust-colored cloud has descended from the stratosphere and laid itself across the desert.

"Sandstorm," Chango cries above the constant squeak of the shocks.

Chavez nods. "Big one. Can you tell which way it's going?"

"Not sure."

Thirty seconds later, when the storm has grown menacingly larger, they're both sure. "Puta madre," Chavez swears. "It's coming right for us." As if he needed another thing to worry about. In another few minutes, they'll be driving blind.

But so will the Fundies.

Suddenly inspired, he taps the map display to life again, scrolling around their location, searching. The shaking and jostling makes it difficult, but finally he finds what he's looking for. At long last, a battle strategy begins to take shape. The Humvee careens over the flat, dry earth. Chavez turns a knob on his hand radio, switching to the wide frequency everyone under his command will hear. He relays a carefully coded message to his squad leaders, then waits as each of them calls back, confirming his instructions.

The battle plan completed, he then addresses the entirety of his rolling army. "¡Compadres!" he booms. "Ready yourselves and your weapons. Don Flaco is counting on us. And remember, los flaquistas have never lost a fight in the desert, and we're not going to start today!"

War cries and cheers rise above the sound of churning motors as Chavez's armada races forward into battle.

CHAPTER 30

Guzmán has been here before, countless times. Waiting in some small anteroom as a crowd gathers outside, the sound of thousands of restless voices coming through the walls, a noise like sustained thunder, growing louder with each moment. A public spectacle awaits, though this time it's not a flaquista rally where the crowd's assembled to hear him deliver a victory speech, celebrating some recent triumph, a new town or turf pried away from the Dallasites. This time it's a different kind of spectacle. This time it's not his words they've come for, but his death.

He sits with his back to the wall, bound hands resting on his lap, unsure how many hours have passed since they brought him here after he'd finished digging his hole. His two silent minders watch over him from across the room, their inked faces expressionless. There's a soft knock on the door, and the old man who offered him a smoke last night shuffles into the room, carrying two steaming bowls of stew.

"Thought you young'uns might be hungry," he tells the guards as he places the bowls on a small table next to the wall.

The guards grunt their thanks, and when the man turns

to leave, Guzmán asks, "What about a last smoke for the condemned?"

The man sneers at Guzmán. "I ain't got nothing for Zara's killer 'cept a nice pile of stones." His thin, raspy voice is full of scorn. "I'll be right up front, sinner," he snarls. "You'll see me right up front."

Guzmán breaks out in laughter. "Well said, viejito!" he cheers, stomping his foot on the floor in mock-approval. "That's the spirit!" The man widens his eyes, offended, then spits on the floor and stomps out of the room. The dramatic exit delights Guzmán. His boisterous guffaws echo off the walls of the tiny space. The guards narrow their eyes and frown at him as they sit down to their meal.

A few minutes later, when Guzmán's minders have finished and set their spoons rattling in their empty bowls, there's another knock on the door, this one loud and strong and insistent.

So this is it, Guzmán thinks, as the taller guard rises from the table and moves toward the door. He notes how strange he feels, or rather, doesn't feel. In his time he's seen the myriad ways humanity greets death's imminent arrival. Some lose it completely, crying and blubbering like a child who doesn't want to be punished. Others panic like cornered animals, scratching and kicking and biting to escape their fate. Some remain frozen with disbelief, unable to utter anything but a constant chanting denial of *no, no, no* right up until the end. But as the shorter guard approaches and grabs Guzmán's elbow to help him to his feet, he finds no rush of fear surging within his gut, no lightning bolt of panic striking his heart. Instead, he's oddly calm, even relaxed.

The door opens and a short Fundie woman with long braids stands in the doorway. *It's time*, she announces, throwing Guzmán a hateful glance before she turns to leave. Guzmán rises to his feet.

It's as good as any other day to die, he decides.

The Fundies grasp him firmly, interlocking their arms

with his and urging him forward. They exit the room into a narrow hallway. The low, rumbling roar of the crowd echoes off the walls, growing louder as they make their way through the narrow, winding passage. Finally they come upon the tall arch of an entryway. Guzmán squints as they exit the concourse and step into the bright sunlight. Momentarily blinded, he feels the familiar heat of the desert sun bearing down on him. A couple steps through the archway, the guards pull him to a stop. Guzmán blinks forcefully and the blur of movement in the near distance coalesces into a mob gathered on the arena floor. Hundreds of heads turn and stare at the condemned man's entrance, and a hush comes over the stadium. The moment lasts maybe a second, a predator's flash of recognition before pouncing on its prey, and then a stampede breaks out, rushing toward Guzmán in a shouting mass of arms and legs.

He instinctively braces himself, but the mob doesn't attack. Instead, they form a tight circle around him, a scrum of mad, screaming faces. His minders hold out their arms defensively, but the crowd seems to know to stay back. The guards hold him there for a minute, letting the crowd work itself into a frenzy. The noise is a deafening, unintelligible roar, assaulting Guzmán's ears. The sound of blood and hate, hollered at full-throated force.

The guards push him forward. The crowd moves in tandem, keeping him within its cage of writhing arms and gnashing teeth. Some of them hold a stone in each hand, knocking them together, making a clacking noise. He slowly walks on, chin up defiantly, eyes forward. They want him to break down in fear or panic, but he won't give it to them.

The stands around the stadium's bowl are nearly empty, Guzmán notices. Only a few spectators here and there perched to watch the scene. Most have come to participate, not to observe. They move forward toward the center of the arena. Directly ahead of them, the crowd parts and the white-suited preacher appears, standing beside the hole, bullhorn in hand.

The preacher brings the horn to his mouth. "Make way, make way, brothers and sisters," he shouts, barely audible above the mob's voice. "Let the sinner through." Guzmán's minders hustle him forward, bringing him to a stop beside the reverend.

"Take your places, brethren, take your places," Wright cries. The raucous shouting dies down and the crowd obeys, untangling itself and reforming into a wide circle with the stoning hole as its center. Around the perimeter of the circle are dozens of thigh-high mounds of rocks, fist-sized stones stacked into piles. Behind each stack, a man and a woman stand, busily passing out rocks to the left and right, distributing them throughout the crowd. An excited buzz fills the air.

Lowering the bullhorn to his side, Wright leans toward Guzmán. "You've certainly got them riled up again, don Flaco. Well done, sir." The preacher then nods at the guards, who jostle Guzmán toward the hole.

Steady, Guzmán tells himself. *Don't give them a damn thing. Don't let them break you.* As they lower him down into the hole, he spots the old man who brought him his pipe and tobacco, grinning at him, smacking two large stones together. With bile churning in his stomach, Guzmán grins back and winks.

Standing neck deep in the ground, he watches as the guards pick up a pair of shovels and drive the blades into the same mound of dirt he excavated hours earlier. They toss two shovelfuls at Guzmán, and the burying process begins. The dirt thuds against his chest and falls to his feet.

Guzmán looks up into the blue brilliance of his desert sky, squinting against the sun as he feels the dirt cover his ankles. As he watches, a pair of dark spots appear in the cloudless expanse above them, tiny black orbs he first takes for retina flashes.

Wright notices him gazing skyward. "You finally

praying for salvation, sinner?" he mocks, laughing. "Asking forgiveness for your—" The reverend stops midsentence, furrowing his brow. He moves to one of the digging Fundies and, still gazing skyward, nudges him with his elbow. "What in the Lord's name is that?"

The man stops shoveling and turns his attention to the sky. There is a moment's pause, a frozen heartbeat, and then he hurls the shovel to the ground.

"TAKE COVER!"

Guzmán instinctively ducks down into the hole as the first rocket hits the stadium.

CHAPTER 31

When the explosions finally stop, Guzmán has a foot of dirt piled onto his head and shoulders. Wrists still tied, he rises unsteadily up through the layer of dirt and out of his hole. Brushing himself off, dazed and ears ringing, he takes in the destruction all around him. There are bodies everywhere. Bodies and parts of bodies, strewn throughout the stadium. The floor of the arena—until moments ago a flat expanse of weeds and dirt—looks as if massive bulldozers have reworked the earth. A huge section of the stadium is missing, reduced to an enormous pile of rubble.

Guzmán climbs out of the hole and coughs. Around him there's no movement at all except a slowly settling cloud of dust and sand. He looks back at the ragged hole, slowly beginning to understand his incredible luck. The grave he dug to be stoned to death in, irony of ironies, has saved his life.

What just happened here? Did Chavez talk the gringos into sending in a drone strike? It doesn't seem likely. Or maybe the techs back in Dallas finally managed to get some of the drones working? He glances overhead, suddenly aware there might be eyes in the sky watching him at this very moment.

The preacher! A sudden sense of purpose overwhelming him, he dashes around the arena, searching for Wright's body. He passes a dead soldier, notices a hunting knife hanging from a belt hook. Guzmán kneels down, carefully removes the knife from its sheath, and twists the blade in his hands to saw at the rope around his wrists. His bonds severed, he grabs the soldier's sidearm, a loaded Sig 320, and shoves it into his pocket. For the next few minutes, he feverishly searches through the grotesque tableau of smoldering rubble and body parts, but he finds no sign of Wright. Perhaps the preacher is buried somewhere, his body hidden under a mound of dirt and rocks. As Guzmán continues his search, he collects another pistol, two semiauto rifles, a decent amount of ammunition, and a tight-fitting pair of combat boots. Near one of the still-intact entrance tunnels he finds a motorbike lying on its side, miraculously undamaged, the motor still idling.

Halfway to the bike a thought stops him, and he scrambles up an undamaged section of the stadium. At the top, he looks out over the remains of Odessa, hands to forehead, shielding his eyes from the sun's glare. Several of the downtown buildings have been leveled, including the old courthouse, black columns of smoke rising from the debris. He turns his gaze toward the southeast, to the Fundie exodus, and what's left of the unlucky vehicles at the rear of that massive caravan. A crooked trail of destroyed trucks and cars extends into the distance. Then, about a mile away, he spies a small group on foot, approaching a Humvee. They enter the vehicle one by one, the tiny figures identifiable as soldiers by their green fatigues. All except one, clad in white, wider and rounder than the others. The preacher. The bastard survived. The white figure disappears into the vehicle and the Humvee lurches forward, heading south to catch up with the surviving fleet.

Guzmán rushes down to the arena floor and the motorbike, grabbing it by the handlebars and hauling it up onto its wheels with a heave that sends a throb of pain through his entire arm. Wincing, he hops on.

Exiting the stadium onto a side street, he brings the bike to a stop and pauses to get his bearings. The street and its dilapidated storefronts are silent and empty of people. The Fundies are gone, the locals—if any have survived—are hunkered down and hiding.

For a moment he considers driving east, putting a safe distance between himself, Wright's Humvee, and the Fundie fleet. He might even run into his own people, who surely by now are speeding across the plains, coming to his rescue.

Guzmán shakes his head, laughing at himself. *You old fool, stop pretending. You know which way you're going.*

Turning the bike around, he points himself southward, then pops the clutch and spins the back wheel. Dirt flies high into the air as the bike leaps forward.

Within a minute, he has Wright's Humvee in sight.

* * *

A hot wind breathes against his face as Guzmán slowly closes in on the vehicle, racing over the flat, parched landscape of scrubland desert. It's a good bike. Nimble and quick, with wide knobby tires and a cushy suspension. Perfect for a desert run. There were four soldiers with Wright. They'd be packing semiauto rifles, for sure, maybe shotguns too. Now that he thinks about it, he should have taken a minute to pull some body armor—or at least a helmet—off one of the dead soldiers back at the stadium. But it's too late to turn back. If he returned now, he might not be able to pick up their trail again.

They haven't seen him yet, he knows, since they haven't opened fire or accelerated to outrun him. His eyes tear in the wind as he closes the gap, maneuvering the motorbike far to the driver's side, out of the rearview mirrors' line of sight. He speeds up until he pulls almost even with the speeding Humvee, a half mile now to his right. His stealthy, patient approach has taken nearly half an hour, and now he's finally in position.

He'll have to hit them very quick and very hard. The odds don't favor one man on a motorbike against a Humvee filled with armed soldiers, but this time *he's* the one with surprise on his side. He speeds up, then angles the bike sharply toward the truck. Within seconds he's closed the distance. He slides the rifle off his shoulder. They still haven't noticed him.

Even over smooth pavement, firing a bulky rifle while steering a speeding motorbike is no easy thing. But with a wounded shoulder, over the jarring, gravelly terrain of the Chihuahuan Desert, dodging creosote bushes, it's a very tricky business. Guzmán knows he has to get close, very close, to minimize the margin of error. He increases the angle of attack, bringing himself near enough to make out the face of the driver. He picks out the wide brim of the telltale white hat in the rear seat. They have Wright in a protected position, sandwiched between two Fundie soldiers. One of them turns toward Guzmán. The soldier's eyes widen in recognition.

Time slows to a silent crawl.

The window of his advantage will close quickly, Guzmán knows. The surprise on the soldier's face will last only milliseconds—no longer than the blink of an eye—and when the shock unfreezes his body, he'll shout a warning to the driver and raise a weapon toward the motorbike. But before that window can close, Guzmán opens fire, and the soldier's surprised gawk is the last expression his face will ever make.

Guzmán sprays the truck's cabin with gunfire, shattering the rear and front windows. The vehicle lurches toward him like an angered bull. He tries to steer out of the huge machine's path, but the truck's bumper knocks his rear wheel. In the next moment the motorbike's no longer under him and he's airborne. He tumbles across the ground and sprawls to a stop in a sitting position. Spitting dirt from his mouth, he scrambles across the ground toward the bike, lying down behind it for cover. The machine's motor sputters and dies, its front wheel bent in half. The Humvee sits idling about forty meters away. Guzmán sees no movement inside the cabin. He's lost one of the rifles in the crash, but the other is still strapped to his shoulder. Lucky. Grunting in pain, he unslings it from his shoulder. The wound he suffered in the ambush aches terribly and he's bruised and scraped all over, but nothing feels broken. He lays the rifle across the motorbike's chassis and peers through the scope. The Humvee cabin appears empty.

He lies still, watching the truck, waiting for movement, his finger on the trigger. A minute passes and nothing happens. Perhaps it's all over, but he doubts he could be that lucky. He filled the cabin with as many rounds as he could in his flash attack, but he can't be sure if he hit anyone for all the bouncing around. Another minute passes. Maybe fortune smiled on him and he hit them all. If the Fundies were still alive, surely they would have opened up on him by now or lobbed a grenade his way. Maybe after all his bad turns, he's finally getting his fair share of good luck.

As he starts to raise his head to get up, a single shot rings out, caroming off the motorbike's handlebars. Instinctively, he jerks away and flattens himself against the ground. Squinting through the scope, he doesn't see anything as the second shot is fired, striking the ground less than a meter to his right. Sand and dirt fly into the air and land on his back.

A pistol, he decides, from the pitch of the fired rounds. With his semiauto rifle, he's got the advantage in firepower, but whoever's shooting at him has the benefit of an entire Humvee to hide behind. He returns fire, a short burst. Small fireworks explode across the chassis of the truck. He waits a long moment, but there's no returning fire. Should he rush the truck? Nothing but flat ground separates him from the Humvee, a long forty yards of open, vulnerable space over which even a poor marksman might be able to take him down. But staying put with his head down, behind the minimal cover the bike gives him, doesn't seem like the best plan, either. He debates with himself as he fires again.

"Don Flaco!" a voice shouts as soon as the barrage stops. Guzmán tilts his head away from the scope, furrowing his brow. The voice from behind the Humvee cries out a second time. It's the preacher, Guzmán realizes.

"What do you want, preacher?" Guzmán calls back.

"You best hop on that bike and get the hell out of here."

Guzmán laughs. "Why would I want to leave this party, preacher?"

"Because I called ahead on the radio," Wright hollers. "I got trucks on the way. Be here any minute."

Guzmán chews on that for a moment. "Hell, preacher, don't you know there's nowhere else I'd rather be right now than here with you?"

He stands and walks toward the Humvee, squeezing off short bursts every few steps. "Why would I want to be anywhere else?" he shouts, laughing maniacally as he squeezes off another shot.

He reaches the Humvee, crouching low. He waits a moment, listening, then springs up quickly to take a look. Inside the vehicle, he finds what he expected: dead soldiers sprawled over the seats, one, two, three, four. Slowly, he moves around the bumper, rifle at the ready. Behind the truck he finds nothing but Wright's hat, crumpled and dirt-stained. Looking up, he spots the preacher, running away, scrambling awkwardly on a pair of old legs.

Guzmán lifts the rifle to his shoulder, and through the scope he aligns the crosshairs on the easy target of Wright's wide back. His finger begins to curl on the trigger, then stops. Releases.

He doesn't fire.

CHAPTER 32

It doesn't take long to overtake Reverend Wright. Even charged with the adrenaline-fueled speed of panic, the old preacher's legs are far older and far more burdened than those of his pursuer.

Guzmán jogs over the sandy dirt, rifle in hand, slowly reeling in his prize catch. The preacher's hands are empty, he notices, the weapon he fired either dropped or discarded. Wright anxiously looks back every few moments, hatless, the top of his pink head shiny with sweat. He's too winded to say anything. Guzmán can hear the preacher's labored breathing, loud wheezes and snorts, and he half expects the man to drop dead from a coronary at any moment. The sun bakes the parched, barren landscape as the two men trudge across the vast emptiness.

When Guzmán closes to within a few feet, he fires his rifle into the air, and the preacher lets out a shriek and falls face-forward onto the ground. The large man flails, reminding Guzmán of an overturned tortoise. Exhausted, the preacher finally gives up trying to lift his bulk. He lies on the dirt, defeated, breathing in wide-mouthed, convulsive gulps. Guzmán towers over him, watching as the preacher slowly manages to get himself into a sitting position. Wright looks up at him, his eyes squinting against the sun's glare.

"They're...coming...for me," the preacher gasps.

Guzmán kicks the preacher in the face with his boot heel, sending the man sprawling backwards. Wright tumbles to the ground, moaning and covering his face with his hands. He rises to his knees, blood flowing from his crushed nose and covering his chin.

"Don Flaco," he cries, holding out a palm. "Stop, please. Listen to me."

The next strike is a fist, a hard blow to the side of the preacher's head. Wright's legs collapse and he drops to the ground again. His white linen suit is covered with dirt.

"Get up," Guzmán hears himself say. He feels a surge of incredible power coursing through him. The throbbing, constant pain of his injured shoulder is gone. He's an angry god, and this is Wright's day of reckoning.

The preacher tries to push himself up, but his tired arms give out and he face-plants into the dirt. Guzmán looms over him, waiting patiently for the man to recover, and when the preacher finally manages to lift his head from the ground, he's met with another kick, this one to the mouth. Wright makes a deep guttural noise and rolls onto his back, face up and eyes fluttering, his arms spread out wide.

"Oh, no, you don't," Guzmán says, unhooking the water bottle from his belt. "You're not allowed to go to sleep on me yet." He tilts the bottle directly over the preacher's face, pouring a steady stream of water into his mouth. Coughing and gagging, the preacher jerks his head away and spits out a mouthful of bloody water onto the dirt, along with the broken remnants of several teeth.

The torturous beating continues for another quarter of an hour, slow and deliberate. A perfectly placed liver punch cripples the preacher for a full two minutes. An uppercut to the chin causes Wright to bite through the tip of his tongue. The preacher's face transforms into swollen, unrecognizable mess of clotting blood and ravaged flesh. Guzmán feels no pain. His chafed and bleeding knuckles don't bother him at all. His vengeance is a seven-course meal he's been waiting to dine on all his life, and he's enjoying every last bite of it.

Lying on his back next to a ragged creosote bush, the preacher begins to make a sound Guzmán at first mistakes for sobbing, but then he realizes it's laughter. Has he literally beaten the preacher silly?

"I told you they were coming for me," Wright says, his speech thick and slurred. "I told you." He lifts his hand and points a shaking finger at some point beyond Guzmán. Turning around to look, Guzmán immediately curses himself. Eight, maybe ten, vehicles speed toward him. He's got perhaps a couple minutes, four at the most, before they're on top of him.

And he'd been so sure the old crook was bluffing...

"You take that truck," Wright spits, motioning unsteadily back toward the Humvee. "It's still running." The beating has left his face grotesquely misshapen. One side of his head is noticeably larger than the other and his eyes are nothing but narrow slits, nearly swollen shut. "You let me live this day, don Flaco, and I will tell them not to follow you. You hear me? We'll let you go on your way."

Guzmán crosses his arms, frowns down at Wright.

"But if you take my life," Wright warns, "they'll chase you down and end you."

Guzmán removes the pistol from the back of his pants.

"Don Flaco, don't!" the preacher pleads, holding one hand up, the other over his heart. "My hand to God, brother, you can live through this."

Racking the slide on the pistol, Guzmán steps closer. He can't hear the engines of the convoy yet, but he knows they'll be in firing range soon.

"Don Flaco, don't do this. I'm begging you—"

The first shot strikes the preacher in the shoulder. He

howls in agony. The second shot hits his thigh. Wright writhes in the dirt, his entire body jerking in spasms as a dark, red stain blooms on his pants leg. Strange gurgling sounds come from his mouth.

Guzmán steps forward, straddling the preacher's torso, then lowers himself on top of him. Sitting on Wright's chest, he wedges the gun into the preacher's mouth, feeling the barrel scrape against a mouthful of broken teeth. Dull-eyed and bleeding out, the preacher's still conscious, but too weak to resist or fight back.

Guzmán leans down, his eyes fixed on the preacher's. "Por mi mamá y por mi Lela." He pulls the trigger. The preacher's body jerks once and then goes still.

A mess of blood and brains fan out over the sandy ground. Guzmán stands and gazes down at the dead man's face.

It's done.

He stands there for a moment, staring at the preacher's swollen mess of a death mask. Then, at the corner of his vision something jumps, and he hears a soft thud-thud-thud. He turns and sees plumes of dirt squirting up into the air. A second later he hears the report of automatic gunfire.

For an instant, he considers sprinting back to the Humvee and trying to make a run for it. But when he looks toward the oncoming vehicles, he realizes it's too late. They're too close to him now.

Another burst of gunfire whizzes past him. He crouches low and hustles over to a shallow gulley, where he lies down on his belly. Unslinging the rifle, he lays out his ammunition in neat rows so he can reload quickly. He peers through the scope, aims, and fires a short burst at the lead vehicle.

It's his last day of life, his last moments, come for him a second time. As he squeezes the trigger again, he doesn't feel any sadness or regret or fear, only a perfect sense of purpose.

Maybe he can take out a few more before they finish him. That would be a good way to end things. The icing on his cake, as the gringos say.

CHAPTER 33

The sandstorm almost on top of him, Chavez watches the approaching horde of Fundie machines through his binoculars. Waves of heat rise up from the desert plain, distorting the horizon. He can make out individual vehicles now: the flat, wide profiles of Humvees, the almost perfectly square silhouettes of Jeeps, the thin vertical smudges of motorbikes. His insides twist with anxiety. They must be nearly in range by now.

As if answering him, a voice comes over the radio, announcing shots have been fired. Chavez gives Chango the driver a steely look. "Keep your head, joven. The hardest thing to do will be to keep your head when the chaos starts. ¿Me entiendes?" The driver takes a deep breath and nods, gripping the wheel tightly.

The chaos doesn't take long to start. Chavez flinches as a round strikes their Humvee with a sharp clank. Far to their right, two explosions burst, orange fireballs flashing to life and sending massive amounts of dirt skyward. A second later the shockwaves pass through Chavez's body, jarring him and rattling the Humvee.

Things escalate quickly. Rounds thud into the truck's steel body. The Fundies close in, their vehicles growing larger, their shapes more distinct and recognizable. Chavez can make out Lincolns with jacked-up bodies and oversized tires. Chevy trucks with machine guns mounted in the beds.

A strong wind kicks up; Chavez lowers a pair of goggles over his eyes and pulls his bandanna up over his mouth. Hot sand blasts the side of his face as the gushing air pushes a cloud of dirt and grit through the truck's cabin. He can no longer see the Fundie fleet ahead of them, their numbers hidden by a rust fog that suddenly blankets the landscape. The West Texas sandstorm has joined the battle.

"We're blind," Chango shouts. The driver leans forward over the wheel, squinting into the dense cloud.

"También ellos," Chavez cries back. The Fundies are, too.

A flaquista martillo motors past, its enormous bulk like a whale suddenly beside them. A monstrosity of a vehicle, the heavily armored bus is blanketed in multiple layers of reinforced steel and sports a huge triangular cow-catcher jutting forward across its front—essentially a fifteen-ton battering ram. Its arrival means the real fighting, the close-in action, is about to begin. Sparks fly from its armor as rounds harmlessly bounce off the thick steel shell. A second martillo bus passes them on the driver's side, blasting its horn in salute as it speeds by. Chavez raises his rifle out the window and fires off a skyward burst in return. The two colossal machines disappear ahead of them into the dust and sand.

Then, in an instant, the world around Chavez goes mad.

Vehicles are suddenly all around them. As the two armies collide, trucks and cars and motorbikes barrel past them in all directions, glimpsed momentarily as they appear out of the thick reddish-brown haze and quickly disappear back into it. Chavez catches the blinking flashes of muzzles firing in the dust cloud. He hears the battle more than he sees it, his ears ringing with explosions, constant gunfire, and roaring engines.

"¡Aguas!" Chango cries, pointing. Chavez turns and sees a motorbike coming up fast. The rider, a skinny kid with bony arms, wears a bulky vest laden with explosives. A Fundie bomb boy, so close Chavez could reach out and touch him. The driver tries to steer away, but the bike—far more quick and nimble than their bulky Humvee—sticks close to them. The truck lurches and Chavez fumbles his rifle as the rider lets go of one handlebar and grabs something on his vest. Chavez scrambles for his weapon, his teeth clenched and body tensed, expecting a detonation any second.

In the next moment the kid flies off the motorbike as if yanked backwards by some invisible rope. He tumbles over the dirt and disappears behind them into the dust cloud. A ball of light flares as the kid's vest explodes. The heat singes Chavez's skin, and the force of the blast lifts the Humvee onto its two left wheels for a dizzying few moments before the driver can regain control. Another Humvee appears next to them; the gunner in the turret salutes Chavez.

"Nice shooting, joven!" Chavez yells, giving the gunner a thumbs-up.

His heart thudding in his chest, he returns to his hand radio, shouting out orders, checking in with squad leaders as bullets fly and engines roar around them. Everything inside the Humvee is covered with a layer of windblown sand and visibility is close to zero as the battle rages. Bullets ping and thud against his door. Wiping grit from the dashboard display, he hunches over the screen and studies their location.

Not yet.

The driver shouts something and he looks up, shouldering his rifle instinctively. He fires furiously at the sudden appearance of enemy cars and trucks, knocking sand from a fresh magazine and reloading. His hands work swiftly, efficiently, as if his movements are being controlled by something outside himself. He fights in another dimension, it seems, inside this cage of sand and dust, this tight, airless space with no up or down, no difference between ground and sky. He takes down a pair of motorbikes with two quick bursts from his rifle. He spots a pickup with a painted cross on its door and fills the cabin with a well-aimed barrage, killing the driver and two passengers. He's not sure how much time passes as the fire-reload-fire sequence repeats itself over and over. He checks the map display again, finally seeing what he's been waiting for.

Now.

He shouts the prearranged signal over the radio, then presses the speaker to his ear and waits for the replies. One by one they come, the voices of his squad leaders, confirming the order. Chavez counts the callbacks until he reaches ten. He waits another minute, listening anxiously, but no more voices come over the radio. *Por Dios.* Only ten of his fifteen squad leaders have called back. He repeats the coded order a final time, then instructs Chango which way to point the truck through the blinding sandstorm.

A minute later, the nose of the Humvee lifts up, pressing Chavez against the back of his seat. The truck climbs up a steep grade. The dust storm still blows hard, and neither he nor the driver can see much of anything beyond their vehicle. He hunches over the map, giving the driver instructions every few seconds. *Left here*, he tells the soldier. *Now keep it straight.* They continue climbing, and little by little the sounds of the battle fade, the staccato gunfire and churning motors growing ever more distant.

"Are we there yet?" the driver asks. They haven't seen or heard another vehicle since they started their ascent.

Chavez doesn't answer, concentrating on the path upward, shifting his gaze between the dashboard map and the narrow swatch of visible ground ahead. "There they are," he says. "Pull up right here." The ground levels out and they come upon a row of parked Jeeps and Humvees. They park at the end of the row and exit the vehicle.

"What now?" Chango asks.

"Flaquistas never lose a desert battle, joven," Chavez answers as he removes his goggles, his face caked with dust.

The old warrior hurries up and down the long line of vehicles, assessing the condition of his troops. He's greeted with smiles and nods, white eyes and teeth gleaming out from dirty, sand-caked faces. The vehicles are beaten up badly, covered with battle scars of bullet pockmarks and puckered dents from shrapnel. He returns to his Humvee and tells Chango to get up into the turret and load the .50-cal. It's almost time, he says with a nod. "Sí, jefe," the soldier replies, obeying the order.

Somewhere far below them, gunfire pops at a near-continuous crackle.

Standing beside the truck, Chavez licks his forefinger and holds it into the air. "Feel that, joven?" he calls to Chango. "The wind is dying." Then he lifts the hand radio to his mouth, ordering his soldiers to wait for his command. Up in the turret, the young soldier holds the large rifle's handles, swiveling the barrel back and forth in a nervous fidget.

The wind stops. Chavez peers downward, though for the moment he still sees nothing but dust and haze. Down the line of parked vehicles, soldiers with black bandannas busily load their weapons as the distant gunfire continues. Finally, the dust cloud begins to break up.

Slowly, Chavez's field of vision expands as the airborne sand and dirt settle. The row of parked vehicles extends for a half mile, he now sees, a neat formation lining the top of the ridge, overlooking the valley below, its floor still hidden under a thinning blanket of dust and dirt. The noise of the battle continues directly below him, the fighting armies also still concealed by the dissipating cloud.

Slowly, the gunfire begins to abate, and then nearly stops altogether. The valley and the ridge high above it becomes eerily silent.

"Look over there," Chavez tells the young soldier, pointing straight ahead. The opposite ridge of the valley, now visible in the near distance, is a mirror image of the one they stand on now. A long line of flaquista vehicles stretches out across the ridge top, overlooking the canyon floor, which finally begins to reveal itself.

Below, a thousand vehicles race back and forth in chaos, scurrying like confused beetles across the valley floor.

Chavez swallows. *Por Dios. Look how many of them.*

The valley is shaped like a football: a wide, flat expanse with a narrow opening to the east and a narrower one to the west. Rocky walls jut upwards from the valley floor at harsh angles, steep and impassable. The young soldier gawks downward. "Did we just drive up all that?"

"We took the long way around," Chavez explains, pointing a thumb over his shoulder. "A lower-grade trail back that way."

A trail the Fundies don't know about because they've never fought out here before. A trail not marked on any map, that he only remembered when he saw the contour lines of Martyr's Canyon on the Humvee's dash display, sparking a dim memory from a scouting trip he'd taken years ago. The timely sandstorm and the valley, with its steep, inescapable walls, provided an opportunity, an advantage he might be able to exploit. The first part of his strategy—except for the loss of his forces, now painfully obvious in the clearing air—seems to have come off as planned. The blinding cloud of dust and sand gave them the cover they needed to lure the Fundie army into the valley with a small contingent of vehicles, while the bulk of his forces regrouped on the high ground, assembling themselves at the tops of the ridges while they waited for the storm to pass and the dust to settle.

But it's the second part that everything depends on, the maneuver they have to pull off in the next few moments, before the Fundies realize what's happening. And now that's he's seen the enemy's numbers up close and unhidden by the storm, he knows this is their only chance. He scans the valley floor through his binoculars, desperately searching. Where are they?

Finally, he spots a small convoy of martillo buses, speeding toward the canyon's narrow western exit.

Come on, close the gate. Apúrense.

The steel-plated vehicles move into the passageway and stop, forming a blockade five buses deep, effectively cutting off the exit.

Good. Now the other one.

Chavez swings his view to the opposite end of the valley, where another group of armored buses performs the same tactic, sealing off the easternmost passage.

The Fundie army is trapped.

Chavez wastes no time giving the order. "FUEGO!" he cries into the radio.

The deafening sound that follows is one he knows he'll never forget: the bone-rattling noise of countless guns firing in unison. Chavez kneels down, taking cover behind a rocky outcropping as the bloody slaughter begins. Below on the valley floor, the Fundies begin to realize what's happening and dozens of vehicles start speeding toward the exits, where they meet the impenetrable wall of the martillos. He watches as the Humvees and Jeeps try to climb around the armored buses at the pass, flipping over or stalling out as they attempt to scale the canyon's steep, jagged walls. The motorbikes, lighter and more agile, try the same maneuver, but none manage to get past the constant barrage of flaquista gunfire from on high.

The bloodbath unfolds with merciless efficiency. The flaquistas, firing from protected positions or laid out flat with only the barest profile visible from the valley floor, suffer only a handful of losses, while the enemy fighters down below die in droves. Panic overtakes many of the Fundie soldiers, who abandon their vehicles and scramble up the canyon walls in desperation, trying to escape the death trap of the canyon floor. Not a single soul makes it out alive. The canyon walls are soon cluttered with hundreds of bodies, tattooed arms and legs frozen in strange, awkward sprawls.

As the firing finally begins to slow, Chavez turns away from the carnage, sickened by the horror of his own design. Never has he seen so much death come so quickly.

Eventually, from somewhere down the line the call to cease fire comes, and an ominous quiet falls over the mass grave of a valley.

The Fundies are defeated.

CHAPTER 34

Guzmán's a better shot than these Fundies are, but they've got firepower on their side. He manages to stop two of the eight Humvees with a pair of lucky shots at the outer limit of his rifle's range, killing the drivers. A pair of *well-placed* shots, he corrects himself, not lucky ones. Because his luck is all gone. He's used up every bit of it—and probably a bit more than anyone could rightly expect on this day.

The Humvees grow ominously larger and closer, hungry wolves charging an injured deer. A volley of rounds whizzes past him, inches above his head. He returns fire, squeezing off a short burst that does nothing to slow the vehicles' breakneck approach. Flashes of distant muzzle fire blink on and off and an instant later the ground around him erupts, sending dirt and rocks high into the air, showering him in falling clumps over his head and back.

A round rips through the bicep of his uninjured arm, sending searing pain through his shoulder and torso. It's only a grazing shot, but from a high-caliber bullet it's enough to render his arm completely useless. He shifts the rifle to his other hand, gritting his teeth against excruciating pain, when another round thuds into his chest like a massive hammer, shattering his shoulder blade. He explodes in agony, convulsing uncontrollably. The edges of his vision go black. He feels himself slipping away.

Immobilized with pain, he gulps in a large breath, determined to get off a final volley before the blackness overtakes him entirely. Without aiming, he manages to move his trigger finger. Before he can fire, the lead Humvee explodes into a brilliant ball of orange.

What the hell?

A second explosion blooms to life and the ground beneath his belly shakes like a flash earthquake, rattling his teeth. Tons of earth fly skyward, the shockwave hitting him like a punch.

His pain-racked mind tries to comprehend what's happening. Maybe he's already dead, and he's dreaming all of this. No, he corrects himself, being dead wouldn't hurt like this. The world around him distorts, sights and sounds stretching and folding unrecognizably as he struggles to keep from losing consciousness. He squints into the distance, where a smoke-and-dust-filled horizon has replaced the approaching Humvees. Coughing blood, his strength fading, he watches as the smoke clears, revealing burnt wreckage and impact craters where seconds before there was nothing but flat desert plains.

Everything goes quiet. He lies there, he's not sure how long—maybe two minutes or maybe two hours—when he hears a high-pitched whine, a sound he at first mistakes for ringing in his ears. It grows louder and more distinct, as if it's getting closer. He wants to turn and look, but he can no longer move his neck. He can no longer move anything.

A pale shape enters his field of vision, which is now reduced to a narrow tunnel, more dark than light. It's a vehicle of some kind, slowing to a stop. Long and white and narrow. An aircraft? He blinks, doubting the certainty of his failing mind, doubting the reality of what his eyes see. People see things when they die, don't they? That's what he's always heard.

The side of the aircraft—if that's what it is—opens and the blurry shadow of a figure emerges. The figure rushes toward him, becoming more distinct as it gets closer. As *she* gets closer.

Soledad.

It's his Reader Soledad. She's next to him now, cradling his head in her arms, gazing down at him, the sun shining from behind her head like a halo. She cries to him, pleading with him not to die. He can barely hear her. Tears stream down her face. A smile forms inside him. His Soledad has dropped from the heavens like an angel.

Is she really here or is he dreaming this? He laughs inwardly, telling himself it doesn't matter. Genuine or illusion, as a final image from his life, Reader Soledad's face is as nice a picture as he could hope for.

He closes his eyes and lets the darkness overtake him.

CHAPTER 35

Yet again, Soledad finds herself at St. Luke's. So many moments of her life have occurred within this building's clean, white walls. Twenty-one years ago, she entered the world in the neonatal unit up on the sixth floor. She returned to its embrace as a child, visiting Doctor Bernard's practice for checkups and booster shots; she recalls his sour breath and bushy white eyebrows. How she hated those visits. And when she returned to Dallas months ago as a flaquista camp runaway, weak and hungry and shell-shocked from her race across the wastelands, it was St. Luke's that once again cradled her in its sterile arms. At the time the Bullocks were still running things, squatting on their final days in power, though they had no idea at the time, no idea the countdown clock was already ticking on their decades-long reign. And as fate would have it, it was in this very same hospital she let loose the technology that brought their regime to its knees, that dropped their defenses so Guzmán's troops could take the city. And now she's here again, watching with worried eyes as don Flaco lies motionless in a hospital bed in this small room, his body roped by tubes and wires to an attentive cluster of machines murmuring to themselves in beeps and tones. She absently fondles her pendant, rubbing the Virgin's image between her thumb and forefinger. A constant murmur of crowd noise can be heard through the closed windows. Thousands of faithful flaquistas surround the building, holding vigil and waiting for any word on their fallen leader's condition.

Keeping his own vigil, Chavez sits in a bedside chair, a station he hasn't left for days except for toilet breaks. As soon as he got word that his jefe, barely clinging to life, had been flown back to Dallas in the Americans' jet, he raced nonstop back to the city.

"Did you eat something today?" Soledad asks, frowning at Chavez's gaunt features, his hollow eyes.

Chavez shakes his head. Soledad cracks open the door and instructs the guard posted outside to send out for some food, then reenters the morose room.

A minute later, Indigo arrives. "Any update?"

Soledad shakes her head. The grim-faced surgeon told them that Guzmán had lost a lot of blood. Medically, they've done all they can, removing bullet fragments and repairing the massive amount of tissue damage, but they don't know if he'll wake back up again.

"He's a tough old critter," the trader says, laying her hand on Soledad's shoulder. "He'll make it, you'll see."

Words of sympathy, not words of conviction. Still, she lays her own hand on top of Indigo's, grateful for the comfort. They stand there for some time, quietly staring at the man, his body broken, his pallid face, bruised and scraped. Soledad shudders, imagining the horrors he must have lived through these last days.

"They're here," Indigo says, finally breaking the silence, announcing the arrival Soledad's been anxiously awaiting.

"City Hall?" Soledad asks.

Indigo nods. "I've got a car out front."

*   *   *

"He'll pull through," G.G. says from the driver's seat, his voice buoyed with confidence. "If he didn't die out there in the desert, he sure as hell won't die in some hospital bed." He turns the Humvee left onto Elm Street.

Sitting in the backseat, Indigo beside her, Soledad stares out the window, wishing she could share the soldier's certainty. She tries to shake the image of don Flaco, prone and motionless, from her mind. She forces her thoughts to City Hall, to the meeting with the Americans.

"Chavez should be there," Indigo mutters.

"He should," Soledad agrees. "I worked on him for half an hour before you showed up, but there was no convincing him." She shrugs. "He's not going anywhere until don Flaco wakes up."

If he ever does wake up. Soledad has little doubt Indigo is thinking the same unspoken thought.

"Are you...chewing leaves?" Indigo asks.

"I suppose I ought to." Soledad reaches into her vest pocket and pulls out a stash of hierba folded up in a cloth. She chews, and the leaves release their familiar bitterness.

They drive on. "Why'd you do it?" Indigo asks.

"Do what?" Soledad answers reflexively, though in the next moment she knows exactly what Indigo's referring to.

The reader sighs. "I don't know." Her hand automatically reaches up and touches her pendant. She's asked herself the same question more than a few times in recent days. Had it been Lela? Had Soledad felt she still owed her late guardian a debt, and by extension owed Guzmán? Or had it been Indigo's story about Prayer Donovan's deathbed regrets that had swayed her? Or maybe it had been the sight of Steffa's scarred wrists, the grim daily reminder of so many others like her out there, still in chains. Maybe it had been a bit of each of those things, in the end. But whatever it was that had moved her, the moment the repaired drone's camera had spotted don Flaco, alone and dying on the dirty desert floor, she knew she'd made the right call.

The truck arrives at City Hall, braking to a stop at the front entrance. Hundreds mill about the plaza, gawking up at the US Army helicopter that had set down on the building's rooftop half an hour earlier. An excited murmur passes through the crowd as Soledad exits the truck. She's quickly surrounded by an awed, adoring mob.

"God bless you, Soledad," a woman shouts, making the sign of the cross.

"Que Dios te bendiga," another woman cries, weeping uncontrollably.

"What do the gringos want with us, Soledad?" an old man hollers. "Why have they come back?"

A security detail arrives from the building, moving the crowd back and creating space for her to breath. Indigo appears suddenly beside her. The two women are ushered through the press of bodies, toward the building. As they make their way forward, Soledad glances upward at the helicopter, at its menacing guns and missiles. She takes a deep breath, readying herself for whatever's about to come. When she pulled her little stunt out at the airport, she knew there would be hell to pay. Now it's time to face it.

They enter the building as the first tendrils of the hierba's effect begin to creep through her mind.

CHAPTER 36

"You kidnapped an American official and held him hostage to repair your drones. Then, after he managed to get a pair of them airborne, you held a gun to his head and forced him to attack a public gathering in Odessa and then later a small convoy of vehicles, resulting in the deaths of untold numbers of your fellow Texans."

Roman Kennedy does not look happy. He stands behinds the table in Guzmán's office, his hands gripping the back of a chair as he glares at Soledad and recounts her crimes. General Bennett is next to him, hands clasped behind her back, her hawklike stare harsh and penetrating. Four security guards hover protectively behind the Americans, wearing their strange globe-like helmets and brandishing automatic weapons. The Americans clearly aren't taking any security risks with this visit. And for their part, neither are Soledad and Indigo, who entered the room moments earlier with the four armed flaquistas now standing behind them and watching the gringos with wary stares.

"Am I missing anything or are there more war crimes you've committed that I'm not aware of?" Kennedy asks rhetorically.

"She also hijacked your jet to go pick up don Flaco," Indigo adds. Soledad reacts by throwing the trader a stink-eyed glance. *Thanks, Indie.*

Kennedy moves his glaring eyes to the trader, incensed by the flippant comment. His chest rises noticeably as he takes in a long breath through his nose. "Indeed. Add to the list theft of our aircraft, which we sent in good faith, by the way, along with an offer of amnesty."

Soledad feels the full power of the hierba now, her perception open wide as she studies Kennedy's knotted features and stiff posture, as she senses the angry vibrations reverberating in his voice. Gone is the wide, magnanimous smile of his first visit to Dallas. And gone with it—or at least temporarily hidden by his rage—is any shred of the sympathy toward the Texans she sensed in him before. A sudden dread strikes her. Did they destroy one enemy only to gain another, more powerful one?

"This will set relations between our nations back years, even decades," Kennedy chides. At the far end of the room, a large square of corrugated cardboard covers the hole in the window. "What you've done is an outrage, Miss Paz. It's nothing short of an international scandal."

The harangue goes on, reminding Soledad of similar ones she's witnessed in this same room. Guzmán chastising Chavez or one of his lesser lieutenants, angered by some new administrative frustration or annoyance. Waving a forefinger at them, Kennedy points out how far he stuck out his neck for Guzmán, how he and the general represented a shrinking minority of those willing to help the flaquista cause. They risked their careers, their reputations. And the thanks they got for it was a knife in the back.

The air in the small, crowded office is tense and thick. But as awkward and strange as it is, standing there being yelled at, Kennedy's prolonged rant gives Soledad a window of opportunity to push into his mind and read him from the inside. She takes a deep breath and pushes in.

An angry mind is hot, or at least that's how it seems to Soledad. The American's rage radiates a palpable heat, as if she's standing a short distance from a bonfire, its uncomfortable warmth prickling at her skin. The movie of his subconscious mind reveals itself in a sudden torrent of quick flashes. She sees an argument in an office from Kennedy's viewpoint, her eyes becoming his. She feels the tightly wound knot in his (her) stomach, feels the rise of his (her) blood pressure as he (she) unleashes a string of profanities at Garcia, who sits with his eyes lowered, gazing stupidly at the tabletop. Bennett's there as well, seated next to Garcia, her features drawn up into a stern glare. Whatever Kennedy's saying doesn't come through clearly, but what's happening is all too apparent. Garcia's getting the tongue-lashing of his life for helping the flaquistas.

Then the American's feelings and images begin to arrange themselves, forming a coherent picture, a story Soledad can understand. There's as much fear as anger coursing through Kennedy's veins, as much panic as outrage. Then she finally sees it, a ray of sunlight suddenly bursting through an overcast sky: the leverage she needs. *Bingo.*

She extracts herself from the oven heat of Kennedy's head, snapping herself back to the moment. A smile spreads across her face.

Kennedy hasn't stopped ranting, but he seems to notice the sudden grin on Soledad's face. He stops, blinking forcefully. "Something about this situation amuse you, Miss Paz?"

Soledad gives Indigo a quick, meaningful glance. Then she looks over at Kennedy. "You can stop all this bullshit now," she says, her voice flat.

The American's eyes go wide. "I beg your pardon?"

"The riot act you're reading us," Soledad says. "Are you getting close to the end? We've got more important things to discuss."

Kennedy's mouth hangs open. He looks as if he's just been gut-punched.

"You're out on a limb, aren't you?" Soledad asks, her smile fading into something more menacing. "Something tells me—call it intuition—that your higher-ups back in the States don't know the whole truth of what's happened, do they?"

Silence. Bennett and Kennedy exchange looks.

"What do you think they'd say," Soledad goes on, "if they found out how Garcia'd helped out? That would be a rather tough conversation to have, I imagine."

"He feared for his life," Kennedy accuses, his ire returning, though lessened, tempered with what Soledad perceives as caution. "Who would blame him for doing what he did?"

"Maybe you're right," Soledad concedes. "Maybe nobody would blame him. Maybe it wouldn't be difficult at all to explain." She pauses for a moment before dropping the bomb. "Unless you've already made some statement to the contrary, unless you've already denied all knowledge of what happened. But I'm sure you wouldn't have done something as shortsighted as that, especially if there might be footage of Garcia loading up an old Texan gunbird with missiles."

She removes a thimble-sized archive from her pocket and tosses it to Kennedy, who's so shocked by her words he doesn't lift his arms. Bennett reaches over and snatches the archive from the air an instant before it strikes her countryman's chest.

Soledad fixes Kennedy with an icy stare. "But I'm sure you didn't do something like that, did you?"

A long, tense silence follows. Bennett turns over the archive in her palm, contemplating it for a moment, then looks at Soledad. "Copies?" the general asks, already seeming to realize she and Kennedy have been checkmated.

"Enough for each senator to have one of their own," Indigo replies.

Kennedy, the color drained completely from his face, stares with horrified eyes at the archive in Bennett's hand, as if she's holding some radioactive piece of toxic waste.

"What is it you want?" Bennett asks, exhaling in resignation. She tucks the archive into her breast pocket.

"We want to put the past behind us," Indigo replies. "We want to make tomorrow better than yesterday."

"We want to find a new way forward," Soledad adds. "That's why you all came here in the first place, isn't it?"

Bennett shifts her gaze between the two of them. Soledad senses her caution, her trepidation, but underneath she perceives something else: an inkling of optimism. A seed buried deep underground, waiting for the right conditions to grow and take root. "Indeed," the general answers. "Indeed it is."

Behind Soledad a muffled voice comes over a hand radio. She turns, sees G.G. standing in the doorway, his expression earnest.

"We need to get back to the hospital."

CHAPTER 37

The following morning, Soledad stands with her arms crossed, shaking her head ruefully at the recent escapee from St. Luke's, still wearing his hospital gown and aiming a Glock at a wooden target thirty yards ahead.

"You look ridiculous," she calls. It's hot out already, even in the shade of the shooting range's tarp.

Guzmán fires the pistol; the recoil elicits a loud groan. Splinters fly as the round strikes the target. As he leans forward, squinting at the result, his ass pokes out of the slit in the gown's back.

Soledad winces at the sight. "Do you really think you should be out here?" she implores, though she knows her reprimands are the very definition of futility.

After he regained consciousness, it didn't take Guzmán long to go stir-crazy. Against doctor's orders, he disconnected his IV tube and unplugged his monitoring trodes and checked himself out. His nurse, after a stern finger-wagging lecture that failed utterly, hid his clothes in a last-ditch effort to keep him in place.

Holding his shoulder and grimacing, Guzmán hands the Glock back to G.G. and wobbles over to Soledad, taking a seat next to her under the tarp. He groans again as he settles himself onto the bench. "Okay, not good enough for shooting yet. But good enough to leave that bed, no matter what that pinche vieja says."

"Terco como una mula," Soledad chides. Stubborn as a mule.

Guzmán chuckles. "That's what my mother used to say."

"Sounds like a smart woman."

"She was."

A Ford truck approaches from the city. Behind the wheel is Chavez; Indigo sits in the passenger seat. Between them is Magnolia, with Steffa riding on the nanny's lap. Chavez parks the truck and the four join Guzmán and Soledad under the shade of the tarp.

"I can see your butt," Steffa chirps, pointing at Guzmán's backside.

Don Flaco adjusts his gown, covering his backside. "They told me you were bringing my clothes, gorda," he teases the girl. "Where are they?"

Holding Magnolia's hand, Steffa juts out her bottom lip and shrugs. "That's Chavez's job."

All eyes turn to Guzmán's right-hand man, who stands there unblinking, his perma-frown firmly in place. He stares at Steffa for a long, uncomfortable moment, then finally lets the girl off the hook with a wink. "I guess I forgot," he confesses.

"How are the ports, compadre?" Guzmán asks, changing the topic to more serious matters.

"All locked down, jefe," Chavez replies. "Everything from Port Arthur to Corpus Christi."

Guzmán nods. "Good."

Soledad recalls the scurry of activity in the aftermath of Wright's death. Once the preacher's army had been decimated, Chavez's next priority was preventing any further arms or vehicle shipments coming in by sea. He wasted no time dispatching troops to all the major ports along the Gulf coast. And not one to take any chances, he even deployed forces into Houston, Fundie ground zero, to consolidate flaquista power throughout the entirety of Texas. Next, he turned his attention to the so-called "debt holders." Over the next days, from all across the Republic, reports were radioed back to Dallas, accounts of child slaves being freed by the thousands, liberated by flaquista soldiers. With the preacher dead and his movement neutered of its weapons of war—not to mention the vast majority of its soldiers—the likelihood of a Fundie resurgence finally seems remote, if not impossible. Ernesto "El Flaco" Guzmán now holds all of Texas, his power uncontested.

A car horn beeps in the distance. Turning, Soledad sees a Humvee rolling to a stop beside Chavez's truck. Roman Kennedy and General Bennett get out. As they approach, Soledad notes a spring in Kennedy's gait, his white-toothed smile gleaming in the sunlight. A pair of uniformed soldiers follow close behind, though unlike the previous morning, they wear no helmets nor brandish threatening weapons.

"Hot one today," Kennedy announces, his tone as friendly and inviting as the day he introduced himself in Guzmán's office. He and Bennett step under the tarp, then they give Guzmán's attire a simultaneous double take.

Guzmán nods at the Americans but doesn't rise or offer his hand. "You're still here?"

All smiles, Kennedy spreads his hands out wide. "Of course. Once we heard you'd taken a turn for the better, we didn't want to leave without saying goodbye in person."

Small talk ensues, a skill which Kennedy has clearly mastered. They must come to the US soon, he insists. How he'd love to host them, show them the sights. And yes, yes, of course, he's sure the State Department will send a team of engineers and AI technicians to help solve don Flaco's infrastructure problems in Dallas. And the American support for the Fundies? No, no, he doesn't think that's anything to worry about, not anymore. The sympathy toward Wright consists of a small, vocal minority, and now that the preacher's no longer in the picture, things will change. Kennedy's confident that once the dust settles, the politicians will soon come around to his way of thinking. The public's attention span is short, and so is its memory. Before long Reverend Wright will be remembered as a novelty, an oddity of a cult leader, if he's remembered at all.

Kennedy and Bennett then make their goodbyes, much in the same way they'd made their hellos. Bennett with her keen, wary eyes, Kennedy with his wide, impossibly white grin.

Indigo at her side, Soledad watches the Americans return to their truck and leave.

"You trust those gringos, Reader Soledad?" Guzmán asks.

"About as far as I can throw them," she replies, then she turns to face him. "But they do want to help. I can tell you that for sure."

Guzmán grunts. "I guess I have to learn diplomacy now. Will I have to sign lots of papers?"

"Stacks and stacks of them," Indigo responds. "But there's also a lot of wining and dining."

"*That* I can do. No hay problema."

Another Humvee arrives, a flatbed model with something hidden by a tarp in the bed. Guzmán's eyes light up. "Ya llegó." The vehicle stops and a Black Bandanna soldier hops out and moves to the rear. He removes the tarp, revealing a freshly painted and polished motorbike. Soledad squints at the chrome plating shining brightly under the Texas sun.

Guzmán stands up on wobbly legs, rubbing his hands together and grinning like a naughty schoolboy. Soledad moves in front of him, blocking his way and giving him a stern look.

She crosses her arms, shakes her head, and smiles.

"Over my dead body, don Flaco."

For free D.L. Young books, new release info, and subscriber exclusives, visit dlyoungfiction.com

ACKNOWLEDGEMENTS

The Dark Republic trilogy was a labor of love, and as I sit here writing this, having just finished final edits, I'm much more aware of the labor than the love.

First and foremost, thanks to my family, who give me the time and space to type up these stories. Claudia, Logan, and Madeleine, your support means the world to me.

I'm also very indebted to my beta readers, who provided some incredibly important feedback on a draft that was, admittedly, a bit of a hot mess. Ira Domnitz, Kristin Mireles, Melyssa Patterson, and Angela Livingston. Many thanks for your time and input.

Juliet Ulman and Eliza Dee were my editors for all three books, and they both did an amazing job. Your help has been nothing short of a godsend.

ABOUT THE AUTHOR

D.L. Young is a Texas-based author. He's a Pushcart Prize nominee and winner of the 2017 Independent Press Award. His stories have appeared in many publications and anthologies.

For free books, new release updates, and exclusive previews, visit his website at www.dlyoungfiction.com.